Donald MacKenzie and The Murder Room

››› This title is part of The Murder Room, our series dedicated to making available out-of-print or hard-to-find titles by classic crime writers.

Crime fiction has always held up a mirror to society. The Victorians were fascinated by sensational murder and the emerging science of detection; now we are obsessed with the forensic detail of violent death. And no other genre has so captivated and enthralled readers.

Vast troves of classic crime writing have for a long time been unavailable to all but the most dedicated frequenters of second-hand bookshops. The advent of digital publishing means that we are now able to bring you the backlists of a huge range of titles by classic and contemporary crime writers, some of which have been out of print for decades.

From the genteel amateur private eyes of the Golden Age and the femmes fatales of pulp fiction, to the morally ambiguous hard-boiled detectives of mid twentieth-century America and their descendants who walk our twenty-first century streets, The Murder Room has it all. ›››

The Murder Room

Where Criminal Minds Meet

themurderroom.com

Donald MacKenzie 1908–1994

Donald MacKenzie was born in Ontario, Canada, and educated in England, Canada and Switzerland. For twenty-five years MacKenzie lived by crime in many countries. 'I went to jail,' he wrote, 'if not with depressing regularity, too often for my liking.' His last sentences were five years in the United States and three years in England, running consecutively. He began writing and selling stories when in American jail. 'I try to do exactly as I like as often as possible and I don't think I'm either psychopathic, a wayward boy, a problem of our time, a charming rogue. Or ever was.'

He had a wife, Estrela, and a daughter, and they divided their time between England, Portugal, Spain and Austria.

By Donald MacKenzie

Henry Chalice

Salute from a Dead Man (1966)
Death is a Friend (1967)
Sleep is for the Rich (1971)

John Raven

Zaleski's Percentage (1974)
Raven in Flight (1976)
Raven and the Ratcatcher (1976)
Raven and the Kamikaze (1977)
Raven After Dark (1979)
Raven Settles a Score (1979)
Raven and the Paperhangers (1980)
Raven's Revenge (1982)
Raven's Longest Night (1983)
Raven's Shadow (1984)
Nobody Here By That Name (1986)
A Savage State of Grace (1988)
By Any Illegal Means (1989)
Loose Cannon (1994)
The Eyes of the Goat (1992)
The Sixth Deadly Sin (1993)

Standalone novels

Nowhere to Go (1956)
The Juryman (1957)
The Scent of Danger (1958)
Dangerous Silence (1960)
Knife Edge (1961)
The Genial Stranger (1962)
Double Exposure (1963)
The Lonely Side of the River (1964)
Cool Sleeps Balaban (1964)
Dead Straight (1968)
Three Minus Two (1968)
Night Boat from Puerto Vedra (1970)
The Kyle Contract (1971)
Postscript to a Dead Letter (1973)
The Spreewald Collection (1975)
Deep, Dark and Dead (1978)
The Last of the Boatriders (1981)

Nowhere to Go

Donald MacKenzie

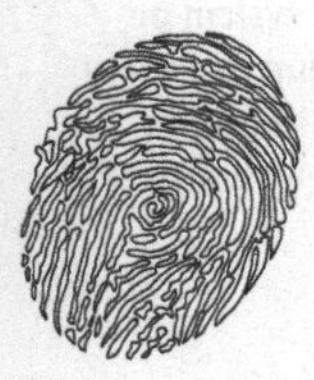

An Orion book

This edition published by
The Orion Publishing Group Ltd
Orion House
5 Upper St Martin's Lane
London WC2H 9EA

An Hachette UK company
A CIP catalogue record for this book is available from the British Library

ISBN 978 1 4719 0559 9

www.orionbooks.co.uk

For B
Whose book it was from the beginning

ONE

THE great studded doors to the main entrance opened inwards to a cobbled courtyard. On the far side, iron gates reaching to the stone archway separated courtyard from prison grounds. This was the Main Gate Lodge. Through it, passed all incoming traffic. Trucks laden with cement and tiles, oats destined for skilly and marked GRADE "A" PIG MEAL, Black Marias with the day's haul from the Metropolitan Police Courts, coaches used to carry convicted prisoners from the Central Criminal Court and the County Sessions.

Those ponderous doors shut out freedom from drunks serving seven days in lieu of a fine, candidates for Preventive Detention and Corrective Training, ten year men and those hustled in direct silence to the condemned cells.

There were two patches of light in the sombre courtyard. On the left, in the gatekeeper's office, were numbered racks hung with cell and pass keys. On a larger painted slate, the legends "Men at Court," "Locking-up Roll," had figures chalked against them. Outside, a rat-faced trusty was stacking loaves of bread on a shelf to be collected by warders going off duty.

On the other side of the courtyard was a room lit by two naked bulbs. Three benches and an evil oil stove were the only furnishings. The decoration was the same as anywhere else in the jail—whitewash and ochre paint. Over the door, the words WAITING ROOM had been inscribed in the tasty style affected by convict signwriters.

It was two in the afternoon and visiting hours. This was the room where those with visiting orders waited till the men they had come to see were fetched from the prison. A thin-faced woman slapped fretfully at two small boys. A tall girl, with bright hair worn in a pony tail, a silver fox jacket and spiked shoes, examined her exaggerated make-up with care. On the bench beside her, a cigarette was smouldering. A stout woman with her head wrapped in a scarf that bristled with curling pins glared at the girl then dabbed angrily at tears that made her ugly face uglier.

One man sat alone, near the door to the yard, reading the early edition of the afternoon paper. As he considered the banner headline, he crinkled his bloodhound face.

GREGORY CASE—APPEAL COURT JUDGES DECISION

He closed the paper suddenly, smoothing the folds with pigskin fingers. Thirty-five, he wore his well-cut clothes with an air of assurance. As he heard the jingle of keys, he stood, showing his extreme height.

The jailer had a scrubbed N.C.O.'s face under a peaked cap. He called names pompously from a sheaf of visiting orders in his hand.

At "Mr. Sloane!" the tall man ducked under the overhang into the courtyard. In the manner of one long accustomed to minor disbursements of the sort, Sloane slipped a half-crown into the hand of the warder. It was transferred to the man's pocket with no acknowledgement.

The Visiting Boxes were between the main lodge and the prison itself—a single-storey building split down its length into sixteen cubicles, each the size of a telephone booth. Visitors used a door on the far side, prisoners one near the cell blocks. Two men came up the steps from the basement level of the jail. The jailbird grey of the prisoner's uniform was drab against the escort's neat blue tunic. The warder rapped with his key on the door to the Visiting Boxes. As it opened, he bellowed as if on a parade ground:

"One man on to you, sir! 1748 Gregory, appeal visit, sir!"

Greg resisted the urge to laugh. This was the stylized language approved by the Prison Commissioners in ball-and-chain days and still passed from one old sweat to another.

"One man coming down, sir!" they yelled to one another though you were going down a stairway with twelve treads. As if you were valuable merchandize to be acknowledged with some magical formula. One that would absolve the screws should you vanish in smoke.

The receiving warder scowled. "Do your jacket up!" he ordered.

Meeting the man's look, Greg fastened the shapeless jacket slowly. He'd have to be careful. They threw you in Chokey for "dumb insolence". Chokey was the same as being on Special Watch or the Escape List. A screw peering into your cell every quarter hour and a light on all night. Worse—the punishment cells were twelve feet above the ground.

The warder was watching Greg, the smile plastered on his face as if he meant it.

" That's better. It wouldn't do to let 'em think we don't keep you smart." He pointed down the corridor. " Number 12."

Steam pipes clanked. Around them, a few of the cons, their visits over, were soaking in the unaccustomed heat luxuriously as they waited to be escorted back to their shops. From the babble of conversation, the flat accusing whine of a woman's voice detached itself. There was a recent case of a prisoner who had smashed the glass in an attempt to disfigure his visitor. The warder followed Greg to his booth, rattling his keys warningly. The woman's voice was suddenly quiet.

Greg's booth was fourth from the end. The warder patrolled the length of coconut-fibre matting, inspecting the booths from time to time—a gesture, since nothing could be passed from one side to the other. His desk was at the far end of the corridor.

Greg let down the wooden flap that served as a seat. Through the glass partition, he could see the windows on the other side of the Visiting Boxes. Beyond that, the wicket in the iron gate. He kept his eyes on it. As the bitter reek of shag tobacco hit his nostrils, his fingers drummed on the raw wood. Why those stupid bastards couldn't wait till they got back to their shops then use the johns! The screw this side was a bad one to start with—if he noticed the smoking, he'd be prowling about this end of the building. What Greg had to say to Sloane needn't take long. But it had to be private.

When he saw Sloane coming through the iron gate, Greg's mouth eased. Boy, you get a friend like Sloane and you really *get* a friend.

The jailer on Sloane's side was one of the old school. One of the " Give me no trouble and I'll give you none " set. He showed Sloane in. " You know the regulations, sir. He ain't allowed to be showed no newspapers or letters."

Sloane's nod was at once an acceptance and dismissal of everything the jailer stood for. He smiled at Greg.

" How is it?" seriously, he asked. " You got the wire?"

Greg moved impatiently. " Yeh. They read it to me. Was there anybody in court?"

Sloane bent his head to the wire mesh that flanked the glass. It was necessary. Either you heard or saw your visitor. You took your choice.

" I went there. They crucified you, Greg. Bryant did his

best but you hadn't a chance. They're not going to bother about *law*, Greg."

Fifteen minutes, Greg kept thinking. "I know," he said. He could smell the other's face lotion, imagine the smooth feel of his linen. "What about Judith—was she in court?"

"I told her to keep away." Sloane talked fast. "There was nothing she could do. She was better with the kids down at Henley." He chose his words carefully. "Greg—Bryant says they'd have given you more time if you'd appealed against sentence instead of conviction."

More time! How much more? If you've already got ten years, what can it matter if they give you fifteen! If you couldn't see the end of a sentence, what difference how long it was!

He waited till the patrolling warder had passed. "They can drop dead," he said flatly, "Bryant, too. A copper, a lawyer, a thief. They all piss in the same pot." Three thousand pounds he'd paid the lawyer—to get ten years.

Sloane spoke sharply and Greg heard his own voice, dangerously high. He nodded. "O.K. Let it go."

"It was the money, Greg," urged Sloane. "Nobody beats them for twenty-eight thousand and walks out of it. *You* ought to know it." Overhead, the round clock on the wall ticked off the minutes. Sloane's voice poured through the mesh in a parody of indignation. "'Not one penny of this money recovered yet the man has the impertinence to appeal!'—that was the Lord Chief Justice, Greg."

It was as if mention of money silenced them both. Greg was first to speak, his words barely audible. "You've *got* to help me, Sloane. You've got to get me out of here." He strained, trying to gauge the effect of his words.

The dark man moved his head and they stared briefly at one another through the glass. Sloane nodded. A shadow moved on the glass and Greg waited till the warder had passed. "I can't take any more chances, smuggling letters out." He was whispering into the grille. "You know the cell number. I'll hang a cloth on the bars. Saturday, Sloane. Saturday?"

Sloane took off a glove. For a second, the two men stood, palms flat against the glass. Once again, Sloane nodded. The jailer stood behind them.

"Five more minutes."

They talked of nothing till the man came back to rap again with his key. *Christ!* thought Greg. *A man and a key!*

" Time's up, Gregory."

He joined the group by the water-pipes and watched Sloane to the Main Gate. As he went through the wicket, Sloane raised a hand in salutation then disappeared.

It was Thursday. He had three days and three nights to wait. Easy enough to rationalize the failure of his appeal. But always there'd been the faint hope that a smart lawyer might have figured out some legal angle. Sloane was right. You couldn't beat them for twenty-eight grand and walk out of the case. This is what he'd bargained for from the beginning. Without any fireworks, the cops had been able to prove his guilt.

Back in the tailor's shop, Greg watched the clock, ramming the blunt needle through the dirt-crusted mail-bag. It was four-thirty and the discipline officer gave the signal to stop work. " Cease Labour " as they loved to put it in their jargon. In the nine weeks that he'd been in Wandsworth Greg hadn't washed in the shop. One bucket of lukewarm water between thirty men, the hell with it! For the rest of the cons, it was a chance to snatch a forbidden word under the nose of the screw. But Greg didn't talk. Even where talking was allowed, on the rings during exercise period, he didn't talk. For an hour each day, Greg made the circuit in complete silence though they made you walk in pairs.

He lined up, arms outstretched, to be searched. The door from the tailor's shop was fifteen feet from the entrance to the cell-block. A bright hanging lamp made a splash of light in the winter murk. Three jailers covered the space between the two buildings as the men filed into their cells.

Greg was located in the " cockpit," D 1/12, on the basement floor of the prison. Without turning his head, he slammed his door shut from inside. The button hit the door jamb and the heavy tongue of the lock shot home. Outside, a white enamelled door handle was now in horizontal position, showing that the door was properly fastened.

He kicked off his shoes and put on the crude cloth slippers. This was the best part of the day—when " they " left you alone. From five, after supper, till seven the next morning, the door would open just once, when a pint of milkless and sugarless cocoa was served and the patrol made sure you were there. At nine, the light in the cell was extinguished from the outside.

Mechanically, he spread the coarse calico cloth on his table. Already they were unlocking the doors for supper. It was the landing screw, Griffiths, who opened the door. He put his red face inside the cell.

" Tea up, Canada." Griffiths was supposed to be one of the " good screws ". " I heard your appeal got turned down." The orderly neared with a bucket of tea and the jailer's tone changed. " Get your woodwork scrubbed, Gregory, and don't let me have to tell you again."

The fiery face vanished. On Greg's table were two tailor-made cigarettes. He considered his supper: 8 oz. bread, ½ oz. margarine, 1 oz. cheese and a pint of tea. He had no complaints. You couldn't starve on the diet. He watched as the door was tried from the outside, heard the spring-loaded handle flipped. The margarine always tasted of fish. He sprinkled it with salt. Salt and water, as much as you wanted, Griffiths always said. Suddenly he stood with his ear against the crack in the door. It was time for the shift of jailers to change over.

In each cell block there were four galleries, forty-eight cells on each gallery. Five cell blocks in the main prison. Up on the other galleries, they were sleeping three in a cell. Three classes of prisoners avoided that final indignity—queers, stir-crazy guys and those doing long sentences. As a location, the cockpit wasn't popular. Often the communal lavatories overflowed, leaving the floors wet with a sickly reek of excrement and carbolic. And down there, the cells were dark, even in the long fine days when first he'd arrived, the cell had been dark. On the credit side, the jail's antiquated heating system rumbled its way through the bowels of the building. His cell was fifteen degrees warmer than those above. There was another and all-important advantage. The night patrol had to pass directly over his head to reach the iron stairway that led to the cockpit. On the stone-flagged gallery above, a loose flag tipped whenever weight was placed on it. And the handrail on the stairs creaked. Some of the screws tripped cunningly on felt-soled slippers once they had reached the basement floor. The flap of the spyhole moved almost soundlessly. With innocent face Greg was accustomed to turn, acknowledging the cold fish-eye with a nod.

He'd have to stop that. Better they weren't aware that you knew they were there. The loose flag and creaking handrail warned him as effectively as any alarm bell.

His plate and cup washed, he lit one of Griffiths's cigarettes, padding from door to window. Without looking, he knew every inch of his cell. In the window there were twenty-four small panes of glass in a cast-iron frame. On the outside, four flat bars of mild steel set so that it was impossible for even a midget to pass through. The basement cell windows were at breast height. On the upper galleries they were high in the cell wall and difficult to reach.

It had taken Greg eight weeks to perfect his plan of escape, going over each detail with dogged persistence. Timing the night patrols both in the cell block and in the prison grounds. He had taken weeks, standing fully dressed in the dark, watching the outside patrol as he passed into the light from the tailor's shop and paused to punch the clock on the wall. Three times, during the night, the patrol made his rounds. Ten p.m., one a.m. and six a.m. The screws varied, the times never. It had been hard work, listening for the tell-tale flag and handrail that signalled the descent of the inside patrol. Leaping into bed, fully dressed, straining to hear the man in the grounds yet watching the spyhole. The clock from the chapel struck at quarter-hour intervals and gave him a time bearing.

It was easier to break into jail than out. To beat this place he needed help. The eighteen feet wall was unguarded on the north where the railway ran parallel for one hundred and fifty yards. For a man on the outside to duck over the fence from the Common, under the bridge and along the embankment was simple. At that point, he would be no more than thirty yards in a direct line from Greg's cell. With an extending or rope ladder, he could scale the wall, avoid the night patrol and reach the dark shelter of the cell block.

Somewhere, Greg had had to take a premature chance in order to give Sloane the essentials. Luck had been with him. A Pole had smuggled out the letter, God knows how or where the guy had concealed the closely-written strips of cigarette paper. But he had delivered them to Sloane and claimed ten pounds. Greg had no qualms—the note had been carefully worded. Of itself, innocuous—combined with Sloane's visits, a pattern for escape.

Quarter to eight sounded with the clank of a cracked anvil. Greg started to make his bed. For the next two nights he needed as much sleep as possible.

The monotony of Friday was broken by an unexpected cell search in the morning before work. It was nine. Outside the window, the cement walks glistened with hoar frost. A vague movement to the end of the block caught his eye. With practised speed, Greg checked the scanty cell furniture. At that hour, a screw outside meant that a block search was under way. Cells and galleries. As soon as the men heard cell doors opening and bells being tested, contraband hurtled from fifty windows. Old newspapers, unauthorized books, razor blades, all the jealously hoarded rubbish that meant loss of remission if found.

It was the outside patrol's job, for the most part done in arbitrary style, to mark the offending windows.

Greg had nothing. But he examined every inch of his cell. Cell doors were open all day with cleaners running about in the blocks. Greg trusted nobody in the place. This was no time for him to foul out. The indicators that marked the source of the cell bells were being tested. The mechanical and ancient system creaked and strained over yards of wire. Suddenly the door opened. They hunted in pairs, as always. This time, Greg hadn't done badly. It was Griffiths and a jailer he'd never seen before. Some of the bums weren't above finding whatever they wanted to find in a man's cell.

"Bring your blankets and sheets outside!"

The stranger sprung the lock and went in, closing the door behind him. On the gallery outside, Greg shook his bedding piece by piece as Griffiths watched.

"How's your wife taking it, Gregory?"

Greg moved his shoulders. When it suited them, the screws accepted you as a human being but only when it suited them. Griffiths was one of the worst offenders. He had a phoney friendliness that came under the heading "Handling the men".

Greg knew that there was one reason why anyone should want to gain his confidence now. They had all tried it. The insurance investigator who had visited him in Brixton while he waited trial. "*We could make it easy for you, Gregory.*" Then Porter and Lee with the monkey shrewdness and glib thieves' patter of Flying Squad officers.

"Why don't you be sensible, Greg. You've got no form in this country. We can do a lot for you."

Sure, they all could, till it came to the pay-off. Then you'd find it was strictly a one-sided bargain. Their side.

Greg knew that to these people he represented £28,000. That and nothing more. That first night in Wandsworth, a stranger had thrown him a half-ounce of coarse black tobacco and a spill with papers and matches. Samaritan, thought Greg, smiling secretly. The next day, after the parade for the Governor and the Chaplain, the stranger picked Greg up on the exercise ring. After five minutes of the man's studiously incurious conversation, Greg interrupted:

"You want to hear about my case?"

The man looked away. "I read something . . ."

"I didn't do it," said Greg.

They walked in silence till they reached the latrines where the man left him.

The strange screw left Greg's cell. The bars and the frame of the window had been sounded, the walls and floor inspected, mattress pummelled. He brushed a few strands of coir from his tunic.

"You want to get those windows cleaned," he told Greg. "If *you* don't want to see out of them, the next man might."

Friday was canteen day. That week, he'd done his task in the shop and no more. At the canteen, he signed for two shillings and bought ten tailor-made cigarettes. After Sunday night, he'd be buying his own.

Saturday morning. Only a half-day to work. When he got back from the shop, there was a letter from Judith. Attached was a mimeographed slip from the Censor's Office.

INFORM YOUR CORRESPONDENT THAT FUTURE LETTERS MUST BE CONFINED TO TWO DOUBLE OR FOUR SINGLE SHEETS. FAILURE TO COMPLY WILL MEAN THE RETURN OF THE LETTERS.

He read his wife's letter carefully, apprehensive of some chance remark that might have intrigued the censor. His mail was read twice. Once by the censor and once by the Deputy-Governor. Greg knew that and more than they imagined. Only Sloane and he were aware that tomorrow night he'd be out of the place. Certainly not Judith. As soon as the hue went out for him, her life would be misery. Each step that she took—even the kids maybe—would be subject to police surveillance. When he was first arrested, it had been like that. And it had continued till they realized that she had no idea what he had done with the money. Nobody knew. That was his strength.

It had nothing to do with trust. Rather, there were different sorts of trust. You trusted a man with your liberty, your wife, your honour. Maybe there were five or six people on the outside he could put in that category. Trusting them with twenty-eight thousand pounds was something again.

TWO

FROM the moment that Greg had met the Nicholson woman, he had accepted the fact that it would be a straight swop. His liberty for twenty-eight thousand pounds. There'd been no chance of a show of innocence. Greg had met the woman casually in Canada House when both had been calling for mail. There was nothing in Mrs. Nicholson's appearance that signalled promise to him. A dour little woman of fifty, she wore sensible shoes and clothes. Beside her, Greg waited his turn at the mail desk.

The clerk riffed through the sheaf of letters with practised speed. " Three for you, Mrs. Nicholson."

She fumbled, fingers clumsy in thick gloves. An envelope fell at Greg's feet. He retrieved it and she nodded her thanks. It was a week before he saw her again. She was standing on the corner of Villiers Street and the Strand. Lost, he thought without interest. As he reached her, he tipped his hat on an impulse.

She braced sturdy legs as the wind whipped her coat round her shapeless body. Surely, he thought, she didn't think this was a pick-up.

" Canada House," he smiled, " You were getting your mail."

Her washed-blue eyes showed recognition. " Of course." They moved to the shelter of a doorway. It was noon. The narrow pavement was packed with office workers. Four-lane traffic moved east and west, the buses bullying, the cabs peevish with thin horns.

She shook her head. " This is worse than Yonge Street."

" Toronto?"

She nodded.

" Me, too," he said.

She hesitated. " Do you know where this place is?" She gave him a slip of paper. " I've been fifteen minutes trying to find out." She said " out " as only a Torontonian will.

The paper she proffered bore the name and address of the best-known numismatist in the country; an address that was on the books of a half-dozen thieves Greg knew, including his own.

In the three safes at Dodds were coins that represented a quarter million pounds, gold value alone. The two moose-jawed brothers who ran Dodds were rich, contemptuous of a vulgar era and no fools. Their safes were impregnable, their office patrolled and their keys deposited each night in the bank.

Greg walked Mrs. Nicholson down towards the river. At the door to the old shabby house, she gave him her hand. "You did that as well as a courier, young man. Come to tea some afternoon if you've nothing better to do." She gave him the number of a house in Green Street.

He walked up to lunch, considering this rugged old battle-axe with a Mayfair address. She was beginning to intrigue him. Three weeks, she said, she'd been in England. He could think of no obvious reason why a woman like Mrs. Nicholson would be visiting Dodds. In Greg's book, anything that wasn't obvious was worth investigating. Already he knew that he'd take her up on the invitation to tea.

It was a small house in Green Street with an Adam door and a wrought-iron railing. His knock was answered by an elderly maid who showed him into a drawing room elegant with Chippendale. Mrs. Nicholson in something that looked like carpeting was incongruous as she poured tea from a Meissen service. After a few minutes grudgingly given to Greg's fictitious account of himself, she started a monologue with frank pleasure. She talked and Greg listened.

Harriet Nicholson was a widow from the Humber Valley section of Toronto. Inheritance of the estate of a second cousin had been an unforeseen event. There was the house in Green Street, enough mining stock to enable her to run it and the Bartrop Collection—seven hundred mediaeval gold coins of value. For twenty years, she had worked five days a week to support a husband with two-thirds of a lung. She talked about his death and her inheritance with the same lack of emotion. All she allowed herself was a regret that the second had not come before the first.

Greg brought her back to the Bartrop Collection. Seven hundred gold coins were cascading through his fingers. His mind was busy; a sovereign, a louis d'or, a five dollar piece. Mrs. Nicholson was easily encouraged. She'd spent a lifetime in a cheap frame house, juggling a secretary's salary against mounting doctor's bills. Not since she was a girl had she owned anything that wasn't of practical or immediate use. Beauty in belongings she didn't appreciate. To her, the Bartrop Collection represented idle capital. Not only was she ignorant of the difference between a groat and a noble. She didn't care, she said. He laughed.

Since her arrival in England, there had been a dozen enquiries after the cousin's collection, dealers, collectors, representatives of the two household names in antique auctioneering. Dodds, where she had been the previous week, had offered her thirty thousand pounds for the coins. Greg watched her bridle, turning down the corners of her thin sexless mouth. Maybe they thought she'd never heard of a dealer's ring! She had a laugh as disillusioned as that of a bartender. Meanwhile, the collection was insured for thirty-six thousand pounds. And for the first time in her life she could afford to wait.

Greg's words came almost without thinking. Instinct prompted him that this was the moment to make his first move. " Funny you should talk about dealers' rings. There's a guy in the business over here—we were classmates at McGill—in six years he's become one of the biggest men in the field. By bucking the rings."

Though she made no comment, he knew that what had been said had registered. They said goodbye if not with friendliness with a readiness to listen to one another. It was the first of many visits to the house in Green Street. The idea that dealers were trying to combine against her grew in Mrs. Nicholson's mind. The offers she had had for the Bartrop Collection were close enough to establish her certainty.

At Greg's third visit, she took him up to the second floor room where coins gleamed bright in glass cases. In the corner was the modern safe that held the most valuable coins. Mrs. Nicholson opened it, pulling out trays where edge-set coins nestled in black velvet. Gold royals, angels and half-angels. A double sovereign that she said was worth eight hundred pounds. She showed him the catalogue, lovingly done in crabbed long-hand. She closed the safe door composedly.

Carefully, he mentioned burglars and she laughed. " Everything's insured. In any case, what would they do, there's an alarm direct to the police station!"

He left the house, uncertain. He had no scruples about robbing her—he couldn't see how it would be done.

Hot jewellery had three values, insurable, replaceable and obtainable. In a crooked market Greg could hope to get a third of the loot's intrinsic worth. As a collection or piece by piece, Mrs. Nicholson's property would be impossible to sell straight. It would have to be crooked. And who the hell would want the stuff except as old gold. The value of the coins in the melting pot would dwindle from thirty thousand pounds to a fraction. Maybe just once in a lifetime a man had a chance like this. There *was* a way to beat this old bag and he had to find it.

From that point it had to be an unequal contest. A middle-aged unsophisticate in a no-holds-barred tussle with someone who knew too many of the wrong answers. Greg was quick to sense that Mrs. Nicholson's cautious greed could be turned to his advantage. Somehow, he had to get authority to market the coins.

For the next few weeks, Greg saw a great deal of the Canadian woman. That first impulsive lie about his friend in the antique business became the framework of his plan. He steered Mrs. Nicholson to the decorous sales rooms off Saint James. They watched as a half-dozen historic homes went under the hammer. Mrs. Nicholson nodded grimly as he pointed out " the ring ". He was merely confirming what she believed already. Casually, he mentioned Bill—the mythical classmate turned art dealer. Always Bill was flying to New York with the pick of the Ludlow Castle tapestries, or buying the Wicklow glass by private treaty. Looting these treasures from under the noses of the ubiquitous ring. Bill's was a simple formula, Greg said. He paid high prices for the best and sold higher. Mrs. Nicholson was cautiously impressed.

Greg gave her lunch at the Ritz. Every day now, he was driving up from Henley, maintaining the fiction of a struggling playwright. More than that about him, Mrs. Nicholson didn't know. Her liking for him showed in her concern at his extravagance. She considered the menu with distaste, ordered an omelette and stared down the wine waiter. Greg's fantasy had him cast in the rôle of a man with a mission. He wanted to do for Canada what the great American playwrights had done for the States. Somehow, in England, he would find the break to make this possible.

As long as it cost her nothing, Mrs. Nicholson was a believer in the advancement of Canadian culture. She sipped her coffee, disapproving of its cost yet determined to have her money's worth. " What happens in the meanwhile?" she asked. " When your money runs out, I mean?"

Through the long windows of the restaurant, the trees in the Park shivered in the breeze. The first brown leaves spun lazily to the ground. " I dunno," he answered, " I certainly don't know. *Anything* could happen." The skin crinkled round his eyes. He was convincing as a gallant tilter at windmills. " For instance, you could give me a job."

" Me? A job doing what?" she asked curiously.

" God knows." He locked both hands behind his head and then met her enquiry. " Selling the Bartrop Collection, for instance."

She was quiet. Almost as though he had voiced some impropriety. Without haste—his eyes honest—he explained. His friend Bill Landers wasn't the sort of guy Greg would ask for money. But for a chance to earn money—that, yes. She knew what she wanted for the collection. Once he had the figure, he was sure that he could interest his friend.

" And if I did," she said slowly. " Would you expect anything from me?"

" Of course." The frank grin always paid off—" That's the whole idea. You get more than you would otherwise and I get a percentage."

" From your friend as well!" She waved a hand. " Don't tell me. I know how these things are done."

He acknowledged her shrewdness. " Look, Mrs. Nick. You're the last person I'd try to fool. But you tell me what difference it could make to you. What matters is that you'd be getting more than you would otherwise."

She settled her monstrous hat. " Shall we go? I feel as though breathing costs money in this place."

At the door to the house in Green Street, she gave him her hand. " Find out if this man is interested first. Then we'll talk about prices."

Greg's nine years in Europe had been packed with larceny for the most part abetted by the sad-faced Sloane, an artist in appropriation. Between them there was the strong tie of men who repeatedly risk their liberty together.

Sloane was cast ideally as the crusading dealer. From the time he made his first appearance, the production gathered speed. He called at the house in Green Street and left Mrs. Nicholson with a feeling of canny approval for him. The money she was asking for the Bartrop Collection was the price for which the coins were insured. Greg gave it a week then relayed the news from the supposed dealer. He was offering a thousand pounds less. Mrs. Nicholson accepted. Nothing happened that demanded references. From Paris, Sloane sent a letter. He would be in London the following week, pay his cheque into the Canadian woman's bank and arrange for the shipment of the collection.

"They're already sold," Greg told Mrs. Nicholson. "I saw him filling out the forms for the export licence. Some American, they're going to."

It was Saturday with Mrs. Nicholson out of town for the week-end. Monday was the day when Sloane was supposed to arrive from Paris. In fact, he had been back in England for a week. It was late on Friday afternoon when Greg reached the office of the Dodds brothers, Dealers in Rare Coins. The Bartrop Collection was for sale, he informed them. He acted as Mrs. Nicholson's agent. He produced the letter of authority he had induced her to give him.

The price asked was thirty thousand pounds, the original Dodds offer. The brothers had a natural curiosity about Greg's part in the sale. In spite of the courtesy with which they negotiated, their inquisitiveness was apparent.

Greg was unknown as a dealer, obviously ignorant of the aesthetic values of the collection he was selling. He was frank. Mrs. Nicholson was a woman with a fixed mistrust of the commercial world. Her suspicion was so dogmatic that she found even interviews with them unpleasant. Greg explained that he appeared as a friend in a sale that was inevitable. The small percentage he would make was with Mrs. Nicholson's approval.

The brothers accepted the explanation. Mr. Ernest—the elder bowed slightly—would arrange for collection. Mrs. Nicholson would make her wishes known about the manner of payment.

Greg shook his head. Had it been as simple as that, the whole thing could have been settled by phone. Smiling apology for the vagaries of a foolish woman, he said that the brothers would be unwelcome at Green Street. On Monday morning, he would deliver the Bartrop Collection at the Dodds' office. Wearing their dignity like a badge, the brothers bowed agreement.

Greg buttoned his coat. One last thing. The purchase price must be paid in cash. Trying to ignore the sudden silence, he busied himself with hat and gloves.

Mr. Ernest cleared his throat. " It's by no means usual . . ."

" Entirely contrary to the firm's policy," his brother supported.

Greg moved a hand. " No doubt. Personally, I think Mrs. Nicholson's crazy. But . . ." His grin showed indifference to large amounts of cash money. His hand on the door, a readiness to take the business elsewhere, if necessary.

The younger brother spoke. " An open cheque, possibly. For our books, you'll understand, Mr. Gregory."

Greg turned the door handle. " You've met Mrs. Nicholson. I'm sorry, gentlemen."

Through the window, a barge on the river below was being unloaded. He kept his eyes on the boom of the crane as it swung out then dipped.

" At what time may we expect you on Monday?" said Mr. Ernest quietly.

" Eleven. Good-morning, gentlemen."

Already, the streets were packed with homebound crowds, their work finished until Monday. Tomorrow was Saturday and according to the rules of the game, there was nothing that could go sour. Over the years, Greg had kept in circulation by putting himself in the other man's place. He reduced the Dodds brothers' concern to two considerations. Whether they were buying genuine articles—whether the seller had the right to sell. Both objections he had met. There had been disinclination over paying cash. But such deals *were* customary—that much he knew. Mrs. Nicholson was away till Monday. Nobody at Dodds could communicate with her till then. And for Monday, he had plans.

Mrs. Nicholson was at Tonbridge. The aged maid at Green Street gave him the number readily enough. No, she said, there had been no other calls for her mistress. Late on Saturday night, Greg rang the Canadian woman. There was the smallest hitch. His friend had phoned from Paris. Her signature was necessary on some papers connected with the export licence. If she could meet the dealer's plane at London Airport, she could fill in the forms and collect her cheque at the same time. He explained that his friend was taking the next plane to Rome.

She was not enthusiastic. Patiently, he explained that this was something nobody could do but herself. No export licence, no sale. The observation impressed her. She agreed to meet the dealer in the main hall at London Airport between eleven and eleven-thirty.

He replaced the receiver. His mouth was dry. One more hurdle, the toughest of all. He slept lightly and was up at seven on Monday. After breakfast, he drove up to London. At ten, he went to a phone booth a hundred yards from Green Street. His first call was to Tonbridge. Mrs. Nicholson had left by road for the airport. The next call was to her house. The maid answered. Mrs. Nicholson was ill, he told the woman. She was to take the ten forty-five from Charing Cross Station to Tonbridge. Certain articles of her mistress's clothing were to be packed and brought. Nervously, the old woman repeated his instructions. He drove directly to Green Street and parked where he had full view of the Nicholson house. In twenty minutes, the maid left in a cab. She carried a suitcase.

Ten-fifteen. There was nobody on the street but a milkman. For two weeks, Greg had been carrying a spare key to the house, lifted from a drawer in the hall. He left the car and crossed the street.

Inside, the house was hushed. As he went up the stairs, a clock behind him chimed. In Mrs. Nicholson's bedroom, drawers in a tallboy had been left open by the hurrying maid. Methodically, he looked for a key to the safe. There would be one somewhere in the house. Twice, Mrs. Nicholson had come from her room with the key in her hand. It was rare that a spare key was not kept for use in emergency.

The pile of stockings and underwear grew on the carpet beside him. He was committed now. If the venture went sour on him, he was in trouble. None the less, if he was unable to find the key, the phone calls, the bogus dealer—there was no way he might explain any of it. This was no sly swindle to be forgotten if unproductive. Greg accepted it as an exchange. Twenty-eight thousand pounds against his liberty. With an insignificant police record, he rated his chances as no worse than a five year sentence. Three years and four months, he'd serve. Nearly ten thousand pounds for every year. He'd waited a long time for a chance this good.

Downstairs in the kitchen the refrigerator clicked loudly. He ran to the open door and listened. A buzzer sounded sharply. Someone was at the front door. On tiptoe, he crossed to the window. It was the milkman. Still, behind the curtain, Greg waited as the man deposited a bottle of milk then walked away. Once, he glanced back as if puzzled.

Working faster, Greg rummaged through drawers and closets

till he found a small black jewel box. Inside was a strange assortment of beads, brooches with elephant hair, a cheap engagement ring and some worthless cameos. In the bottom section of the box was a thin bright key with an intricate business end. It bore a superfluous label—" Safe ".

Like a hurdler, he went up the stairs. The small museum was open. At the back of the safe was the switch that controlled the burglar alarm. The button was down. For a second he was irresolute. Occasionally, alarm switches were fitted upside down. An extra precaution. A thief lacking the knowledge whether the alarm was already set ran further hazard. It was too late to worry about that. His hunch was that Mrs. Nicholson, away for the week-end, would leave the alarm switched through to Savile Row Police Station.

He flipped the button up and took the safe key. One full turn to the right then a half turn. There was the dead feel of an open lock. Turning the brass handle, he pulled the safe door. The coins gleamed bright in their velvet bed. He'd brought a canvas hold-all from the bedroom. He started to pack the trays of coins. Against his will, he was wasting time. Running to the window that overlooked the street. Nothing outside had changed. Twenty yards up, the milkman was going about his business unconcerned.

The collection he delivered to Dodds had to be complete. The showcases holding some of the coins were locked. He broke the flimsy fastenings. As he bent over the glass, he saw his reflection. He was still wearing his hat. Blood oozed from an unfelt cut on his thumb. The usual precaution of wearing gloves had been useless. From Canada House to Green Street, his true identity had been established as positively as any fingerprints could do it.

Again the hall clock chimed. Ten forty-five. He went down the stairs, staggering under the weight of the gold. Using the phone in the drawing room, he called Dodds. Mr. Ernest answered. The brothers were waiting. The dealer's voice sounded unstrained, without suspicion.

Greg left the canvas bag in the hall and brought the car to the door. He drove carefully. He had maybe an hour before all hell broke loose. At the office near the Adelphi, two boys were waiting to help with the bag. He wore his gloves now to hide the blood-soaked handkerchief on his thumb. He followed the bag into the brothers' office.

There was a chair in front of a felt-covered table. With an effort, he took the glass of sherry the younger brother proffered. The three men were alone in the office.

Almost reverently, the dealers lifted the trays from the bag. Greg let the heavy wine roll in his mouth, controlling the shake in his hand.

Mr. Ernest's voice was flat and accusing. " What made you do this, Mr. Gregory?"

Slowly, Greg turned. The dealer was holding the bag with the coins that had been loose in the cases. Greg made no reply.

Shaking his head, Mr. Ernest took each coin from the bag, laying it on the felt table top with delicacy. " Completely irresponsible. Surely you realize the damage this sort of handing does. A scratch—the slightest blemish—and the value of a coin is dissipated." He grumbled as though at a child. " No apparent damage, thank goodness."

It was almost eleven-thirty. A secretary was taking the particulars that Mr. Ernest dictated. The younger brother checked each coin against the list with terrifying slowness. It was five to twelve before the catalogue of coins was complete. Greg refused the second sherry. He had to meet Mrs. Nicholson immediately, he said.

The package the girl brought in was about twelve inches in height, eighteen across. Mr. Ernest broke the seal on the banded brown paper to expose six thousand five-pound notes. Black and white symbols of success. Sight of them eased Greg's nervousness. There were sixty packets, each containing a hundred notes. Apparently, Mr. Ernest was ready to count each one.

The thumb was paining him now. Thought of what was going on at the airport persisted. Time. He still needed time. He had no illusions as to what Mrs. Nicholson would do as soon as she realized the implications of the scheme.

He addressed Mr. Ernest. " I suppose this comes from the bank?" He pointed at the stacked money.

The dealer bowed slightly.

" Then let's consider it counted." The bow was repeated.

The canvas bag was to carry the notes. Greg signed two receipts and left the office. Somehow, he resisted the urge to run. Backing the car, ready to drive north, he took a quick glance at the office window. Something at the curtain moved. He could not be sure if it were a hand or a face. Slamming into first gear, he sent the car roaring up the narrow street.

He garaged at the back of Covent Garden market, sitting in the car until the attendant had gone. All but four of the bundles of notes he packed in two large cardboard files. Carrying these, he walked east to Kingsway where he took a cab. Three times, he changed vehicle, doubling his tracks. By one o'clock, his job was done. They could arrest him as soon as they liked. The money was safe.

He walked quickly along Oxford Street, treading the gutter to make better time. A block north, he rang a doorbell. Sloane opened the door, his dark face creased in welcome. Inside the flat, the big man gave Greg the half-caress, half-shove, that acknowledged victory.

" No trouble?"

Greg eased his back into the chair and closed his eyes. A red stain had spread on the yellow of his glove. " No trouble." He went into his pocket and threw the two packets of notes on the table. " There's two grand there. It's certain the bank will have the numbers. You're on your own with it now, Sloane."

The other man nodded. " I've made arrangements in Paris. Brulfert's ready to pay three thousand five hundred francs for a fiver." He looked at Greg curiously. " Where are you going now?"

" Home," said Greg. " If I get there."

Sloane moved round the room, drawing curtains as if he could shut out impending disaster. " Have you had any food?" Greg shook his head. " Then you'd better eat first," said Sloane.

He was tired and his thumb ached. Maybe a piece of the splintered glass remained. " Sloane!" he said suddenly.

The dark man turned, filling the doorway with his bulk. His face was incurious, almost expressionless. From the chair, Greg watched him.

" The law's going to pick me up before I get home." Greg's voice was flat. " They'll take me to Savile Row. Stay away from the court but see that there's a lawyer there."

Sloane moved a hand. " What about the money. Your end of it, Greg?" His voice was concerned. " I'm clean enough. I can be in Paris and back by tomorrow. Brulfert'll take the lot for the same price."

Greg closed his eyes again. " By the time I get out, those notes and the numbers will be history. They're going to pay me a hundred cents on the dollar." He stripped the glove from his left hand. Under the blood-soaked handkerchief, the flesh was ripped from first to second knuckle.

Sloane fetched warm water, cotton and tape. As Greg dressed his wound, the big man fixed ham and eggs. When Greg had eaten, his friend took the tray.

" You're sure you don't want me to do anything with Brulfert?"

Greg looked at his watch. Three o'clock. " Not a thing. When the time comes, I'll take care of things. In the meanwhile the money's safe enough." At the front door he turned. " Savile Row. And see the lawyer's there."

The big man's pressure on Greg's arm was reassuring, friendly. Suddenly Greg was grateful for Sloane. For the certainty, the solidity that the man represented.

" Don't worry. He'll be there." Sloane looked at him with affection. " Be lucky," he said, and closed the door.

Greg picked up his car at the garage. Any moment now. A call to the licensing office and the police would determine the number of his car. He drove out at speed on the Great West Road. He passed through Slough and Maidenhead without incident. At the bottom of the long hill down into Henley, a figure stepped into the road, hand outstretched. Greg braked sharply. This was it, he thought. Under the trees, in a driveway, a police car waited. The man showed a warrant card.

" You're Paul Gregory?" Greg nodded. The man placed a hand on his sleeve. " You know what this is about? "

Greg kept his eyes on the man's face. " No. But I want to bet you do."

THREE

HE tore Judith's letter into small pieces. Not that it made much difference. The police would check every address on his visiting and correspondence list since he'd been in jail. They took a break from a maximum security prison with seriousness. His photograph would be in the *Police Gazette*, in police stations, railway terminals, all the ports. In the newspapers, maybe. Every busybody in the country would be falling over himself to do a little amateur detection, eager to sneak meanly into the headlines. On the run, in this small country, a man lasted just as long as his luck. Sloane was his ace-in-the-hole. There wasn't a cop, a jailer, who knew where the man lived. Each visiting order Greg had sent to Sloane had gone to a pick-up address.

There was a clatter of keys on the gallery outside. The screws were back from their lunch-hour break. In a minute, his door would be unlocked for the afternoon exercise period. He started to put on his shoes. Lacing them up, he found himself whistling. He remembered Sloane.

During the week, after the five o'clock lock-up, the cell blocks were quiet for no more than an hour. At six, the social and educational life of the jail erupted on to the galleries. Convicts attending French classes, handicrafts and choral singing had their doors unlocked. With the troubled in spirit who somehow managed to find lipstick in jail, the Choral Society was popular. They went golden-haired and powdered, in the best-fitting uniforms their admirers were able to produce with boot-leg tobacco. Once unlocked, they undulated to the assembly point where a gravel-gulleted jailer called their names from a roster. The fluting responses evoked a chorus of catcalls from the neighbouring cells.

For the men who were left in their small worlds, " screwed-up " was a word that could be understood in many contexts. The next two hours made a time of comparative peace. The patrols had keys but short of a swoop on a suspect and a special search, a suicide or one of the monotonous smash-ups, the patrols tended to forget their charges. Smash-ups—the methodical destruction of windows and cell furniture—worried the authorities. They were psychopathic indications that spelled trouble. To a hundred men behind locked doors the sound of a comrade being forcibly removed to the punishment cells meant but one thing. The screws were beating him up. Nine times out of ten, this was an accurate assessment. From every cell within earshot came the pounding of tin jugs and earthenware chamber pots. It ceased only when the jailers rattled their keys threateningly against the iron banisters. Through this inferno gyrated the ministers of the gospel, the priests and " unofficial visitors " bent on their charitable missions.

Saturdays and Sundays, the evenings were quieter, if longer. There were no evening classes and the traffic in the block was little. Later, the dreary shuffle of despondent men in ill-fitting shoes announced the arrival of the day's receptions, to be watered, warned and locked up.

On his back, Greg stared at the whitewash on the arched ceiling. After nine weeks in Wandsworth, his senses were heightened. Like those of an animal whose use of them was the difference between life and death. In a jail, as in a jungle, to have quick warning of danger was imperative. From the cell on his left, a faint ticking sound filtered through the foot-thick partition wall. Greg was able to identify it readily enough. The man was using a makeshift but forbidden tinder lighter.

The cocoa count was taken by one of the young jailers he feared and detested. An ex-N.C.O. whose cap peak had been cut in Guards fashion, shading his eyes in a way that was vaguely sinister. The jailer crashed back the door, pushing his face into the cell.

" All right?"

Greg nodded. " Yes, thanks—sir."

One long month ago, he would have ignored the ridiculous enquiry. It had taken that time for him to realize that it was not enough to be there when the jailers took the count. He had to make it appear that he was grateful for being there. As the door closed, Greg heard the man's voice.

" Forty-six."

And the next would be " forty-seven " till at last the count was squared with the tally and the locking-up was signed.

I HAVE INSPECTED THE CELLS, LOCKS AND PRISONERS ON D I GALLERY AND CERTIFY THEM TO BE CORRECT AND IN ORDER.

He took off his jacket and trousers and got into bed, pulling the sheets to his neck. It seemed endless till he heard the loose slate on the gallery above tip under the weight of the night-watchman. Then the handrail creaked. Seconds afterwards, eyes closed, Greg heard the spyhole moved cautiously. Then the light button was snapped and his cell in darkness. From the cell on his left came the usual rhythmic snoring. Another hour before the outside patrol passed on his rounds.

He got out of bed and put on his trousers, sitting under the window. Though the heating had been turned off for the night, the pipes were still warm to his body. By flattening his face against the wall, he was able to follow the angle of the building with his eyes. Between the cell block and Tailors' Shop, the bright arc high on a bracket threw a light that penetrated the edge of the dark exercise ground. On the wall, at shoulder-height, was a wooden box. Inside, Greg knew, was a key on a chain.

Ten sounded from the chapel clock, muffled by the sleet that spattered the window panes. Like an actor who steps into a spotlight, the Yard Patrol appeared round the end of the cell block. He wore rubber boots, an oilskin and a protector that covered his cap, pulled down over his ears. His flashlight travelled the length of the building, hovering on windows and bars. Three times the light passed Greg's cell, aimed at the galleries above him. As the beam hit the basement, Greg moved from his window. For a second he waited then, cautiously, returned to his vantage point. The patrol blew on his fingers, punched the clock that was slung round his waist and disappeared clumsily into the obscurity.

Moving carefully in stockinged feet, Greg took his dish-cloth and tied it to the lateral bars outside his window. He put an ear to the wall that separated him from his left-hand neighbour. The snores were full and regular. On the other side, the cell was completely silent.

He had a sudden picture of a man who knew too much in there. Someone who was duplicating his movements. Who stood, as he stood, listening. These bastards were as much a hazard as the screws. In nine weeks, Greg thought, he'd witnessed every conceivable type of treachery among the people he had to live with. Impelled by greed, fear and hatred, they sold out one another to a common enemy and with great cunning. The anonymous notes addressed to the Governor, the Chief Officer, the Visiting Magistrates—these bits of paper were found in the locked boxes placed at the end of each cell block for prisoners to mail their letters. Usually, they were acted upon. A chance word overheard on the exercise ring, on the line that waited to use the lavatories, and a man found himself hauled from bed, stripped and searched.

As Greg moved back to the window, the quarter-hour chimed. He lit a cigarette, holding the flame cupped in his hand. There must be nothing—no unfamiliar sound or sight that could give anyone an urge to investigate. Twice in his short stay, men had been caught trying to tunnel out. Both times, it had been their comrades who had been first to detect the attempted break—who had drawn the attention of the block patrol by violently ringing their cell bells.

Something had to be holding Sloane! At the open pane in his window, Greg tried to see past the wet and the darkness to the prison wall. Sloane might come over at any point for a hundred yards. It was impossible to see past the brilliant light at the end of the block. *The dishcloth.* Tied as it was, near the end of the bar, it would be difficult to distinguish from outside. He moved it to the centre of the bar. It whipped in the wind with the sound of a pistol shot. In his hurry to control the flapping rag, his shoulder was rattling the loose window fixture. In spite of the cold, his mouth was parched.

Jesus! He ran to the door, ear at the crack. There was nothing to be heard but the wind. Then somewhere else, a window slammed loudly, echoing in the tall empty building.

For Sloane—in the certainty that his sad-faced partner would be over the wall—Greg had a childlike faith. Now, with a child's uncompromising insistence, he cursed Sloane's delay. This time-table represented hours spent standing through the night, sore-eyed with fatigue, till he knew for certain the movements of the patrols. Sloane's was the soft touch. He was on the outside, with every resource at his command. All he had to do was climb an eighteen feet wall with a rope or folding ladder. And avoid the patrol in the yard. It was Greg's time table that had made the last leg foolproof.

Nervously, he stubbed his cigarette. Almost without seeing now, his mind registered the scene outside. The hanging light, the sleet that drove the darkness against his window. Suddenly he flattened hard against the wall, following the definite change in the pattern of light and shade at the end of the building. A figure moved swiftly into the brightness then vanished into the basement area that flanked the bottom cells.

Greg waited, head averted. Something hard hit his window. He heard the pebble bounce on the concrete window ledge. He looked down. In the area, Sloane's face was barely discernible. He wore dark clothes and a cap. Greg moved a hand through the bars. Sloane crouched then sprang, both hands catching Greg's window ledge. Taking his weight on his right hand, he pushed a small flat package on to the sill. Then he dropped to the ground and stood motionless in the shadow. Standing on the water pipes, Greg put his hand through the loose iron frame and took the package. He waved once, then stood back from the window. Immobile, he waited as the other ran along the area and was lost in the gloom. Neither had spoken.

Greg undressed completely. In bed, he examined the package under the sheets. There was a note wrapped round the hard length of the parcel. He would have to wait till morning before he could read it. Through the heavy, oiled paper, he could feel the outline of twelve highspeed hacksaw blades. Putting them under his pillow, he turned on his side. He was asleep before his spyhole moved cautiously, some time later.

Sunday in Wandsworth, with the accent on godliness, gossip and a marked improvement in the diet sheet. Attendance at chapel was compulsory. Under the scrutiny of jailers seated on platforms, the congregation shuffled nervously at some visiting cleric's harangue. The kitchen tables dispensed a slice of recognizable meat and a couple of roast potatoes per man, carried to the cell and wolfed in a hurry. In the afternoon there was a concert. Earnest amateurs sang " Keep Right on to the End of the Road " and the prisoners tried to see the legs of the women in the party.

There was a skeleton staff of officials, adequate since for only an hour were the convicts out of the cell blocks. The one Medical Officer left on duty resented as a personal affront any complaint that could not be dealt with by one of the jailer-orderlies.

On D 1, a line of bored men waited to empty their chamber pots. The noon meal was collected, cafeteria style, to be taken to the cells. For breakfast, as Griffiths the jailer put it, there was room service. A basket of bread, two cans of porridge and a can of tea were placed where he could observe them from his desk—in the lavatory. Any sneak raid on the provender would meet with the jailer's scathing anger. He picked his teeth, abstractedly watching for cavalier disposal of chamber-pot moisture. As Griffiths repeatedly told his wife, he knew how to deal with prisoners. Psychology, he said. For most of his charges he had a contempt that he rarely showed. He was a jailhouse snob, using the same values as most of the convicts he guarded. The successful thieves impressed him. In the Officers' Mess, he bragged about Greg being on his gallery. The word " good " figured much in his vocabulary. He liked a " good " thief, was a " good " screw. His bonhomie deceived most. He was an undercover security man for the Governor, charged to detect corruption among the staff.

His slops emptied, Greg filled his water jug and took his cell card to Griffiths. " Put me down sick, will you, Mr. Griffiths?"

Griffiths took the card and copied the particulars into a book. Sunday morning applications were reduced to a minimum. If a prisoner had information to pass on, he might obtain an interview with the Governor or Chief Officer on Sunday. Otherwise not. In theory there were no approved hours for complaining sick. According to the rule card, a prisoner could ask for the Medical Officer at any hour of the night or day. Doing so was an easy way of landing yourself in a great deal of trouble.

Griffiths's face wore its usual shifty good humour. He gave Greg a wooden disc with a red cross painted on it. " Stick that on your door, Canada." Without change of expression, he roared at a man trying to scuttle from cell to lavatory, unobserved. " PUT YOUR SHOES ON!" He shook his head at Greg. " Dirty bugger," he commented. " Slopping about in his slippers." Idly his eye travelled to Greg's feet. He shook his beefy head again as he saw the shapeless grey slippers. " You and me's going to grow old together, Canada. You're going to have to change some of your ideas."

Greg hung the disc on the outside of his door and slammed the heavy wood into place. The Medical Officer made his rounds late on Sundays. The disc was a warning not to unlock Greg's cell till the doctor had been. After breakfast, Greg read Sloane's note. It was brief.

The rope will be immediately behind the Tailor's shop 10.5 *prompt. This side, you'll find a bag in the grass on the embankment. Be lucky!*

It was unsigned but he burnt it, throwing the ashes from the window. Whatever he did now was with certainty. He knew that he was going to beat this jail. He let his mind run on

Sloane. Maybe once in a lifetime, a man had a friend who would do what Sloane was doing for him.

After the breakfast patrol had gone his rounds, Greg sat at his table, angled close to the door. It was impossible for anyone outside to see what Greg's hands were doing. He had the hacksaw blades in front of him. They were in eight-inch lengths and had been carefully chosen for flexibility and strength. Twenty-four teeth to the inch, the best cutting gauge for the mild steel he had to deal with. He detached one side of the writing slate issued to every cell. The wooden slat made a perfectly fitting grooved holder for the blade. He threaded string through the holes in the ends of the blade and bound it to the wood. There could now be no lateral play.

He had to make four cuts in all. The bars were three inches wide and a quarter-inch thick. All he knew about the time this would take was what he had found in the *Mechanic's Handbook.* The librarian had been facetious when Greg had asked for the book.

" Something new for you, Gregory, isn't it? Don't tell me you're going to learn a trade!"

In a chapter headed " Working with metal ", Greg found what he wanted—USING THE HACKSAW. The book had been returned but not before Greg knew every word in the paragraph.

It was nine-fifteen. He heard Griffiths unlocking the cells with his companion. The spyhole did not move but a flat hand slapped the door. Griffiths's beery voice said, " Off that bed, Canada. You're not dead yet."

Automatically, Greg put the framed saw and spare blades in his bedding. He stretched himself out on the blankets. The men were going into chapel. The iron plates on their heels screeched on the slate flags on the upper galleries. They were good for a couple of hours. Greg had been the only man to complain sick that morning. Apart from the few who professed no religion on reception, he was alone in the block.

" Chapel all correct, sir!" The Principal Officer's shout echoed flatly, then the chapel doors were closed.

Greg's door opened. It was a tall jailer with a tight mouth and the Maltese Cross worn on the sleeve of the Hospital Officers. He spoke with lofty indifference.

" Stand up! Drop your trousers and lift your shirt up. MEDICAL OFFICER!" The jailer stood to attention inside the cell and closed his eyes as if praying.

The Medical Officer was a Scot with thirty years' service. He carried disbelief and resentment at his lot like banners. The stethoscope round his neck swung wildly as he bent at Greg's table, the Sick Book in front of him.

"Name?"

"Gregory, Doctor."

"What's the matter with you?" The doctor had his back to Greg. The jailer looked from one to another. Ready to anticipate the doctor's command or deal with any lack of respect by Greg.

"A cold, Doctor."

Like a goaded bull, the doctor swung round with lowered head. "*I'll* tell you what's wrong with you. Put out your tongue."

"Put your tongue out," echoed the jailer, rocking on his heels.

Greg opened his mouth and the jailer pushed in a thermometer. "No temperature, sir." The man made it sound as though he had suspected as much.

The Medical Officer was writing rapidly in the book. "One of those gentlemen who doesn't like chapel, I think, Mr. Murphy."

The jailer's mouth turned in appreciation of the sarcasm. "Tired, I think, sir. There's a concert this afternoon, sir," he added happily.

"Aye," said the Medical Officer dourly. "Aye, so there is. *Mist Alba*, Mr. Murphy, and we'll keep him in for twenty-four hours. Confined to cell, Mr. Murphy." He stamped from the cell.

The jailer waited, determined that Greg should drink the laxative. "No concert, Gregory, and no exercise. A pity. Next time you complain sick, perhaps it won't be on a Sunday." The door slammed.

When Greg heard the gate close at the end of the block, he went to work. The yards were empty and the cells that faced him across the exercise rings. Ninety-five per cent of the prison population was occupied with its soul. In the same auditorium, that afternoon, a concert would be given. Under the Medical Officer's instructions, Greg was allowed no further than the lavatory for the next twenty-four hours.

He had four hours in which to cut through the bars. Standing on the water pipes, he pushed his left hand through one of the two openings. In it, the framed blade. Then his right hand through the other space, grabbing the free end of the blade. It was an awkward position but it enabled him to bring pressure to bear.

He made his first cut, starting on the far edge of the bar. One stroke every second. Once the cut was under way, Greg increased the length of his stroke. The blade bit into the metal, singing. With anyone in the cells next to his, it would have been impossible for them not to have heard.

He was sweating now. His knuckles were scraped where the saw had slipped. Three times, he snapped a blade. Nine left and the first cut not yet made. He worked with more care, lifting the blade at the end of the stroke so that the teeth did not drag.

Outside, black clouds obscured the sky. The wind freshened, driving the first flurry of sleet in his face. It was dark in the cell. Four times, he heard the chapel clock strike before he completed the first cut. The bar was almost severed. It hung on a sliver of metal that would break with a pull. He filled the cut with black cobbler's wax. It was unnoticeable. The second cut took only three-quarters of an hour and he broke no blades. He gave it the wax treatment.

By now it was completely dark in the cell. He lay down on the bed till the shuffling overhead signalled the return of the men from chapel. Freezing rain was bouncing on the concrete walks outside.

Griffiths's voice boomed in the block. " Exercise in twos, not threes. *Anti*-clockwise."

Greg's spyhole moved. " No exercise for you, Canada. You've got to stay in. Do you want your light on? "

Greg waved a hand from the bed. " No thanks."

He lay warm in his blankets till lunch time. The saws were beside him. As the exercise passed his door, it built a kaleidoscope of conversation.

" My old woman . . ."

" . . . that f. . . . . . judge . . ."

" Innocent but this copper . . ."

" . . . Gregory—'im that 'ad the thirty grand . . ."

He shut his eyes, forcing himself to think of nothing. After a while he slept. Griffiths woke him with the noonday meal. The jailer lifted the top of the aluminium tin and sniffed with delight. " Roast! Two veg! My old woman can't afford to give me a meal like that."

" No," said Greg. All he wanted was peace till the afternoon. Two more cuts and worst was over. Only a nick in the window frame itself was necessary. The cast iron would go like matchboard.

Griffiths looked at him curiously then closed an eye swollen with self-indulgence. " Cheer up, Canada. It's the first five that's the worst."

He said b . . . . .! under his breath as the door closed. The cell was completely dark now. It was impossible to see the print on a book. He went back to bed till the time came for the men to be unlocked for the concert.

One after another, the cells on D 1 were crashed open. Once more, the heels scraped the slates overhead as the men filed into the chapel. He stayed on his bed, flat on his back, staring at the ceiling. Outside, the sleet had been replaced by rain that lifted in sheets in the wind, cascading down the small window panes.

On the stairway outside his cell, the tell-tale handrail creaked. In the dark cell he sensed rather than saw the spyhole move. A voice he did not recognize asked the inevitable question.

" You all right?"

The blades were gripped tightly in his hand. " All right," he answered. He waited. If the door opened, it would be for one reason—a special search . . . There was the click of sticking paint as the man put pressure on the door. The handle was spun. Then whistling, the jailer climbed the stairs to return to the Centre. The jail was like a wheel with the boundary walls the periphery, the cell blocks the spokes. The hub was a glass-walled office that controlled all the galleries. It was the Holy of Holies, the nerve navel of the jail. The Centre.

There were still two cuts to make in the bars. He fitted a new blade in the holder and went back to work. The sound of the biting steel was lost in the drumming of the rain. As his arms moved in the narrow window space, the wet oozed from the stuff of his sodden jacket.

Up in the chapel, a fiddle scraped out the Londonderry Air, echoing drearily through the block. His cell was one of hundreds —a cage remote from the attention of the centre office. The Governor and Deputy were both at the concert, nodding in the choir stalls. The chaplain, his eyes closed in concentration, was composing his ' Thank You ' speech. Bright with relief, he would stand facing the congregation.

" Men! I'm sure you'll wish me to thank mumble-mumble and his concert party for coming along and giving us such a splendid show. This afternoon, we've heard etc. . . and now, show your appreciation in the usual manner. No whistling, please."

He would crane with lifted chin in the attitude that had earned him the jailhouse nickname, " Chicken-neck Charlie ".

With the Governor present, the jailers were stiff in their raised seats, eager to smell out indiscipline, ready for any sign of the mob mutiny that could break without warning whenever the prisoners were assembled together and out of their cells.

In his cell in the cockpit, Greg fitted a new blade in the frame and started on the last bar. The lashing rain and gloom outside gave him a feeling of security. His cramped muscles drove the blade with confidence and surely it ate through the last inch of steel. When both cuts had been filled with the black wax, he wrung the water from his jacket sleeves and wrapped the tunic round the hot pipes.

He still had the four nicks to make in the cast-iron window frame. Under one sharp blow with a heavy weight, the frame would collapse. Its purpose was merely to hold the small squares of glass. Security lay in the steel bars beyond, set flat at an angle like an open Venetian blind.

Another new blade and he nicked the movable iron frame at each corner. Finished, he replaced the wooden slat on the cell slate and went back to bed. In a quarter-hour, the bawling of jailers announced the return of the men. The light in his cell was snapped on from the outside. There was the rattle of cans then Griffiths opened the door. He put the small loaf and piece of margarine on Greg's table.

" Tea up, Canada!" He looked round the cell incuriously. Then as he caught sight of the water pipes, his voice changed. " What's that jacket doing on the pipes?" Any article on the water pipes was an affront to his orderly mind.

Sawing a slice from the loaf with his tin knife, Greg kept his head down. The knife slipped, clattering on the plate. He leaned across the doorway, trying to block Griffiths's vision. The blades in his sock were working up. If he took a half-dozen steps, he felt that he would litter the cell floor with hacksaw blades. Griffiths looked over Greg's shoulder, tea ladle in his hand.

" The jacket? It's wet," said Greg. " I upset the water jug."

Griffiths hesitated for a second. Suddenly his neck swelled. From the corner of his eye, he had caught sight of the prisoner who carried the bread basket. The man was busily pushing crusty loaves to one side.

" Stop sorting that bread out!" shouted Griffiths. " I'll take it as it comes. We've no favourites here and don't you forget it, mister! If I catch you doing that again, you're on report." His sense of fair play and hygiene satisfied, he remembered Greg. " See me in the morning. I'll get you another jacket from the Part Worn Stores. We can't have you catching cold." He closed the door.

Greg sipped the hot sugarless brew. He had no appetite. It was going to be a long evening. Four and a half hours till Lights Out. Another hour till he made his move. Wandsworth had given him the ability to do things mechanically. He was able to work, finish a chore, without mental effort. If you kept yourself free from thinking, jail lost most of its unpleasantness. It was worst at night. There were the long hours of remembering. A beach bright with sunshine. Fresh-cut grass spilling in front of a mower. The oddest things forced themselves into your consciousness, insistent with bittersweet memory. It was things rather than people that he remembered. Maybe because people mattered less to him than things.

He washed and dried the tin plate and earthenware mug. The plate went face down on the table, the mug on top of it. In front of them, the spoon and the knife in the neat Saint Andrew's cross that Griffiths demanded.

He took up a book but reading defeated its purpose. Every paragraph held some keyword that sent his thoughts scurrying. Movement of any kind was better to kill these hours. He started walking. From door to window. Five paces, turn, then back. He was still walking when he heard the cocoa cans being carried down into the cockpit.

When the door opened, Greg was standing ready, his mug in his hand. As he saw who was there, Greg lowered his eyes. It was one of the ex-Guardsmen. A discipline officer in the Tailor's Shop the week before, the man had made plain his dislike of Greg.

He held the mug steadily, waiting for the cocoa to be poured. This guy was poison. One wrong answer—one look that might be construed as Dumb Insolence, and he'd find himself on the way to the Punishment Cells.

The jailer's cuffs were turned back daintily to avoid being splashed. A prisoner held the steaming can as the jailer dipped the measure. As he recognized Greg, the jailer smiled.

" Mr. Gregory! A full pint, Mr. Gregory?"

Greg answered cautiously. " Yes, please."

The jailer waited. " Sir," he suggested.

" Yes please, sir." Greg forced the words, making them stand for that and no more.

" Much better. We're learning, aren't we?" The man gave the mug back to Greg. As it changed hands, the jailer tipped it slightly, spilling some of the hot greasy liquid on the floor. His smile broadened. He slammed the door shut and pounded on it from the outside.

Greg's hand was shaking. The pool on the polished floor would mean normally an hour on his knees. Working the scarred surface back to the mirror finish required for the Deputy Governor's Monday morning cell inspection. Somehow he had resisted the urge to let the man have it. To turn the grinning face into a scalded mask of fear. This was the worst type of screw. One who had saluted for his breakfast since he had been a drummer boy. Himself brutalized by years of discipline and unable to understand in what way convicts differed from cattle.

In the yard outside, the wind had freshened still more, scudding the rain in sheets, buffeting the loose slates on the roof till they skated through the night to crash on the concrete walks.

Under the blankets, he listened as the jail stretched before sinking into grateful unconsciousness. " Beating 'em for eight " as the cons had it. The sleep of the unjust was no different to any other. Soon the half-strangled cries, the groans, the snores, would be heard only by the night watchman, long since accustomed to them.

Propped on his elbow, he stiffened as first the flag tipped on the gallery above. Then came the cautious creak as the watchman padded down to the cockpit. The spyhole slid back and the lighted gallery outside showed like a bright penny in the door. A shadow moved across it. The cover dropped back into position. His fists were tight balls and the scar on his thumb throbbed. He relaxed, pushing deep under the blankets.

What had seemed simple had suddenly become fantastic. It had been part of his attitude to his imprisonment that you could beat any jail in the world. Provided you had someone on the outside to help. Even the tough American jails, where scaling a wall was offering yourself for target practice to a ready machine-gunner. As long as you had just *one* person ready to furnish the means, you could probe till you found the inevitably weak spot. Jail wasn't a prison camp where men were bound by loyalty and discipline. With an escape committee and determined comrades ready to pool their efforts. A jail was a jungle where dog ate dog. Where sharing a secret was the same as confessing it to the Governor.

In the darkness, he remembered the weakness in the security of British prisons. They were old. The walls were comparatively low and with no watch-towers. At night, you could play tag with the Yard Patrol who, himself, was unable to get into the cell block until a gate was opened from the inside. For that, the Orderly Officer had to be called. Even the night watchmen in the blocks were themselves prisoners, without keys. From ten at night till six the next morning, the only man with keys in the block was the Orderly Officer, a senior warder whose shift was spent in a room off the centre, fitted with camp bed and gas ring. There, the Orderly Officer napped, drank tea and read. If a cell had to be opened for any reason at all, it was to this office that the night watchman was forced to come first. The room was a hundred and fifty yards from Greg's cell. What Greg had to do to his window frame was going to awaken the entire cell block. But first the watchman had to locate the noise, investigate it—then fetch the Orderly Officer and return to Greg's cell. The worst way for Greg, this manoeuvre would take five minutes. The best way, ten.

As soon as the chapel clock struck the hour, he put on the dried jacket and went to his window. Punctually, the Yard Patrol rounded the end of the building. He stood in the light as he punched his clock. He stepped back. Slowly, his flashlight sent a beam, the length of the block. As it reached Greg's window, he stopped breathing. The light moved on. Hunched against the rain, the Yard Patrol disappeared.

Ten-five. Sloane had promised the rope for then but once Greg was through the window, it would be too late for him to change plans. He gave Sloane ten more minutes. He worked swiftly in his stockinged feet, stripping the bedding and mattress from the iron bedstead.

The frame was heavy tubing, strong but manageable. As the clock struck the quarter, Greg hefted the bed to his shoulder. Taking the length of the cell at a run, he rammed the end of the bed against the window frame. Glass shattered and the bars that were still sound rang under the impact. The frame stood unbroken. Already, as he made his second run, the man on his left had started to rap on the wall. Yells from the cell above him echoed in the block. As the bed hit the window, the frame snapped, leaving an open square, marked by the notches he had scored. It hung by one corner. He dropped the bed and tore at the window. Through the opening, he forced the back of his chair, prising it under the bottom bar and levering up. It quivered then snapped. Behind him, the spyhole spun furiously. Greg had pasted paper on the inside of the glass with soap. It was impossible to see through. The door handle was rattled menacingly.

" What's going on in there?"

Greg worked on the second bar. It snapped as he heard the watchman pounding up the iron stairway. By now, the block was bedlam. Under the impression that he was demolishing his cell furniture, men in the adjoining cells shouted advice and encouragement. In the yard outside, everything was still quiet, only the noise of the rain and the wind.

He went through the window, feet first and dropped into the area. His shoes sounded on the cement. He kicked them off and ran in his stockinged feet. Past the light and round the Tailor's Shop. The wall was twenty yards away. It was impossible to see more than a couple of feet in front of him. He ran left, trailing his hand till it hit something that was suspended from the top of the wall. The rope had been knotted every foot. He went up it, using forearms and knees as he had done in the school gym. Fear gave him added drive. At the top of the wall, he straddled it. The rope was attached to a hook. He pulled it up after him and dropped it to the ground outside. He took one last look. His cell was a patch of light in the darkened cell block. Window and bars gaped where he had used his hacksaw. He could even see the uniform caps of the men inside the cell. Beneath him lay the grass of the railway embankment. Certainly they would search the prison and yards first. He had left no indication that he had come over the wall. Still, he had no time to spare. He still wore prison uniform and there was the bag to find. Quietly, he dropped to freedom.

FOUR

It was a steep embankment. At its top, a narrow footpath followed the line of the prison wall. At its bottom, a double set of railway tracks ran east and west. On each set, one of the rails was live. On the far side of the tracks, the embankment climbed to the backs of forlorn Victorian houses, hideous with dripping laurel.

An electric train rattled by, brilliant against the wet darkness. It illuminated the bank beneath him. A dozen yards down, he could see the canvas bag that Sloane had left. He picked it up and jogged east. There was a bridge there, Sloane had said. It crossed the tracks, making a brief tunnel. He would change there. Another train passed, travelling in the same direction. The sudden scream of its whistle quickened Greg's lope. Once he stumbled, a knee squelching in the mud. He covered fifty yards before the prison wall took a right-angle turn to the Main Gate. He followed the path straight ahead till he reached the bridge.

Thirty feet over his head, traffic moved on the road that passed the front of the prison. At the mouth to the tunnel, there was sufficient light from the sodium arcs on the road for him to dress. Sloane would be home by now. His car would have been useful but dangerous. There was always someone to remember the number of a licence tag—some amateur detective to recall a car that had stopped to pick up a man on the Common near the prison.

On the road above, buses ran frequently. No more than ten minutes had passed since he had gone through his cell window. The hunt would be on but still in the grounds of the jail. Prison governors were in no hurry to hand over the chase to the police. First they made sure that their prisoner was not holed up somewhere in the jail.

He unzipped the bag. There was a ready-made sports suit of good quality. He had vetoed the idea of one of his own suits being left. Too many guys had been trapped by a tiny tailor's label with their name written on it. Shoes, shirt and underwear. A dark blue stormcoat and a soft hat.

He shivered as he stripped to the skin. Using the prison shirt he wiped his wet, filthy feet. The rope he had carried, he stuffed in the bag with the prison uniform. These Sloane could send back to the Governor. At least Greg would avoid the technical rap—" Stealing Government Property ".

Stuffed in the pocket of the jacket Sloane had left were five one-pound notes, a Yale flat-key, some letters addressed to a Norman Bishop and a couple of club membership cards in the same name. In the trousers, he found some change, cigarettes and a lighter. Some guy, Sloane. He thought of everything. There was a scrawled message in the storm coat.

Be careful going into the flat. Use the entrance on Flood Street. Past the main door. The door will be unlocked. Be lucky.

" Be lucky." Sloane overworked the phrase. What Greg needed was some organization and his money.

In dry clothing, he felt a different man. *Was* a different man! There wasn't a cop in town who could pick him as a guy who'd bust out of jail within the last quarter-hour. When they started, the police were going to be looking for a man aged thirty-five, about one hundred fifty pounds, five ten, wearing prison grey uniform. Brown hair, blue eyes, speaks with a Canadian accent. American, they would probably say—they never knew the difference. He'd just keep his mouth shut as much as possible. At the bottom of the description on the WANTED sheet, they'd write " no distinguishing marks ". Involuntarily, he looked at his left thumb. The scar showed, a purple zigzag from knuckle to knuckle . . . He'd have to remember that as well.

He moved lightly and quietly on the crêpe-soled shoes. Through the tunnel, he climbed a fence on to the Common, dripping and desolate with stunted bush and bracken. Stepping through bramble snarls, he found himself on a footpath that led to the highway. The bus-stop was at the end of the bridge under a light. He waited, the bag at his feet. A couple of hundred yards away, he could see the swaying lights of a bus coming towards him. A pedestrian stopped under the light. He turned to Greg.

" Does this bus go to Streatham?"

Greg moved away, hiding his face and avoiding an answer. He was still far too near the jail. This might be some off-duty screw who would recognize him. He boarded the bus and took a seat upstairs. They were going south. Back past the Main Gate to the prison. As they neared, he looked. The great studded doors were shut tight. No cars were parked in the forecourt. In the Governor's house, lights were still burning. Good deal, he thought. Right this minute, every available screw in the place would be out in the rain, beating the yards, searching the lavatories, shops and peering between the rows of cabbages. Nevertheless, it would only be a short while before the Governor notified Scotland Yard. Idly, he wondered how he would figure on the Roll Slate at the Main Gate. Whether they'd mark him " Discharged " or promote him to some special niche for jail-breakers.

He sat up and put his feet on the canvas bag as the conductress came along the bus. She was a blonde with a mouth like a parrot's and wore platform shoes with her slacks. She rattled her money bag with the air of dispensing largesse.

" Fez pliz!"

" A twopenny."

Her nose lengthened and she showed long teeth stained with nicotine. " There ain't none." Greg stared. " There ain't none," she repeated. " Not since eight weeks ago. It's tuppence 'apenny now." The corrugated waves in her hair jerked like spring wire. He gave her the coin.

At Trinity Road, he left the bus and took the subway, booking to Charing Cross station. He took a seat at the end of a warm coach in the first train. After nine weeks in jail, the unfamiliar was full of charm. Opposite were a couple of girls who discussed Sinatra with interest. Greg found himself staring at their legs, slim in nylon. The cheap gaudy clothes, the obvious scent, the tasty accent—all of it fascinated him. And he remembered it had been three months since he had held the softness of a woman's body close to his own.

It was going to be tough on Judith until Sloane was able to straighten things out for him. All he could let her know was that eventually she and the kids would be able to join him. From now on, she'd be watched incessantly. At the movies, the hairdressers, collecting the kids from school. When she slept, there'd be someone waiting outside. Someone hidden, biding his time till Greg felt himself safe and made the classic blunder.

If he'd been able to talk to her—explain this thing from the beginning. Tell her that he'd taken the first chance to make a real killing he'd ever had in his life. Convince her that he'd done if for both of them. To put an end to the insecurity of furnished houses, hurried trips with a hundred creditors yelping on their trail. To tell her all this would have taken time. He hadn't had the opportunity to shake the sullen resignation she'd shown at their last meeting in Brixton Prison, the day before he'd gone for trial.

" Don't you trust me, Greg?" she'd asked deliberately, as if his answer would hold great significance. He'd *had* no answer.

It was the same old wail. Everything had to be shared. Worries became lighter, joys fuller, if only you shared. Marriage meant a complete surrender of individuality—the way they wanted it. You were meant to think, act and emote as one.

The train jerked to a halt at Kennington. A group of Teddy Boys joined the coach. Spindle-legged with string ties and coats like Mississippi gamblers. Greg closed his eyes. Even bums like these, drugstore villains, he had to avoid. A word or a look could lead to an argument, a brawl and the police. His identification would never stand close scrutiny. From then on, while he was in England, it mattered as much what the other guy did as how he himself reacted.

Once out of England, things would be different. With twenty-eight thousand pounds, a man could start a new life in fifty places. One of the banana republics, maybe. He had a quick picture of a white, shaded house with lawns stretching to the jungle where a jaguar crouched, sending chattering monkeys in flight. Or Sweden, where an honest people assumed everyone else's honesty. Maybe he could run some business up there. There were plenty of places for a man with money and a past to lose. First, he had to collect his loot. No matter what Sloane or anyone else said, that was one thing he would do himself. Twenty-eight thousand pounds represented ten years if they ever got hold of him. The days were gone when in England a jail-breaker was safe if he stayed free till his sentence expired. The Criminal Justice Bill of 1948 had changed all that. Now, if a man was " unlawfully at large ", his sentence was suspended until his rearrest. If he stayed in England, he wouldn't be safe even at ninety.

Without his money, Greg had as much chance of another life as the sorriest bum he had left in the jail behind. Without Sloane's help, no better, either. He had to see that Sloane was well-fixed. A guy in a million. Sloane was able to call on a dozen men to pattern an escape route from England. He knew the right people. No, without Sloane, he would have been a gone goose.

At Charing Cross, he changed to the District Line and doubled back to Victoria. He walked up the steps to the main station, through to the Grosvenor Hotel and out the front entrance. On Buckingham Palace Road, he flagged a cab and gave an address on Chelsea Embankment. When he paid off the cab, he went to a phone booth by the river. There was no answer from the number he dialled. It was what he had been told to expect. It had stopped raining. Across the sucking black river, the deserted Festival Gardens looked like some derelict movie set. He walked north on Flood Street till he came to a red brick apartment building. There was a central courtyard that was a through way to another street. The block had a dozen entrances. In the lighted portico of the main entrance, he could see two doormen chatting. He walked on. On the left was an emergency door with a push-bar arrangement to lock it. He stepped into the shadow and waited till a woman had clicked by. Very carefully, he scanned the parked cars, searching for anyone who might sit there in darkness. The idle onlooker to observe and remember an incident that would hold significance later. He hoped his trail had been broken at Wandsworth. If not, it must be broken before he entered the block. The street was dead.

He pushed on the door and it gave. Stepping inside quickly, he lifted the bar. He waited. Nothing moved. He was in a furnace room. Lagged steam pipes ran round the walls. Gauges quivered above a boiler. A mechanical feed ticked as if anxious to perform. Through a door, a red arrow pointed along a corridor. 112-150. He followed the passage to the end, up a short flight of stairs and through a service door. There was a small self-operated elevator. He stopped it at the sixth floor. The sound of the television service closing down came from a few apartments. It was eleven-twenty-five.

Using the key Sloane had left in the pocket, he opened the door of 125. There were some letters on the mat and he picked them up. They were addressed to Norman Bishop. The name on the letters in his pocket. Sloane had taken this flat furnished for a month. The one room had a divan, some Chinese prints, a good rug on the polished floor and cottage Chippendale chairs. By the bed was a table with a telephone. Behind it, the picture of a girl about twenty-five. It was not a beautiful face. One by one, the features were unremarkable but the whole gave an appearance of great sincerity. The eyes were serious, belying the smile on the sensitive mouth.

There was little to explore in the flat. A bathroom and lavatory and kitchen. In the kitchen, a back door led to a fire escape. That had been Greg's idea. Pulling aside the curtain, he craned down the fire escape. Thirty feet beneath, it touched the roofs of a neighbouring studio. If necessary, he could be down and over the roofs, a block away before the door to the flat could be broken in.

He went back to the sitting room and bolted the front door. From now on, it would open only to Sloane. He wouldn't use the phone except to take incoming calls. Not even then unless he heard the buzzer sound three times then go dead and ring again. There was food in the refrigerator. Milk, fruit, bread and books. This was better than a cell in the cockpit. Though this door was locked, he'd locked it himself. He turned back the cover on the bed and stretched out. In minutes he was asleep.

It was eight before the slamming of the elevator gates outside disturbed him. He awoke suddenly to take in the unfamiliar surroundings. Stretching, he pulled a cigarette from the pack beside him. He sucked the smoke deep into his lungs, locked both hands behind his head and stared at the wall. Someone was moving around in the flat next door. A back door slammed and footsteps scuffed on the iron service stairs. He could hear the chink as the milkman set down a crate of milk bottles. Then the footsteps receded. Idly he wondered whether Sloane would fetch more milk. He had a list of things for the other to bring.

In a block like this, Greg felt safe. Here, there was no communal life. Flat-dwellers slammed their doors on the day behind them and included their neighbours. If anyone had noticed Sloane when he came to the flat, it was unimportant. They could only assume that he was the occupant.

He made an arm for the radio. There were no pyjamas in the place. He could well stand sleeping in the raw after the alternative offered by the jail . . . a dirty shirt. He remembered Griffiths's jocularity. " Now you get *two* shirts, Canada. One off—one on. But you can only send one to the wash. What you had on you last week does as yer night-attire." The man had been pleased with the phrase.

He turned on the set. Pips—then the eight o'clock news. A pompous voice started to outline news of weather, strikes and politics with the same condescending promise of rare treats to follow. With no change of tone, the voice continued.

" A prisoner serving ten years has escaped from Wandsworth."

Cautiously, Greg increased the volume. In the reprise, the announcer gave details.

" Paul Gregory, thirty-five, a prisoner sentenced to ten years at the Old Bailey in October for theft, succeeded in escaping from his cell in Wandsworth Prison late last night. A thorough search by prison officers failed to find the man who is now believed to be at large. Gregory, a Canadian, was dressed in dark grey tunic and trousers and a blue-striped shirt. He is thought to be without shoes. Gregory's home address is at Henley-on-Thames. Police in the Metropolitan area and Home Counties are intensifying their search for the fugitive."

He turned the dial, silencing the set. It was no more than he had expected. He intended to disregard every police bulletin that he heard—every news of his escape that the press printed. Whatever he learned, that way, would be what they *wanted* him to learn.

He got out of bed, slapped the sheets straight and replaced the cover. He stretched, looking at the girl's picture. It was a face you could trust. Hands on hips, he did a tottering knees-bend then overbalanced. There he went with that word again—trust. Without a doubt, she'd be the same as the rest of them. Born to possess completely, to probe and share. That's what *they* meant by trust. He went to the sitting-room window and looked down at the doorman, white-capped and yellow-mackintoshed against the inevitable rain. The flat had been well chosen. There was no window to overlook within a hundred and fifty yards.

In the kitchen, the back door and windows were curtained. He put a kettle on to boil. Still yawning, he turned on the bath. His face showed haggard in the mirror-backed cabinet. It had been weeks since he had looked at himself in a normal light. Older, he thought. This last couple of years he'd grown so much older. His beard stubble was flecked with grey. In the cabinet, he found a razor and tooth brush. Humming now, he let the steaming water rise round his buttocks and sank, letting it lap on his chest.

This was the life! No more, the one bath a week ordained by the Prison Commissioners. Nine inches of water at a temperature of sixty-five degrees Fahrenheit—bath to be occupied for fifteen minutes. Once, he had been brash enough to ask the Governor if it were possible to have an extra bath. Staring straight at a spot over the Governor's head, he explained the lack of washing facilities in the shops. The filth of his hands, black with mail-bags that had been dragged through the spittle of countless railway platforms. He had not asked twice.

"This is a prison, not a beauty parlour. Get out!" the Governor replied.

He soaped himself slowly. Maybe he was getting too sorry for himself. Better ease up on this business of remembering jail and its indignities. Only ex-cons and prison reformers showed heat in discussing jail conditions. The run of citizenry—the "Square Johns" whose ranks he hoped to join—were either indifferent or indignant at any suggestion that something in *their* backyard stank. He'd have to watch how he talked on the subject.

The phone in the living room buzzed three times then went dead. Immediately it started to ring again. Insistent and menacing.

He wrapped a bath towel round him and ran to the sitting room. Gingerly he picked up the receiver and waited.

Sloane's voice came breezy and matter-of-fact. "'Morning, Mr. Bishop. I'm in Chelsea at the moment. I'll be up in three minutes."

Greg replaced the instrument without answering. He dried himself hurriedly. Against the well-scrubbed flesh, the scar on his thumb was violent. He wrote the word "Gloves" on the list he had prepared.

There was no ring at the door-bell. Only the flap of the letter-box fluttered, tapping gently.

"Who is it?"

Sloane kept his voice low. "OK, it's me."

Greg drew the safety bolt and unlatched the door. It might be an idea to add another couple of bolts. Something that would hold the door long enough for him to use the back stair-way. He said "Hi" to the big man who threw a large paper sack on the bed.

"Hello, Greg," said Sloane. He looked round curiously. "Everything all right?"

Greg took the proffered cigarette. When it was lit, he said: "Did you hear the news this morning? On the radio?"

Sloane was whistling softly through his teeth, plucking the edge of the bed cover. "I heard," he said finally. "That's not all." He pulled a newspaper from the paper sack. "You've got yourself a lot of publicity, Greg."

It was front-page news, repeating what the radio newscast had given. There were two additions. A recognizable reproduction of Greg's mug shot—the picture he had taken in jail. The general description given was amplified. " Has an irregular scar between first and second joints on the left thumb."

Sloane's eyes were brooding. He tapped the bag beside him. " I brought you some gloves."

" What about the passport?"

" I don't know yet. It should be all right. There's a man coming down from Manchester tonight. There's just one thing . . ."

" What thing?" Greg hitched the towel round his middle. He found Sloane's deep voice reassuring. The unhurried way his partner moved, his careful assessment of values, gave Greg a feeling of security. It was like having an intelligent bloodhound to care for you.

Sloane smiled back at him. " Why don't you put something on—you look like a refugee from a steam bath!" He leaned his long face on his hand. " I dunno. This man from Manchester—it's the one with the contact in the Passport Office. He wants one and a half."

" Well, give it him." Greg was definite. " I'm not going to argue about a hundred and fifty pounds now."

" It isn't that. He's got to have a picture of you for the passport. The name doesn't matter—nor the signature. I'll fix all that. But he's got to have a picture."

The smudged print on the front of the newspaper was bad but it was a palpable likeness. Greg threw the towel to the floor and threaded a leg through his trousers. He talked to himself rather than in answer to Sloane. " Even if he didn't know *who* he was getting a passport for before, with this goddam thing in every paper, he certainly will." He swung his head as the implication hit. " No matter *where* I go to have a picture done, it'll be the same thing."

" I doubt it," Sloane said easily. " Think of a picture that you saw in the paper—can you remember what it looked like? Could you pick a guy from one? It isn't the picture that bothers me. I can take one of you up here and develop it myself. Once this guy knows, Greg, knows who you are—he might get ideas!"

" I'm worried less about the money angle than whether he's solid, Sloane. *Is* he?"

The big man was emphatic. " Christ, yes. I could ruin him

if he turned copper and he knows it." He put a hand on Greg's shoulder. " You don't have to make your mind up till tomorrow. If you don't fancy it, I can get you a ship from Tilbury. No papers but a guaranteed ride to the Argentine. *And* you'll be put ashore."

Making fresh tea, Greg moved restlessly from kitchen to sitting room. Secretly, he felt that his departure from England should have been arranged. But the idea was impractical. For a passport a picture was obviously necessary, no matter in what name it came, and he'd had none. His own passport was still in the hands of the Yard. Anything might have gone wrong with his break—it could have been delayed. No, Sloane would always do a little more than the best.

" How's Judith?" he asked suddenly.

The big man was apologetic. " I've never told you, Greg. But I'm not too popular there. I think she blames me for you being pinched." He turned a hand and studied it. " You know the way they are," he said at last, " I sent someone down there this morning. He drove past the house. The place is stinking with coppers. Is she all right for money?" he finished curiously.

Greg poured tea the way they both liked it. Orange, hot and sweet. He gave Sloane a cup. " Why shouldn't she be?" He blew on his tea. " I put thirty-five hundred in her bank two months ago."

The other's broad shoulders moved easily. " I just wondered. When it comes to shipping her and the kids out, it's going to take money."

" It'll be there," said Greg steadily.

Sloane got up. " Right. You don't want to move out of here today. As soon as we know what to do with you, we'll move you at night, by car."

" Sure." Greg was not listening. " Is your man in Paris still good?" Sloane moved his head. " I'll have three grand ready for him. In the fivers. I want two thousand for them. Used one pound notes and both deliveries here in London. Can you do it?"

Again Sloane nodded. " I should think so. You're asking less than he paid me. But he'll have the business of getting the fivers back to France." He gave his lugubrious smile. " He's used to it. When shall I say that you want the cash?"

" Tuesday." There was a momentary silence. " Don't worry about my end of it, Sloane. It's safe enough."

Sloane tipped the paper bag he had brought on to the bed. There were magazines, a packet of cigarettes, milk, bread and fresh underwear. The gloves were pigskin.

"A going-away present," said Sloane.

"What about callers here?" asked Greg suddenly.

"There won't be any. This Bishop's in Spain for a month. Nobody here knows the flat is occupied. I duck everyone coming in and keep my eye on the driving mirror. By the way—the law's been round to the pick-up you used for the visiting orders. They work fast but they drew a blank." He buttoned his top-coat, tucking the polka-dot scarf round his neck. "If you want me to drive you tomorrow, we'll chance it."

"Drive me where, for example?" Their eyes held steadily.

Sloane grinned affectionately, made a huge fist and rapped Greg's bicep. "Who knows! The Bank of England or wherever it is that you stashed your loot. Jesus, Greg! Don't be so touchy. Nobody's going to beat you for your end!"

Greg's voice was flat. "I'm taking care of that, Sloane. Not a single one of the bastards."

He unbolted the door quickly and Sloane stepped into the passage.

"Tomorrow, same time," whispered Sloane.

Greg nodded and closed the door.

The day dragged on. Rather than cook, he broke out a can of beans from the groceries Sloane had left. He ate in the warm kitchen, spooning the beans from the can. There was gin and scotch in the place and he considered going to bed with a bottle. The idea of drinking alone was without charm. He dumped the can in the disposal unit and prowled round the flat, opening locked cupboards with a bunch of keys that he found in the writing desk. A dozen suits hung above as many pairs of treed shoes. Not bad, thought Greg. Whoever the guy was who owned the place, he spent his money in the right quarters.

There was a dog-leash in the chest in the hall. A dog—a cat, something living that didn't represent a threat would have made this waiting easier. There was no room for much furniture in the small flat. But from the Persian rug, lustrous with deep colour, to the William and Mary writing-desk, everything had been chosen with taste. Almost too much taste for a man, he thought. The eye for colour, the gift of creating an atmosphere in this box of a flat, belonged to a woman.

The writing-desk was dark with generations of polishing.

The unlocked drawers were empty. He lifted the desk top, grinning as he found the wooden peg. Secret drawer! It never failed. The cavity gaped. Pushed to the back were a bundle of letters and a pile of photographs. He carried the prints to the window. All were of the same girl—the girl who looked steadily from the frame on his bedside table. Hair plastered wet to her head on a beach white with sunshine—leaning with pride—confidently astride a rawboned hack—serene—in an old-fashioned garden.

Two of the prints showed a man with her. Tall, about thirty, with flat pale hair and a sullen mouth. A jerk, Greg reasoned immediately. From Knightsbridge to the Ritz Bar and back there were hundreds of the type. All arrogant about something. Their looks, their brains, or their money.

Already the short day was disappearing. He drew the heavy curtains, switched on the fire and lamp and took a seat with the letters. Reading the mail of a stranger, he rationalized, wasn't the same as peeking in a friend's letters. He was still reading, an hour later.

The letters were signed " Bridget ". Some were written on crested notepaper from an unpronounceable place in Wales. The rest were from an address in Cadogan Street. All were love-letters with a difference. There was something almost incestuous about the tone. It was neither mother nor sister but a relationship that had something of each. " Who cares *what* they say, Norman!" she said in one letter. " We'll never be able to explain to Mummy or Daddy. It seems hopeless even to try . . ." A girl with a good emotional digestion, thought Greg as he read. In an envelope at the bottom of the pile were two press cuttings. In bald prose they set out the arrest, conviction and fine of Norman Bishop, for importuning at South Kensington Station.

Greg read through the correspondence again. It covered the period before and after Bishop's arrest. The second time of reading brought more understanding. This was a record of loyalty. An acceptance of fact that he found impossible to agree with. The third sex were no strangers to him. He had met the best and the worst of them. If they and their critics thought less of themselves as being abnormal, there'd be not so much suffering on the one hand and fewer expressions of manly indignation on the other. One that he'd known—rudderless in search of the affection he craved—had once said to Greg:

"If you'd been born this way, you'd realize that it's like having two heads or a hare-lip. You *need* no defence and no apology."

Greg put the letters back where he had found them. Be all that as it may, he didn't get the idea of any normal woman being in love with a queer. He let his mind wander bawdily on the possibilities the situation suggested.

Merely because he had nothing else to do, he took another bath. Shaving again, where the persistent bristle sprouted anew along his jaw-line and under his lip. Tomorrow or the next day, he'd have to chance the streets. That meant a cab. It had nothing to do with mistrusting Sloane. Let's say, rather, in this he mistrusted everybody. Included, the people on whom he would stake his liberty. This was money and a great deal of it. He was going to collect it himself with no outside help. From then on, it would never be inches away from him till he arrived at his ultimate destination. Every hack driver in town was a potential copper. He knew it. They were avid newspaper readers and reward-conscious. They would be on the alert. Maybe a disguise would be best. Tenderly, he massaged the back of his shoulders. That goddam place had given him rheumatism in nine weeks. Sure, a disguise but not one of those beloved by lady novelists. Personally, he'd never seen a false moustache that didn't look like one. It would have to be something outstanding about his appearance that would catch the attention of these amateur sleuths. Drying himself, he had the solution. In the airing cupboard were racks made of wooden slats, three feet long. He pulled two of them from their screws and ripped a sheet into strips. The slats he bound firmly round his right leg in splints.

He had to sit on the floor to put on his trousers. He got up, splay-legged. He tried walking, admiring the effect in the long mirror. He rapped the splint with his hands, pleased. It was a perfect imitation of a man with a wooden leg. Already his mind was busy with a story to account for it. You bet—that's what they would remember, the brown-nosers and glory-seekers, a man with a wooden leg. And they'd get fat on it. With gloves, glasses maybe, he'd be safe enough to travel the short distance necessary.

The clock in the living room said six. He switched on the news bulletin. The same voice read the same details of his escape. One piece of information was added.

"A watch is being kept by the police on all ports."

Greg moved round the room, accustoming himself to the lift-drag motion of the strapped leg. Let 'em watch, he thought. One of Sloane's contacts would be able to square a trip to Eire. No papers and no cops to pass. Once there, he'd use his passport. Take an air taxi from Dublin to Paris. In unconscious self-reassurance, he nodded again. From Paris, with his bank-roll, he could go anywhere in the world. If the passport was impractical, no matter. They said that the Argentine was a good place to live.

He resisted the urge to write to Judith. All she need know was that he was safe. Anything more meant starting something that could easily backfire. He could get Sloane to see that the message was delivered. It struck him that no longer could he be sure of Judith—how she would react. Once, long ago, in Canada, he'd seen a message printed in a newspaper. It was from a woman whose husband had broken out of prison.

"*Give yourself up, George, for my sake and your own.*"

Well, maybe for *her* sake. And Christ knows what story lay behind that particular piece of wifely advice. Who knew, perhaps Judith would dig deeper in that vein when the time came.

During the next half-hour, the phone rang twice. Not with Sloane's warning manoeuvre but with foreboding that Greg found hard to ignore. His ear was becoming accustomed to the sound of the elevator. The door slammed on the cage outside but he paid no heed. In a chair by the fire, his right leg at an ungainly angle, he tried to make sense of the magazine article he was reading. The pages were glossy but the language abstruse.

In the door behind him, a key turned in the lock. He swivelled on his good leg and climbed upright. He could feel the colour leaving his face. Held by the bolt, the door rattled then the key was turned once more. He limped down the corridor towards the back door. There was no time to get rid of the splint. At the kitchen door, the sound of a girl's voice halted him. He turned. Slowly, the flap in the front door was being lifted. He stood to one side out of sight.

"Norman!" The bolt creaked under pressure and the girl called again, "*Norman!*"

He stayed where he was. Maybe this bitch would blow if only he kept his mouth shut. The light in the flat might well have been left on, she wasn't to know. Then he remembered the bolt. Somebody had to be in the flat. Irresolutely, he moved towards the front door.

Suddenly, he had to know who she was—what she was doing here. He made his voice unconvincingly English.

" Who's there?"

There was silence outside then the door flap was moved up and down . . . " Who are you?" the girl called. " What are you doing in there?"

His back itched as if with prickly heat. He had a picture of porters being brought—an attempt to explain what he was, why he was there in the flat—the arrival of the police.

He pulled back the bolt and opened the door. The girl was tall, with brown hair to her neck, pulled back behind her ears. She wore a dark blue suit with a setter in diamonds on her lapel. He had the impression that he'd seen her before. As she came into the room, he recognized the girl in the photographs.

In the flesh, she lost none of the composure that her pictures promised. She gave the impression of being aware without being afraid. Hobbled a little by the tightness of her skirt, she stalked by Greg into the flat. She passed close enough for him to smell her sharp, expensive scent. She inspected the room, taking in every detail. The ill-made bed, littered magazines and overloaded ash-trays.

" What *is* going on?" She turned to face him. His back to it, he closed the door. Over the bolt, his hand hesitated. He left it. Her lipstick had been used as an aid, not a disguise. When she spoke, she showed good teeth. " Where's Norman?"

Almost, Greg felt, as if he were supposed to have the guy in his pocket. " You'll have to excuse me—it probably looks a bit odd. The fact is, a friend of mine took this place for a month. I'm simply spending a couple of nights here."

She watched him curiously as he limped towards her. " But *why?* I mean this is all news to me—I'd no idea that Norman was away."

He shrugged.

" In Spain. For a month. That's what I understand." There seemed to be something more than enquiry in the voice. Jealousy, almost. Maybe she had him pegged as one of the lovers!

" I drove up from the country today," she persisted, " Norman hadn't left a message. He always does. Besides—he's never let the flat before." She was still dubious. " I phoned here twice this evening but nobody answered."

He smiled ruefully. " I was in the bath." He let his right hand fall. " It's a bit difficult for me to get around. I've got a tin leg."

Between her dark eyebrows, a small furrow was showing. " Please sit down," she said quickly. " I didn't realize . . ." He pushed a chair behind her. With the tightly bound splint on his leg, it was impossible to move comfortably.

She took the cigarette he offered. " You're an American, aren't you?"

He had kept his left hand out of sight. " No light," he said suddenly. He went out to the kitchen. When he returned, he had matches in his gloved left hand. Let her think what she liked. Already the story had taken shape in his mind. A pilot shot down, beat-up and burned.

" That's right," he said. " I'm a writer. Philip Drury." The grin was wholehearted. She was good to grin at.

" I'm Bridget Selkirk." She had the complete social ease of one very sure of herself. She dragged at the cigarette a couple of times then stubbed it into the ash tray. Her hands were strong without being masculine. Her nails, a tribute to time or expense. " I must go," she said suddenly.

Deliberately, he looked at her. " Please don't." With any luck, he reasoned, he'd be able to build up this false personality. Lull any suspicion that might still remain. If she'd driven up from the country, the chances were that she wouldn't have looked at a newspaper. If she had, there was no reason for her to associaate him with a man on the run. Sloane had been right. Nobody remembered a face once seen in a newspaper.

He held out the cigarette pack, unsure why he really wanted her to stay. " Please don't," he repeated. He went on impulsively. " You probably came here ready for dinner. Right?"

She put both ankles together and considered them. " Yes, I did."

" Then why not have it?" He continued before she had a chance to interrupt. " Imagine it's Mr. Bishop." She looked hard at him. " It's difficult for me to get around with this." Warming to the rôle, he succeeded in looking woebegone. " Why not eat a meal with me?"

She made a sound halfway between amusement and exasperation. " That's ridiculous!"

" Is it?" he asked. " Is it? Or do you mean that you're not in the habit of eating meals with fresh Americans?"

She was relaxed again now. Indifferently, she took a fresh cigarette from the pack he still held. " Either you're mad," she said, "or conceited to a degree. Probably both." She waited as he held a flame to her cigarette watching as the smoke curled away from her. " Who looks after you here?" she asked suddenly.

He frowned, pretending to consider. " Women bang on the door all day long. I ask them in to look at my garbage collection."

Completely feminine yet without affectation, she put a hand to her neck, lifting her hair and shaking it back. " All right." She looked at him coolly. " I'll cook you a meal. Have you anything to eat?"

She used the drawers and cupboards in the kitchen with the ease of familiarity. He leaned against the door jamb, watching her. She knew this flat inside out. He was beginning to dislike Bishop. And, he told himself, with a reason, now.

She cooked without fuss and with an economy of movement that fascinated him. They ate ham and eggs, fruit from a can. They were still eating when the phone rang. It was the normal continued buzz. He kept eating. Her mouth full, she looked at him enquiringly. He made a token movement to get up. She beat him to the instrument. As he looked at her, she wiped her mouth. " Wrong number."

They drank gin. Already, for him, yesterday seemed remote. There was a sense of normality about being here with this girl. Yet he knew with certainty that with one false move she'd be gone. Only a girl of this type would have been able to handle a whore's dilemma like a duchess. With the unaccustomed liquor dulling his control, he pulled himself together. The girl's eyes were still clear and her gaze level.

" What kind of books do you write, Mr. Drury?" She spoke quietly and with interest.

" Cops and robbers," he decided. " Epics with honest cops and dastardly robbers."

" Are they good books?"

He blew out his cheeks. " God knows!"

" They probably are." Without letting her eyes leave his face she nodded assent. " Yes. You look as though you do whatever you set out to do."

" Not always," he said. The quizzical look was on its way before he remembered. But if she noticed, she showed no sign of it.

There was a friendly atmosphere in the room. One that had nothing to do with gin, he told himself. There were the long silences that come when two people are content to sit, without question and answer. They finished two-thirds of the gin bottle. He was in the kitchen getting more ice when she called.

" Do you know any rich bitches, Mr. Drury?"

He called back to her. " No! It's a contradiction in terms."

" No, but *have* you?" she insisted.

When he came back into the room, she was walking about in stockinged feet, opening drawers then shutting them. Once she belched without comment.

" Rich bitch," she chanted. " Spoiled brat. Buy what you want." For the first time he realised that she was slightly drunk. " Can you do that, Mr. Drury? Buy what you want?"

He put the small ice squares on the tray. " Not often enough."

She shook her head, sending the long straight brown hair swinging. " You can't. In four letter words, Mr. Drury, B . . . ."

He was suddenly sick of it. He wanted no significant discussions with this girl. With any girl, even sober ones. Any time Judith had touched on fundamentals, he had taken his hat and gone. He was already wondering what he was going to say to Sloane. If anything. With conscious lack of reason, he blamed the girl rather than himself for his mental disloyalty to his partner.

As though she had understood that their moods had changed, she wriggled her feet into her shoes. " I must go. Thanks for the meal, Mr. Drury." She gave him her hand. It was a shake and no more.

" So long. And thank you for staying."

He held the door slightly open for her and waited as she went to the elevator. She turned, lifted a hand and stepped to the cage. He shut the door and rammed home the bolt.

He was glad it was over. He washed up the crockery and threw the empty gin bottle under the sink. In the living room, the telephone books were by the bedside. He took S-Z. Against Bridget Selkirk's name was an address and a number. He wrote both on a piece of paper and pocketed it. Taking the splint off his leg, he went to bed.

With the lights out and the curtains drawn back, he watched the lights in the sky for some time before he dropped off to sleep. Her scent was still sharp in the warm room.

FIVE

He awoke to leaden skies that whipped rain against the windows in vicious bursts. He stirred uneasily, unable to recognize the unfamiliar outlines. He propped on an elbow and lit a cigarette. He wanted to go back to sleep. To avoid recollection of the previous evening. A dozen accusing memories clamoured in his brain. The publicity attached to his escape was certainly not finished. It was possible that Bridget Selkirk would read something, hear something and in turn remember.

At the last, he thought, that jerk Bishop had been on her mind. Drink—the certainty that she was with someone she would probably never see again—had caught her unguarded. He had admired her poise. Now, vaguely, he resented the idea that she had been on the brink of denying it. Of admitting a breach in her defences.

Christ, he thought, what a life! To be so fond of a queer as to be willing to marry him. What was she trying to prove? Defying every convention save that of the *milieu* that was ready to welcome them both. A world of sad bastards whose talk was never of things but of people.

It was almost eight. His brain, still obeying the jail's insistent morning bell, woke early. He switched on the set beside him. The voice droned but had little to offer about his escape.

"There is still no further news of the whereabouts of Paul Gregory, the prisoner who escaped from his cell in Wandsworth Prison. The police . . ."

Throttling the volume, he tuned in on one of the French stations. He went into the bathroom, dragging his right leg a little and whistling. Even without the splint, his leg was stiff.

He took his time shaving and was eating his breakfast when Sloane's warning combination buzzed from the sitting room. Greg took the call. Sloane was on his way up.

Almost complacently, Greg made his toilet. He wrapped the linen strips round the splints on his leg. The good feel of the grey sports suit had gone. In Paris, he'd stock up on shirts and shoes. And there were English and American tailors there who made suits in a hurry. For a thousand pounds, he could buy the sort of wardrobe he had coveted. That was an idea—maybe in Paris he'd let Sloane's man take some more of the fivers. Enough to produce a year's living without Greg taking a chance with the stuff himself. It was impossible for the numbers to have been circulated throughout the entire world. In places as remote as Mexico or the Argentine. And once out of England, he'd have no trouble with police. For his money, INTERPOL was about as effective an organization as Clancy's Army. Not a single working cop in the outfit. It was nothing but a clearing-house for police statistics—an excuse for high-ranking cops to career round the world attending conventions. The only time INTERPOL need bother a man on the run was when they had a known destination or a passport number. With him they'd have neither, if Sloane kept on the ball.

The thought was arresting enough to interrupt his dressing. Tie in hand, he worried about Sloane. For years, Greg had taken him for granted. Sloane had always been there, like the Rock of Gibraltar. Never a ball of fire when it came to ideas, the big slow man had been completely dependable. Now, it occurred to Greg that he knew little about his partner. Maybe Sloane was one of these inarticulate idealists. Maybe his feet weren't as squarely on the ground as Greg had imagined.

He finished knotting his tie as the door flap lifted behind him. Hand on the bolt, he waited till he heard Sloane's cautious voice then opened the door.

The big man came in shaking the rain from his hat. He warmed his hands at the fire, watching quizzically as Greg limped after him. They sat deep in their chairs, like old clubmen wagging their heads at the world.

Sloane spoke first, the furrows round his eyes and nose deepening as he smiled his appreciation. " That's quite a production. What have you got on it, plaster?"

Greg rolled up his trouser leg, rapping the slats with his knuckles. " It'll do. What's the news on the passport?"

Lazily, Sloane lifted his weight as he reached in his pocket. He lit his cigarette, squinting along its length. " Your worries are over, friend. I'll be up to-night to take the picture. I'll have it developed by tomorrow morning." He blew a casual cloud of smoke. " This guy from Manchester's all right. I've done some more checking. He's been inside himself."

Greg came up straight. " What the hell are you talking about! Every informer in town has been inside. That makes him all right?"

Sloane flipped his ash to the floor, shaking his head. " No, but he could easily go inside again. With a slight shove, and he knows it."

It was a new side to Sloane. An unprecedented affront to the code that forbade using an informer's own weapon to defeat him. But it was an effective one.

" And the boat?" The passport would be useless till he was out of England. His description and picture would be at every port.

" A banana boat," Sloane grinned, " leaves Avonmouth—Bristol—Thursday night, gets into Cork the next morning. I'll take you down by car."

" What about getting on the boat? There are dock police and Jeez knows what at the gates!"

" You don't have to bother about them. The boat's anchored out in the Channel. My man's the bo'sun. He'll take you out by dinghy. You'll be locked in the ship's stores till you get to Cork. He'll get you off." Sloane linked his hands behind his head and closed his eyes. " No cops. No immigration. You'll see nobody."

Now that the decision was made, there was a feeling of anticlimax. Embarrassed, Greg avoided looking at his partner. " You've done the hell of a lot for me one way and another, Sloane. I intend to see that you're taken care of before I leave."

Sloane shrugged indifferently. " Isn't it what you'd have done for me?"

The grey prison uniform, still damp, and the rope were in the canvas carryall. Greg brought the bag into the room and started to unpack.

" Get these clothes back," he instructed. " Send 'em to the Governor. This guy can register them from Manchester when he gets back." He ran his hand along the sodden rope. " Pity. I'd have liked to keep this as a souvenir."

" I will," said Sloane. " It's my tow-rope. Leave the rest of the junk in the bag."

" I need the bag," Greg spoke steadily. They looked at one another for a second. " I need it today," he repeated.

" You're going out?" asked Sloane.

" That's right. I'm going out," answered Greg.

The small flat had become refuge. Once on the street he was a man on the run. The doorman who tipped his hat, the stranger who asked for a light. Out there, everyone represented a threat. He was suddenly envious of Sloane, two thousand pounds the richer and with no fear of a tap on the shoulder. Those long hours, Greg remembered, when the cops had tried to break him, he'd kept his mouth shut. Their interest in Sloane had dwindled with the realization that their case against Greg was open and shut. Sloane had no worries.

" Do you want me to drive you?"

" I'll grab a cab. One of us has to be in circulation if anything goes wrong. That's another thing. You better hire a car for this trip on Thursday night. Don't use yours."

" Right." Sloane busied himself packing the rope and uniform into brown paper. " I'll be up about eight with my camera." He hesitated. " There's nothing else you want me to do, Greg?"

Yes, get the hell out of here and leave me alone, he thought. Sloane's calmness was beginning to irritate him. The notion of leaving the flat put him back in the desperate seconds when he had gone through his cell window. He was vulnerable. Afraid. And he wanted to be alone.

" See that Judith gets a message that I'm all right. You don't have to go yourself. Just see she gets the message. Tell her I'll contact her through Mary when the time comes and tell her what to do. She'll know who I mean."

Carrying the package, Sloane waited by the door as Greg limped across. He touched Greg's shoulder. " It'll be done."

He stood a long time at the window, watching the street. The pavements under the rain shone like black glass. Against the grey of the King's Road, the neon sign of an espresso bar glowed. A nursemaid, in old-fashioned cape, trundled a child into the block. Three art students, their sex indefinable from their clothes, walked bravely into the rain. None of the parked cars looked suspicious.

He buttoned the stormcoat under his chin, pulled his hat down and unbolted the door. If he went to the end of the corridor, Sloane had said, he'd hit the service stairs. There was a small swing door at the bottom, unguarded and unlocked during the day. Carrying the canvas bag, he made the descent. It was impossible to negotiate the steps in normal fashion. He stood sideways, lowering the stiff right leg from one step to another. At the bottom, a cleaner was on hands and knees, washing the mosaic. As she heard him, she looked up. Her pale inquisitive eyes softened. She wiped her hands and pulled the door open for him.

There was no cab in sight. He knew fifty people in Chelsea. On the King's Road, he might run into any one of them. The Chelsea Police Station was only a block north. All day long, the squad cars wheeled in and out of the police garage. Every man on the crew would be on the alert for him.

He turned south, away from danger. Behind him, two hundred yards up the street, a car pulled away from the kerb. It moved after him, travelling slowly.

A cab was paying off at the bottom of Flood Street. Greg flagged it down. He opened the door, dragging his leg but averting his head.

"Oxford Street. Corner of Orchard will do."

The driver spun his cab north towards the King's Road. As they went towards the block again, Greg made himself small in the back. It was impossible to be seen or to see from the nearside window. As the cab had turned, the following car had been parked again. Before the cab reached the top of the street, the car was travelling in the same direction.

Through Knightsbridge, north to Park Lane then east along Oxford Street, the two vehicles kept their distances. Once, the car behind accelerated on the amber to stay within reach.

Greg paid off the cab without waiting for change. As he went through the swing doors, it was eleven o'clock. It was a store with a tradition of American salesmanship. A busy store, thronged by determined shoppers. The safety deposit vault was in the basement. Greg had had a box there for two years without anyone knowing of it. Even Judith. He paid his yearly rental in an assumed name. Always, when he left, the key was sealed in an envelope and left with the vault guard. Greg signed the book to redeem it. The Dodds money was in two cardboard files in his box, less what he'd given to Sloane.

He knew enough of police procedure to be sure that they would cover every vault in the city—checking on people who had recently rented boxes—scanning the lists of holders. He, better than anyone, could be sure that the money he had left there was safe.

Twice, forcing his way through the crowds to the lift, he rammed someone into the counter. Only his limp saved him from unpleasantness. He went to the back of the lift, making himself inconspicuous till they reached the bargain basement.

A half-acre of marked-down socks, household appliances, garden hose, paint and " genuine simulated alligator handbags " were spread out around him. Harassed sales girls clutched desperately at their gentility under a barrage of enquiry. The stairway to the vault was at the far end of the basement. Through bronze doors where the first of the security guards checked names against a register.

He dragged round the outside of the crowds to make better time. His leg was paining. The bandages had been too tightly wound, preventing the blood from circulating properly. To adjust them, he would have to lock himself in the lavatory. There was no time for that.

Near the vault entrance, the floor space had been cleared of counters for thirty feet. There was a no-man's land, skirted by indifferent bargain hunters. A few yards away, Greg stopped, joining a group of bystanders surrounding a gadget demonstrator. The vault guard was no longer alone. A fat man in a macintosh was standing near him. Greg watched the byplay. Without moving their heads or looking at one another, the two men were carrying on a conversation.

Greg moved round so that, his back to them, he watched every move that they made, in a mirror. The fat man unfolded a newspaper and held it in front of him. Still without moving his head he was watching the passing crowd.

Limping faster, Greg pushed his way back to the lift. It might be a store detective. Men and women, there were fifty of them in the place. It could well be a man from the Yard or merely a plain-clothes hack from one of the nearby stations. One thing was certain. Whoever the man, he was not looking for Greg. But by now, his face, his description, could be in the mind of every member of the Metropolitan Force. They could even have his picture in their pockets. He *had* to assume it. The guy could stand there for three hours. There was no way of telling. Tomorrow had to be another day.

At a push, he could get Sloane to collect the money for him. If he had to trust anybody, it would be Sloane. It came as a shock to realize that nobody but he *could* collect. The vault security officers were unlikely to accept an authority given to somebody else.

Doubling on his tracks like a hound-ridden hare, he rode the lift to the top floor. Then rode it down again. Changing cars, he went to the fourth floor and came down on the escalator.

On the street, he stopped a passing cab and asked to be driven to Paddington Station. As the cab moved off, he peered through the darkened back window.

He stopped the cab on Praed Street, opposite the station. Railway terminals were popular with cops on detail and for those on a roving commission. As at dog tracks and prize fights, there would be two or three Flying Squad cars parked in the vicinity of the station. The days were gone when you could tell a squad car by the squat nickelled nose of the Railton. Now they used Jaguars, Bentleys, Wolseleys. In them, the picked men of the Yard—the " Heavy Mob." They'd be in there, scanning arrivals and departures with as much interest as a train dispatcher.

He walked twenty yards south towards Sussex Gardens and found another cruiser. He gave the driver a random number on Chelsea Embankment and leaned back. He lit a cigarette but it tasted stale. A second was no better. Bile embittered his mouth and he wanted to be sick. Yesterday, any sort of movement had seemed preferable to being screwed up in the small apartment. Now, every screaming nerve in his body waited for the door of the flat to close behind him. There were two more days of it. He decided to be at the vault in the morning at opening time.

He paid off the cab, lingering till it had disappeared. He walked north along Flood Street, leaning into the rain squalls. He entered the block in the same way that he had left it. He met no one. It was noon. He stowed the canvas bag in a closet and picked at a lunch he ate standing, the top of the refrigerator his table. When he had eaten, he took the splints from his leg. The flesh was ridged and livid. He sat for an hour, kneading the cramped muscles till the blood flowed freely again.

He slept. When he awakened, the room was in darkness. He went to the window. The rain had stopped. The lights of the King's Road threw sharp shadows round the red-brick apartment building. Sick of watching for some vague danger that he never wanted to recognize, he drew the curtains and put on the light. On the wall, the clock said eight. He went back to the window, yanked the thick stuff to one side and flipped the light button. The fire glowed, warming the darkness.

The phone came to life like a bee in a bottle. It was Sloane. When the flap in the door moved gently, Greg drew the bolt. Sloane barely had space to squeeze his bulk by as Greg closed the door and refastened it. They sat in the chairs, facing one another across the fire.

" What's the matter, the light gone?" Sloane's voice cracked and he repeated the last three words.

" I like it," said Greg. Unaccountably, he was impelled to vent the frustration of the morning on Sloane. " Is there anything wrong, having it out? Wanting to sit in the dark?" he asked impatiently.

" Nothing," said Sloane.

They sat for a while in silence. He felt the anger rising, a driving urge to destroy blindly. " Don't just sit there!" his voice pitched high. " Where's the camera? Let's get it over. Christ, Sloane, but I'm sick of this set-up." Eagerly, he fastened on the opportunity to attack. " That was a great idea you had, telling me to use those back stairs. I almost fell over some bag on her knees. If she hasn't been at the Yard all afternoon, picking out my picture, it won't be your fault."

Relaxed in his chair, Sloane kept silence. The bars of the fire glowed, silhouetting his broad shoulders. He pulled up his legs, taking their weight on his toes.

" There isn't going to be a picture, Greg," he said. " There isn't going to be a picture, a boat, *nothing* until I take that money."

Three times before, possibly, Greg had heard the same flat finality in the other man's voice. Unalterable decision backed by two hundred and fifty pounds of savage endeavour. In a brawl, Sloane lost none of his certainty.

Greg bent forward, touching the switch for the top half of the fire and hiding his face. He chose not to understand, forcing the fear from his voice.

" Money for what? The passport? If the guy wants it now, *you* give it to him."

The lights in the next door flat went on. In the reflected glow at the window he could see Sloane's mouth, the white of his teeth as he spoke.

" F . . . the passport," said Sloane pleasantly. " I want the money you got from the vault this morning. I'm taking it if I have to belt you bowlegged to do it. I've waited a long time for this, Greg."

Greg made no answer. Without thinking, he brought his hand near the flame of the fire, watching it. He knew he had to laugh. Like some Victorian melodrama, he thought. With the next line, " He who lives by the sword . . ."

" That's great," he said nervously. " Yeh, that's a good thing to learn. What a friend you turned out to be! OK, Sloane. I'm going to make your name stink wherever you show your face." Hate drove him on. " You big bum! You never had a brain in your head that I didn't put there. The money's right where it was. I changed my mind, Sloane." Dimly, he realized he was shouting. " Changed my mind!" Digging his heels into the rug, he drove his chair backwards then came to his feet, a cut-glass ash-tray in his hand.

" I followed you," Sloane said simply. " You went in with the bag. You came back to the block with the bag." Deep in their folds, his eyes were unwavering. " For years, you've used me as you use everyone else. Even your wife. Everybody. Two lousy grand while you get twenty-eight," he said bitterly. He got to his feet.

Greg backed behind his chair. " OK, Sloane. OK. You want the money. And I'm telling you it's not here."

As swift as a clawing bear, Sloane's foot shot the chair at Greg's middle. He grunted as the heavy glass tray struck his forehead. The blood running into his eyes, he shook his head and came on. White-lipped, Greg managed to avoid Sloane's outstretched arms and kicked viciously at the big man's crutch. Sloane took the foot on his thigh. Lunging forward, he caught the back of Greg's neck in his left hand. Pulling Greg on to the punch, he smashed with his full weight. The blow took Greg on the side of the head. His knees gave. As he started to drop, Sloane hooked him, once with the left, once with the right. Greg went down to the floor. Very deliberately, Sloane stepped over him and drove his right foot into Greg's side.

Pain tore at his head and his side. He lay on the floor, unable to move yet conscious. He could hear Sloane's heavy breathing as he scattered clothes and linen in the closets. The tipped chair had fallen against the bars of the fire. Slowly, like petals of an opening flower, the polished surface was cracking and peeling back.

When he opened his eyes again, Sloane was standing over him. The chair was upright but the room stank of smouldering wood. He started to struggle upright, licking his lips but the words would not come. " You . . . bastard," he gasped.

Delicately, Sloane put the flat of his foot on Greg's chest, pinning him back on the floor. " I ought to break your back," Sloane snarled. He dabbed with a blood-soaked handkerchief at his forehead. A flap of skin hung perversely, like a dog-eared book page. "*What did you do with that money?*" He brought the edge of his heel on Greg's gullet. Slowly, Sloane increased the pressure. Greg's hands drummed on the floor. Sloane took away his heel.

" Didn't . . . get . . . it." The words were croaked. " Foxy . . . Sloane." Somehow, he managed to twist his swollen face into a sneer.

The big man pulled up a chair and sat down in it. Leaning across Greg, he spoke very distinctly, dropping the words with emphasis. " Now you listen. You can go no place without me. There are a hundred thousand of them out there, all ready to blow the whistle on you. You better remember that. Tomorrow morning, we're going to collect that money, together." He grinned down at Greg. " I'm a better friend than you think, Greg. Didn't I get you out of Wandsworth? And listen—I'm going to stake you to everything. Passport, a ticket from Dublin to Paris and a hundred pounds to bankroll you." He shook his great shoulders and got to his feet. " Sloane," he mimicked. " Good old reliable Sloane."

The sharp peal of the doorbell interrupted him. They waited, not moving, then the bell rang again. Like an uncertain animal Sloane turned his head from the door to Greg.

" Open it," whispered Greg.

Light from the corridor outside spilled through the barely-opened door. From the floor, he watched as Sloane talked to someone outside. It was a woman's voice, cultured and diffident.

" I hope you'll excuse me, I live next door," she began. He heard her drawn breath as she saw Sloane's forehead. " God! How awful! You've hurt yourself . . ."

Sloane put his hand to the wound as if he had just noticed it. " No, thanks." He cleared his throat. " I mean, yes. I was fixing a light in the socket and got a shock. I landed on my head. It'll be all right. I was just going out for a doctor."

Concern sounded in the woman's voice. " You must. It looks simply terrible. We heard a bang. Then I thought I smelt something on fire." She hesitated, letting the amusement creep into her voice. " My husband wouldn't come. He said it sounded just like two people rowing."

" Good-bye," said Sloane, closing the door. " It'll be all right. Thanks for your kindness." He stood still by the door till he heard the woman go back into her own flat.

Now that the danger had passed, the enmity between them was once more a ponderous thing in the dark room. " I'll be up in the morning," said Sloane. "Nine o'clock. Be ready. If you do what's necessary, you'll have your passport before night." He turned at the door. " Sleep well, dasher!"

For a long while, he lay where Sloane had left him. In the half-light, he could see the time. It was nine-fifteen. With an effort, he got to his feet and went into the bathroom. For ten minutes, he stood straddled over the lavatory bowl, his forehead against the cool of the pipe. Suddenly he was violently sick. He poured himself a shot of whisky and sat on the edge of the bath. He had two large lumps over each ear, one on his temple. Sloane's toe had left its mark on his side.

But the damage that Sloane had done to Greg went much deeper. It was a door that had always been open, now slammed suddenly shut. For years, Greg had been sure of his partner. A gentle giant, incapable of treachery, Sloane had been unable to understand it. He hated any evidence of it with the classic venom of his calling. Time and again, these past years, Sloane's strictures of an unethical thief had been more final than Greg's. For the guy who held out on a partner—the police informer—the pimp—the man who made a play for a woman whose lover was in jail—Sloane had but one criticism: " Rat!"

With any personal interest and faced with the outcast, Sloane struck swiftly and savagely, the only way he knew. Battering his opponent senseless with religious fury. These were the occasions when Greg had seen the same finality on his partner's face that had been there that night.

There had been no compromise with Sloane. Lacking imagination, he was unable to accept an excuse for whatever the Code deemed inexcusable.

Greg held his head in his hands, tenderly touching the swelling. The big bastard hadn't a brain! Every play had always been called by Greg. That crack about " using people ". *Using* them! If it hadn't been for him, Sloane would still be where Greg had found him. Odd job man for the con mob. A dogged retriever who barked to order. Greg had taught him to order a suit, to own a car, to harness his dependability.

He moved his head wearily. Finished, he thought. In some unaccountable way, it was Sloane who possessed the initiative. A rat who from now on had to be treated as such. With one eye on the clock, he bathed his head, wincing as the cloth touched the contusions. One thing, Sloane's forehead would need stitches. It was a pity it hadn't been his throat.

In the mirror, the swellings extended to both his cheekbones, giving him an asymmetrical Mongolian look. He had to leave the flat as soon as he could. This woman next door—maybe she would call one of the porters, the building management or somebody. A thing like that might end anywhere. After tonight, this place was about as safe as the steps of Savile Row Police Station.

He moved round the flat in his gloved hands. Every surface that might offer a possible fingerprint, he rubbed with a damp cloth. He ran a bath full of boiling water, dumping into it crockery, ashtrays, household utensils. The small articles that would take too long to wipe. From now, he had to outsmart Sloane. His partner—ex-partner—would hardly be likely to do any open coppering. With Greg in jail, the big man had no chance of collecting a nickel. Once he found Greg missing, Sloane would make for the vault. He knew that it opened at ten. And there he'd wait till he got tired of it. Sloane's brain handled ideas cautiously. But once accepted, they were unshakable. Exposure, a chance of escape. These were the things that Sloane thought his strength. Somehow, Greg had to nullify both threats.

First, he must find a place where he could stay the night. Hotels, the steam baths, these were the places the police would be watching. The all-night cafés in Soho—the ones used by whores and their escorts, were always being turned over by the cops. And they were stiff with the scum of the West End. The card-players, weed-peddlers, bandsmen and thieves. The fringe of the underworld with every man out to earn a dollar the best way he could. Preferably by informing. The Maltese and Cypriot owners of Greasy Spoons, ready to turn any trick that would keep their places free of police surveillance.

This was what Sloane had done for him, he thought bitterly. For the first time, he had to consider who there was in London he could trust with his liberty. It wasn't much of a list. Three, maybe four. There was Judith, of course. But the house at Henley was under a twenty-four hour a day watch. And how sure *could* he be of this new Judith?

Still aware of the passing minutes, he sat in the chair in the sitting room. Money. He took stock. Just over three of the five pounds remained. He'd have to get some from somewhere.

He picked up the phone and dialled two numbers. There was no reply from either. Each time, before replacing the receiver, he spun the dial from force of habit. The manoeuvre destroyed all chance of anyone recording the numbers he'd dialled, as long as it was a local call. The third call was answered. A girl's voice told him that Cameron was still at the Club.

He put on the stormcoat, switched off the light and opened the door. The corridor was still. Tiptoeing past his neighbours, he went down the service stairs to the floor below. He would have to take the lift to the basement and hope that he met nobody. The door that he'd used in the morning was shut at night, locked.

He left the cage gate open to avoid making noise. The brightly-lit passage that led to the boiler room, with its rows of pipes painted red, blue and yellow, was like a gangway aboard ship. He moved along the wall silently, eyes on the arched entrance in front of him. He was through it before he saw the old man who was watching him. Bald, in oil-soaked jeans, the furnace man sat in a canvas-backed chair, a newspaper in his lap.

Greg waved a hand vaguely. "A dog," he said. "Black retriever. Have you seen him? Just taking him out and he bolted." Past the shining brass and trembling gauges, on the other side of the room, he could see the door to the street. It was shut tight.

The old man made no answer. He sat staring at Greg's face. Then he swung his knee to the ground and the paper fell to the floor.

Greg flexed his right hand in his pocket. He gathered the loose change in his fist. He was taking no chances. It was a street fighter's trick, one that gave crushing force to a blow delivered with the clenched fist. He took a step towards the furnace man.

"I know you're talking to me." The old man blinked. "But I can't 'ear a thing. I'm stone-deaf, sir."

"Door," breathed Greg. "Black dog." He pointed across the room.

The furnace man wagged his head. "Door, sir? Over here. Lorst a dawg, 'ave you, sir?" Mumbling to himself, he shuffled in sneakers to the barred exit and lifted the bolt.

SIX

OUTSIDE, it was dry but colder. The sky was filled with bright stars. He stood where he was for a moment. Only one car was parked near the apartment building. It bore no lights. Forcing himself, he walked forward towards it. It was a different make to Sloane's and empty. He pulled up his collar, fastening the tiny strap across his mouth. Most of his face was covered. He walked quickly east, past the cloistered quiet of the Royal Hospital and into Lower Sloane Street. The illuminated sign of a free cab pulled from a side street. Stopping it, he asked to be driven to the Dutch Air Line Terminal. Outside the K.L.M. offices, he paid off the driver and walked straight through the swing doors. Out through at the far end of the Booking Hall and into the alley that ran parallel. Looking neither left nor right, he climbed the slope to Lowndes Square and crossed.

In front of him was a small block of shops with an arcade in the middle. He walked in. A tall negro doorman swung a lazy salute. Greg climbed the short flight of stairs to a closed door with a small plaque on it.

MARS BAR—MEMBERS ONLY.

He turned the handle. He was in a small ante-room. On his right, an elegant array of furs, coats and hats were behind a counter. A membership book lay open on a small round table. Two girls, alike with their Italian hair style and uniform of orange sweaters and black trousers, looked up as he spoke.

" Will you tell Mr. Cameron that I'd like to see him?"

The girl at the table answered. Her "r's" had a Latin quality that made her accent dubious. " Are you a member, sir?" He shook his head. Her smile brightened to the meaningless mask used by those who handle the public. " I'm afraid Mr. Cameron . . ."

" Just tell him Paul," said Greg.

" Certainly, Mr. Paul."

He took a seat by the mirror. The ante-room was lined with pictures of people looking arch, important or decorative. The inscriptions on them fitted the faces. Greg studied them. Many of the faces he recognized. Theatre, films, the Bar and what New York called " café society " were represented.

Behind her counter, the other girl was looking at him with interest. For the first time, he realised he was still wearing his hat. He removed it. In the new uncertainty, he was reluctant to part with anything that left him unready to move at speed. Through the open door, he could see that the downstairs bar was crowded. Beyond, were candle-lit tables where people were eating. To the right of the vestiaire, a red-carpeted stairway followed a mural of beckoning satyrs and nymphs.

" Eat, drink, and for God's sake be merry " said a sign over the rope handrail. From upstairs came the sound of a calypso band. In the downstairs bar, a mulatto with a guitar sang chansonettes. He gave the lyrics impudent suggestiveness.

In five years, Greg thought, Bill Cameron had done all this. Cameron had taken his last corner as a con man and gambled with the lease to a deserted theatre club. For two thousand pounds, he had an upstairs auditorium that seated three hundred and a tea-bar downstairs where women in flat shoes and knitted dresses had discussed Kafka. It had been a good score, that last one of Cameron's. Three of them had cut up five thousand apiece. With the rest of his money, Cameron had made down payments to interior decorators, bar builders, and firms supplying kitchen equipment. From the moment his club had opened, Cameron had made money as fast as a paper mill. As he put it, he'd been selling gold-bricks to suckers for thirty years, too bad if he couldn't sell them good liquor. Every stick in the place, even his reason for being there, reminded Greg of the twenty-eight thousand and his own urge to respectability.

As Cameron followed the girl into the ante-room, Greg got up. The small fat man came through, his tiny feet treading delicately as if testing rotting boards. He wore an expression of general welcome that changed as he recognized Greg. His voice sounded natural.

" Good evening, Mr. Paul. I'm afraid I forgot that you were coming." He had the pleasing accent of someone from British Columbia. " Will you leave your hat and coat?"

He nodded at both girls and, taking Greg's elbow, steered him through to the bar. Cameron passed among the crowd with a compliment for the women, a smile of congratulation for the men, tolerance for the witless joke. Behind the guitarist was a table by the wall marked *Reserved*. They went to it.

Cameron moved the candlestick to one side. A blonde girl, her high breasts pushing the stuff of her orange sweater, hurried over.

" Two large whiskys from my bottle," ordered Cameron. When the girl had gone, he lowered his voice. " Christ Almighty!" he said with feeling. " What made you come here?"

Greg shifted the weight of his feet. In the soft light, the bruised lumps were less prominent but he kept his head between his hand, leaning across the table. Faced with the fleshy elegance of the other, he felt dirty—unwashed and aware of his soiled shirt, his empty pockets.

" You've got to help me, Cameron." He waited as the girl put the drinks on the table.

The fat man spoke to the blonde. " All right, Rosa. We'll eat in a minute. Come back." The girl included Greg in her swift smile.

Cameron touched flame to Greg's cigarette. Then he rolled his glass, studying the wash as it neared the rim. Suddenly he emptied the glass down his throat. " You listen to me, Greg. I'll do what I can. You know that. But it was a liberty to come here." In their sheaths of fat, his bright eyes were never still. " Why didn't you call me at home?"

" I did," answered Greg. " They said you were here."

Cameron nodded as if remembering countless hurried exits of his own. The guarded knocks at dead of night on the door of a friend. " Suppose you're pinched here—how do you think I come out of it? We're both Canadians. I've got a record. Harbouring an escaped convict, the law'd put me out of business overnight."

" That's for the birds!" *Begging*, he thought bitterly. Crawling to a guy who had been loud in his gratitude in the years that had gone by. " It isn't likely that the Squad's going to burst in here, looking for me."

Cameron flipped his fingers at the blonde girl. " Two more and we'll eat." He smiled at a woman on the dance floor, a brunette with the fashionable look of a cadaver. " You don't think so, eh? Well, let me tell you something. I've got everyone coming here. Reporters, debs, judges and bankers. If one of the Squad comes in here on a social call, he gets a drink on the house. A dozen if he wants them. They leave me alone and I give them no trouble. It isn't like the old days, Greg. Not for me, it isn't." He pointed a finger. " The only people I don't want here are grafters. I don't need their money."

Greg left his second drink where it was. It seemed the best thing to do. " You've changed your patter quite a bit," he said sarcastically. " Twice, I stuck my neck out for you in the past. For friendship, Cameron. Dear Old Pals. Both times, you could have gone inside." His laugh was offensive. " Whatever you do for me will be paid for."

The fat man's face was concerned. " What are you talking about now? he complained. " Don't get your bowels in an uproar about nothing. I wasn't talking about you. It was just that . . . well, for the last couple of days the police have been turning over everyone in town, looking for you. And seeing you stroll in . . ." He leaned across the table in turn, making his words tell. " You need a place for tonight? Somewhere safe to stay?" Greg nodded. " I can't have you home and you can't go to an hotel."

The blonde girl busied herself, putting silver and plates in their places. Cameron's eyes watched the play of her forearms and as she looked up, he smiled at her. Hungry, Greg ate his scampi and allowed the fat man to pour him some hock. Cameron dabbed at his chin with the napkin, making small prissy movements. " I've got it," he said suddenly. " We've got to get you off the streets tonight. Tomorrow we can arrange something definite. You'll have to blow, that's for certain." He looked up curiously. " What about Sloane?"

" Put Sloane at the top of your shit list. He's got to be taken care of."

Cameron turned down the corners of his mouth and raised his eyebrows. He dug no deeper in that vein. " What about money? Ready cash?"

Greg held up two fingers. " Hundreds?" asked Cameron. " Ones," Greg replied.

The fat man reached for an inner pocket then changed his mind. " Tomorrow will do. You won't need any tonight."

" I won't?" asked Greg. " Where am I going then?"

" With Rosa." Cameron silenced the other with upraised hand. " She's a good kid. An Italian. She worked sixteen hours a day. Washing diapers for a family that paid her three quid a week. Here, she makes fifteen. She'll do what I want without asking questions. Tomorrow, we'll make other arrangements." He creased his face, showing his teeth. " Unless it turns out that you like it there."

" I want a bed not a mattress," said Greg. " When do I go?"

Cameron dusted the ash from his trousers. " You'll have to wait till we close. If you sit here, you're out of the way. Blow the candle out if you like. If I let Rosa go now, the others will wonder why. I'll have a word with her. You can leave here with me and she'll be outside with a cab. I'll give her some story." He pulled himself up and trod away on the balls of his feet.

For a second, Greg had the impulse to follow. To grab hat and coat and move. But any place would have given him the same sense of being hemmed in. Trapped with no exit and the hunt drawing nearer. He drank some more of the hock, trying to feel and act normally. The table was tucked in a corner with only one other near. There, a man and a girl were intent on their meal. Rosa, her legs slim and straight in their tight black trousers, was serving them. He expected that she would look at him, but she paid him no heed. Cameron couldn't have spoken to her, Greg decided.

His tension relaxed with the wine. He ordered another bottle of hock from Rosa. Cameron had left a blank signed bill. As Rosa poured, Greg noticed the summer tan, still warm, on her arms and neck. Milan, he thought, with that colouring. He wondered what had brought her to England in the first place. She wrapped the napkin neatly round the bottle and set it by him. He said, " Thank you, Rosa."

Dark blue eyes, faintly amused, she said, " Thank *you*, signor." The look told him that Cameron had spoken to her. He was uncertain what the fat man would have said.

For an hour, he sat at the darkened table, watching the dancers. The guitarist had been replaced by a pianist with the style of Oscar Peterson and hair that bothered him. Half a dozen people watched as he gave a hard, brilliant rendering of the Cole Porter classics.

" Good evening, Mr. Drury."

It wasn't the name that brought his head round, it was the voice. Bridget Selkirk stood watching him. He floundered to his feet, remembering too late the splint he had worn when last he saw her. Her long hair was drawn back and she wore a black dress that looked simple and wasn't. The man she was with was like an escort in any smart bar. She had been one of the group round the piano. Now she stood by Greg's table, cradling a glass of champagne in her hands. Leaning forward, she sipped the wine.

" I thought of you leading the life of a hermit in Norman's flat," she said at last. Her look was quizzical. " I think your life must be fascinating." She hesitated. "*Bonne chance*, Mr. Drury."

He stood, awkwardly silent. Afraid and ashamed. What she said might be innocent enough. He had the feeling that she knew who he was—that he was both thief and liar. He wanted to be able to defend himself, to explain. This was no longer a question of moral judgement. This was The Chase. An endless dark forest where silent hunters awaited him. Somehow, if only he had time, he thought he could enlist her sympathy. Her understanding. He said " Thanks," as she moved away and watched as the man with her collected her coat. The pair went out without looking back.

It was nearly midnight. The grille at the bar was down. The Irish barman slipped a few favoured customers the last drink through the open hatch. Cameron rounded up an elegant drunk, arm round his shoulder, kidded him to the door. With the last customer gone, the fat man became less jovial. He checked the cash in the registers, had an eye for the rows of bottles behind the bar.

The cloths had been whisked from the tables, the candles extinguished. Only one light remained behind the bar. Greg had not moved, letting the darkness surround him like a shield.

His shadow moving in front of him, Cameron tripped across. He had undone the neck of his shirt, pulled down the knot of his tie. He stood at the table, looking at Greg. " Are you fit?" he asked.

It had been pleasant, sitting there for a while. Relaxed in the knowledge that this fat man represented a new lease on freedom. The need to think had gone. He got up wearily, a head taller than Cameron who patted his back.

In Canada, Cameron's impulsion to fondle and pat had earned him the unjustified nickname, " Bill the B. . . . ." It had taken three thousand miles and a hundred women to rid himself of it.

He watched Greg shrug into the storm coat. " You'll need clothes," he said casually.

Greg moved his head. It was good to let someone else take decisions for you. With Cameron, he knew where he was. That slap-your-back routine fooled nobody. For years, Cameron had beaten suckers, patting their backs on their way out. What counted was his debt of loyalty to Greg. It would be discharged.

Still, that crack about paying Cameron for his trouble had not been idle. The business they had thrown each other's way had established one certainty—Cameron never gave, he invested.

The stairs to the street were in darkness. The negro at the door had gone. It was still dry outside. The trees in the deserted square were forlorn and bare. A cab with the flag down waited at the kerb.

Two uniformed policemen stepped from a shop doorway. Instinctively, Greg swung his body in the opposite direction. Only Cameron's muttered assurance stopped him from running. One of the men shone a flash on the club entrance then acknowledged Cameron in broad Scots. " Yon was one o' ye're guid nights, Meester Cameron." With the dignity of sergeant's stripes, he admonished his junior. " It's no always the same, ye'll find oot." The pause that followed covered countless cars parked illegally, gin-fired extravagances that Cameron managed to keep out of court.

" To keep you warm," said the fat man. He reached in his pocket and produced two pound notes that the sergeant pocketed.

" Aye," said the Scot dourly. He looked briefly and without interest at Greg. " Ah weel, Meester Cameron. We've a bit walking to do tae keep us warm. We're away."

They waited till sergeant and constable had crossed the square. Cameron pointed. " I'm parked there. Rosa's in the cab. Don't leave her place till I give you a ring in the morning."

" OK." He looked at the cab. The girl was not in sight. " What did you tell her, Cameron? Why does she think I'm going back to her place?"

The fat man patted Greg's sleeve. " I told her you liked her. And that you are someone I've got to keep sweet." He took his hand away. " Rosa's a good kid, Greg. Be nice to her."

As he opened the door of the cab, Greg saw the tail-lights on Cameron's car round the square. The girl sat in the corner. She wore a camel hair coat and no hat. She smelt like a lady not a whore, he thought. The cab was still stationary and he leaned forward.

" He knows where to go." There was little trace of the accent that Cameron found desirable in his girls.

Greg shut the partition and the cab moved off. Now that his eyes were accustomed to the interior, he could see her face. She gave him her slow smile. " Hello!"

He smiled back, wincing as the skin over his cheekbone

tightened. If she'd been there because she wanted it, things might have been different. But she was an alien with pressure on her, a bar girl doing right by her boss's friend. Her ungloved hand had moved nearer—to be fondled or ignored, as he pleased.

He covered it briefly with his own then lit a cigarette, striving for time. Less to know what to say than how to say it.

They were in the stream of late night traffic, going west on the Old Brompton Road. He didn't care where she lived—as long as it wasn't in Chelsea.

" It's not so far. In South Kensington." She had trouble with the " th ". " What shall I call you?"

" Call me Paul," he answered and was silent.

South Kensington was dangerously near to Chelsea. Remembering, he told himself he'd get Cameron to have Sloane taken care of. This was a false-pretence country when it came to gunmen. They were either pistol-bluffers who carried no shells or lunatics blazing magazines at some thick-skulled cop who was chasing them. But there were a hundred tearaways on tap who would break a man's legs for a couple of hundred, slice with a razor into cheek or neck. The pleasure of dealing with Sloane was one he would have to forego. Best leave it to some spiv from Shepherd's Bush or somewhere. Someone to whom Sloane's bulk on a dark night would mean nothing. Coldly, his hate assessed the chances of getting the big man killed. Wishful thinking in England, he decided.

The cab turned north up Queen's Gate then into a mews. The driver braked outside a cottage with a dwarf tree in a pot in front of it. Greg fished for change.

Rosa put her hand on his arm. " Mr. Cameron has paid." She opened the door. A fat black cat rose to greet her, arching his back. Greg followed her up the steep stairs. Without removing her coat, she went into the tiny kitchen. He could hear her in there, pouring milk, talking to the cat.

He inspected the room. It was a small cottage with a hall downstairs. Upstairs, the room he was sitting in and through an open door, a bedroom. The kitchen backed the bathroom. Both overlooked the mews. At the back of the cottage were two windows. He peered through a chink in the curtains. It was difficult to see. He was able to make out the bare walled gardens of the houses on Queen's Gate. These he knew well. Tall endless houses with magnificent staircases, now turned into flats and " chambers " for people who wanted a room with a good address.

Rosa came out of the kitchen. Without her coat, she looked younger. The bones of her face were good, whether by breeding or chance he could not tell. She yawned.

" I'm tired," she said simply. He nodded and she went through to the bedroom where he could hear her drawing the curtains and lighting the gas fire.

There was a bowl of freesias on the table beside him. Their scent made him think of Bridget Selkirk for some reason. He called the girl's name sharply. She seemed to have left her clothes where they fell. Already she was in candy-striped pyjamas with legs too long for her. She stood in the doorway, brushing her hair over her eyes.

" Sit down, Rosa," he said. He unbuttoned his stormcoat and threw it over the back of a chair. With the obedience of a child, she sat down opposite him. So that she could see, she pushed her hair back but went on brushing, slowly, firmly.

He kept his eyes on his shoes, untying the laces. " You can forget what Cameron told you about me, Rosa. I don't want to sleep with you." He floundered, remembering that no other reason could account for his being there. " I mean make love to you."

Her eyes serious, she tried to follow him. " You think that I am virgin?" She managed to sound modest yet forthright.

He shook his head. " Hell, no! Yes." His voice was rising. " How in hell should I know! It isn't that. Rosa, you've got to understand that I didn't come here for that. I came because I wanted to be with you." He hoped that she would be sufficiently Latin to accept and not try to reason. If she did, maybe she'd have him tagged for some kind of pervert—if she knew what the word meant. In any case, it didn't matter.

He started to kick off his shoes. " Is there a bed I can use?" he asked.

She was obviously at a loss. " I have a bed. You can see."

He looked round. There wasn't even a sofa. She pointed. " There is the bathroom. I am sorry . . ." she finished.

He threw his jacket on top of his coat. " For Christ's sake don't be sorry! Just say it's nobody's fault. We're both tired. Let it go at that."

In the bathroom, he smeared her toothpaste on a finger and rubbed his gums. In the morning, he'd have a hot bath, at least. His whole body had started to ache anew. The lights in the bedroom were out. Only the gas fire still burned. He pulled back the covers and got in beside her.

He could see her face in the bright light from the fire. Her eyes were dark, receptive. The need to conceal and the urge to confide were fighting it out in his mind. He turned on his side so that they faced one another. Her hand, warm and friendly, found his. They lay like that till the wavering shadows on the ceiling were still and they slept.

It was the cat that disturbed him. An unfamiliar weight kneading his legs, purring its pleasure. Beside him, her hair fanned on the pillow, the girl slept heavily, her mouth slightly open. The gas fire still burned. In spite of the open window, the room was stuffy. It was five a.m. He slid his legs carefully from under the covers and crossed the room. He switched off the fire then stood at the window, gulping the fresh damp air. The curtains had been pulled back, giving an uninterrupted view of the mews outside. He stood there for a minute more.

Then he saw the car. Its lights extinguished, it was travelling slowly towards the cottage. It stopped thirty yards away. He waited long enough to see five men leave it. The mews were a cul-de-sac, a high blank wall closing the end. Two of the men walked back to the mews entrance. The other three moved in the shadow of the houses, headed towards the cottage. It was the quasi-military manoeuvre of the dawn arrest.

His brain signalled wildly. *Cameron!* Without stopping to analyze the fat man's treachery, Greg broke for the sitting room. He pulled on his trousers and coat in desperate haste. The stormcoat and hat he left where they lay. Now the police would have an accurate description of every article that he was wearing. He knotted the laces in his shoes, hanging them round his neck than ran back to the bathroom window. The three men were standing underneath in silence.

As he lifted the catch to the rear sitting-room window, he heard the door downstairs shudder under the impact of a shoulder-charge. He put a leg through the window, then closed it behind him. Hanging from the sill, he dropped twenty feet to the garden below. There was a house in front of him, shuttered and silent. On either side, a brick wall, a dozen feet high. Using hands, knees and feet, he scaled the one to his left, crashing through the cold frame the other side. He had put two more gardens behind him before he heard the window in the cottage being thrown up.

He dropped where he was, burrowing into the dank leaves of

a dead bonfire. Without moving his head, he raised his eyes. One of the Squad men stood framed in the lighted window. Peering into the gardens, searching the gloom in front of him. Without haste, the man put a whistle to his mouth and blew three blasts, two long, one short. Immediately, a police whistle answered from the direction of the mews entrance. In a few seconds, it sounded again, a little further away. A second detective had joined the man at the window. One after the other, they dropped to the garden.

They were out of Greg's sight, screened by the intervening walls. He got to his feet, running blindly from the sound of their pursuit. Forty yards away, the detectives crashed through the bushes, whistles still shrilling. Off to the right, a light at the top of one of the houses went on. He could hear someone shouting enquiry, the answering shouts of the police. They sounded further away now and he realized that they'd gone right instead of left. The shouting continued. Here and there, more lights were showing in the tall houses on Queen's Gate. Some of the cottages in the mews had come to life. He could see the silhouette of a man crawling over the roofs.

Almost soundlessly in his stockinged feet, he climbed wall after wall, leaving behind the commotion. He had no way of telling whether the police had the block surrounded. It would not be easy. Queen's Gate was a wide thoroughfare, half-a-mile long. The last wall was higher. Above it, on the other side, he could see the street lamps of an intersection. In his mind, he saw the long black shape of a Squad car parked behind the brickwork. The men in it, silent and listening.

Somehow, he had to get under cover. The police could search all the gardens. It was unlikely that they would search fifty of these enormous houses. It was still dark. He was re-acting like an animal, flaring his nostrils at the wind that whipped the leaves at his feet. This was a well-tended garden. A hard court surrounded by netting led to a flight of stone steps and a French window. On his left, a brick building looking like a garage. He crept towards it. The windows of the house were silent and curtained. The garage was square with one small dirty window. The garden door to it was locked. He shinned himself up but could see nothing except the drawn catch. Far-off, now, he could still hear the police whistles.

The catch to the window had to be prised back. He dare not risk smashing the glass. Not even if he muffled the sound with his jacket. The damage might be noticed. Beside him, at the foot of the steps, was a bed of bulbs thrusting up green spears. He bent down feeling the moist earth with his fingers. At the edge of the bed, a small wooden stake bore a metal ticket. He tore off the strip of tin, doubling it and pressing it flat with a stone. Picking up an iron garden seat, he carried it to the window. Standing on the seat, he pushed the strip into the space between the sashes. It was a rusty catch and did not budge.

In spite of the cold and the damp, sweat was soaking into his shirt back, running salt, into his eyes. He shoved with both hands on the top sash, taking advantage of the fractional play. The catch moved slightly, vertically. He tried with the piece of tin once more. This time the catch moved back stiffly. He opened the window then carried the iron chair to where he had found it. He was careful to replace the feet in the pits they had left in the soft grass. Pulling himself up, he went through the window and dropped into the garage. He slipped the catch back again.

It was a two-car garage and both stalls were used. A large Humber limousine flanked a Dodge station wagon. There were two naked bulbs in the roof and a wire-cage inspection lamp on the bench beside him. He felt round the walls till his hands found a stack of old newspapers. He doubled a couple and stuffed them against the window. Still more, he rammed in the cracks at the bottom of the door. The light now screened, he moved round the garage, investigating. There was a work bench with a small lathe and tools. New spark plugs in their cases were piled against the wall. Four new tyres in their wrappings. In the corner, a tap dripped. A piece of red soap and a hand towel were near it. A chauffeur's cap hung on the wall.

He tried the cars. Both were unlocked. The clock on the dash of the Humber showed ten minutes past six. On the driver's seat, neatly folded, was the uniform topcoat. Either he could stay in the garage, chancing the use of either one of the cars or stow away in the trunk and chance its inspection.

He looked at the cars speculatively. Or drive one of them away. There were no keys in sight. Most people, he thought, kept a spare set of ignition keys in the garage. He spent a useless quarter hour looking for them. There was a locking device on the steering wheel of the Dodge. The Humber was free. Both petrol-gauges showed to be half-full.

Frantically, he tried to remember the dodges of car thieves, the expertise involved. He knew the principles. It was necessary to bridge a gap in the ignition circuit made by the turn of a key. He felt under the instrument panel. All the cables were concealed. Making a breaker was simple. All he needed was a length of wire. But it would take him hours to find and bare the right cables. He was no electrician.

His eyes lightened as he saw the thermometer hanging on the wall. This was right back in the old days. The ace-in-the-hole to be guarded jealously and used only in an emergency like this—if you had the luck to find a thermometer. It was a cheap model. A tube of glass set against calibrated wood and with a blob of mercury at its base. He pulled out the staples and broke the glass tube on the bench. The mercury ran on the oil-stained wood, liquid and silver. There was a can of putty on the floor. He rolled a pellet of the soft stuff. Tearing a piece of cardboard in two narrow strips, he folded one down its length. With the other, he scraped the mercury into the little trough.

In the driving seat of the Humber, he bent at the ignition lock. With care, he lowered the trough so that the mercury rolled down. Finding the slit of the lock, a small quantity passed inside.

He wiped his forehead on the back of his sleeve. With an eye-dropper, he'd have been able to blow this stuff into the lock in one shot. This way, there was no force. He gave the cardboard trough more elevation. The mercury rolled to the lock and spilled back. But each time, some remained inside. At last, none remained. He sealed the lock with the blob of putty. Inside the lock were two points, positive and negative. The liquid metal should find its level, completing the circuit. He touched the starting button. The motor purred to life.

From now on, there was no way of stopping the motor except by stalling it. His foot off the accelerator, he put the car into top gear and let in the clutch. The heavy limousine jerked then stalled.

He washed his hands, face and feet under the icy water. He could do nothing about the stubble sprouting from his chin. The chauffeur's topcoat was a reasonable fit. The cap settled comfortable over the bruises. They seemed to have gone down. It was a quarter to seven.

He stood at the door to the street for a while then cut the light in the garage. The doors opened outwards and he followed the swing of the door with his head. The street was empty. The big car rolled easily down the slight grade. He put a few of the tools from the bench in his pocket and got into the car. The Humber moved quietly away, throbbing with latent power. Once in Queen's Gate, he sent the car up the incline towards the gate to the Park. He drove with one eye on the driving mirror. Behind him was a long line of cars, parked overnight. A milkman glided up beside him, standing in his delivery float like a charioteer. Back in the direction of the mews, what looked like a furniture truck was parked in the middle of the road.

That would be them, he thought. The Yard had fifty of these observation vehicles, disguised as laundry, delivery and furniture trucks. Under their hoods were souped-up motors. In the back, enough room for a squad of men and a radio operator. Obviously they were still covering the area.

Greg kept going, towards the lights. The car in front had pulled over to the outside lane for no apparent reason. Then Greg saw the block ahead. The automatic signals had been switched off. A uniformed constable was directing the traffic into one lane by the kerb. A group of detectives was checking the occupants.

To the left, a block of apartments had a ramped driveway to the portico. Without haste, he turned the Humber on to the smooth tarmac and stopped at the entrance. There was a porter polishing the brasswork. His thin face knowing, he looked up as the car stopped then came over, snapping his cleaning rag. He greeted Greg with the camaraderie of those who serve the rich.

" Christ, mate," he said. " They got you out early, ain't they?"

Greg could still see the police, beyond the brick wall, as they inspected the cars. One on each side, they were scrutinizing the interiors. A third man walked to the back testing the trunks.

Greg nodded, handkerchief to his mouth. The porter showed no desire to go, absent-mindedly polishing the windshield with his rag. " Ah," he said conversationally. " All on the go, it is ain't it, mate?" He stepped back, head on one side. " Lady 'udson's, ain't it?"

Greg nodded again. This short driveway curved to the side of the building. He remembered another entrance to the block on Knightsbridge. If he followed the driveway round, he would avoid the police check. Even though the cop directing the search knew every inch of the neighbourhood, he'd never be able to have a man covering every driveway and alley. They must have cordoned the main streets leading from the district on the chance that he had been picked up by a car Ten minutes had gone by since he had moved the Humber from the garage. It was unlikely that it had been missed yet. When it was, it would take still more time for the Yard to get the numbers on the air.

The porter looked at the grey sky, shivered and started collecting his cleaning material. " Get the sack, I will. " 'anging around. Them b...... made me all be'ind to start with." He stabbed a finger in the direction of the group of police.

Greg mumbled something through the folds of the handkerchief. The porter blew hard in disgust from one cheek. Still looking at the police he said, " Silly bleeders. Stopped me coming down to work." He affected a mock pompous voice, " 'oo are you? says one. Where do you work? says the other. They've 'ad a burglary down in the mews," he added importantly. " I got it from the milkman." He hunched his shoulders, disassociating himself from everything but his world in the block and went inside.

As unobtrusively as he could, Greg edged the limousine forward. The northbound traffic on Queen's Gate was a single line, ten cars long now. He followed the line of the block till he reached the second portico. Through the entrance in front of him was Knightsbridge. There was a forecourt with a dozen parked cars. The entrance hall was lighted but he could see no one. Putting a cigarette in his mouth, he strolled to the street. The traffic was normal. Loaded buses barrelled down the slope to the West End. On his right, he could see the checked cars filtering into the main stream. He took a quick look at the windows of the apartments. He had to get the plates from one of the parked cars and change them for those on the Humber. Seven out of ten drivers never knew their licence tag numbers, anyway. There was a heavy Rolls with the same type of plates. With a wrench from the Humber, it took him three minutes to unbolt the plates and make the exchange. When the Humber was missed, the police would be trailing the Rolls. It all added to the confusion. Gained time.

He turned the Humber into the traffic. As he passed the top of Queen's Gate, the detectives were still at it. Turning north, through the gate to the Park, he drove over the bridge to the Serpentine and slid the car under the trees at the edge of the lake. There were a few people on the grass, walking their dogs. Hungry swans sailed near to the concrete walk where an elderly man was feeding them from a paper bag. The boathouse was deserted.

He thought about Cameron for the first time since he had left the cottage. He couldn't be sure whether that girl had been in on the deal. The lousy stinking deal. He couldn't be sure of anything or anybody. Maybe that fat copper had used her to bait the trap. He should have realized that the whole production had been too pat. The girl—the cottage—the safe place to stay for the night and the promise of help in the morning. Cameron was much too smart to have had him picked up at the club. He'd have done it cunningly. Probably phoned in from some booth on his way home, giving the girl's address. If she had known, she'd tell the cops anything Cameron told her to say. If not—well, she was an alien, in the country for domestic service. They'd put their own interpretation on Greg's night at the cottage.

He could never know why Cameron had turned copper. Fear, hate, jealousy. Maybe it was just because respectability had given the guy the heart of a rat. He could easily have said no to Greg's plea for help and let it go at that. Before you turned in a man on the run from a jail, you had to have some sort of strong motive. Even the Square Johns—the technically honest—wouldn't do as much. Many of these would neither help nor hinder, but stand on the sidelines with no cheer for either side. Spectators.

He touched the starting button. Pretty soon, the Park would be filled with keepers, the Park police, the nursemaids and busybodies reading their newspapers. This business this morning had put new life into the story of his escape. Too late to catch the dailies, the account would make the early editions of the afternoon papers.

He drove east to Marble Arch, keeping well inside the Park speed limit. He had to wash and shave somewhere. Public lavatories, the Lyons Corner Houses, these were danger spots. He bought a cheap razor and blades and a toothbrush at a chemist's in Oxford Street then turned south into Grosvenor Square. He parked the limousine in front of the American Library and sat there till he saw it being opened. He bundled the chauffeur's cap and uniform topcoat under a seat, left the car and went up the steps to the Library.

SEVEN

INSIDE the slightly decrepit exterior, the old town house had been allowed to keep much of its graciousness. The great drawing rooms, carpeted and lined with bookshelves, offered deep armchairs to those seeking information on the American Way of Life. There were thirty thousand volumes. Americana at its best. Mencken, Hemingway, Faulkner, Capote. Expensive scientific tomes, the progress of industry, the printed record of the greatest success of all time. A gentle heat, thermostatically controlled, lulled even the sceptics. From the record library they might choose from twenty great concert orchestras or the folk music of the Sioux and Chippewa Indians. Books, maps, films and photographs were there to be borrowed. Free of charge and by courtesy of the United States Information Services.

Past the man at the desk on his right, Greg bent at the drinking fountain. Nobody had followed him in. He went down to the lavatories. It was an aseptic world of gleaming tile, soap and hand towels, hot water that spouted from gleaming faucets. There was nobody there. He took his time at the bowl, shaving in comfort. His cheekbones were less swollen. The Oriental look had gone. The slight swelling left gave him the appearance of a seasoned club fighter. When he had washed his teeth, he stripped to the waist. It was still early and he had been first in the library. He whipped soap into the bowl and kneaded his nylon shirt clean. After ringing it in a clean hand-towel, he went into the lavatory and hung it on the wall-heater. Then he locked the door and sat down to wait for it to dry.

By now, Sloane would have gone to the flat in Flood Street. When he found it was empty, he'd break a leg to get back to the vault before it opened.

Greg pulled the nylon straight at the stitching, coaxing the puckering collar. At a push, he could last here in the library for days. There were few visitors, most of them brown-skinned negroes and Hindus, fine-boned Malays and the short-sighted Burmese. All the improbable holders of British passports, oblivious to everything but the pursuit of knowledge. The

English who used the library stayed with their heads in their books, indifferent to their neighbours. For a cop who was looking for Greg, it was the least likely place in London.

It was the nights that were going to be difficult unless he was able to get things straightened out in a hurry. It seemed crazy to plan days ahead—how to get out of the country—when you had no idea where you'd sleep that night. He couldn't even chance a trip to the vault. Sloane could do nothing except squat there waiting for him to appear. There was a limit to the length of time Sloane could do that. Somehow, thought Greg, he had to work out a new deal. One that allowed for some reasonable way of reaching his money—getting rid of as much as he needed for his expenses—and arranging some way of getting out of the goddamned country. He needed someone crooked. Someone with ability, imagination, someone who could thumb his nose at the cops. And Greg had to make it worth his while.

He held the shirt in his hands, stroking the last crease from the front and the collar. It was warm to his back. He shrugged into it and went to the mirrors. It would do.

One man in London could help him, he decided—if the guy wanted to—Danny Sullivan. Greg knew three of the man's intimates though he had never met Sullivan personally. Maybe ninety-nine in a hundred who claimed to know Sullivan were name-dropping.

Over twenty years, the name Danny Sullivan had been inscribed with monotonous frequency on charge sheets, "WANTED" notices and, latterly, in his banker's credit balance. A shrewd, determined thief, Sullivan served a half-dozen jail terms before he realized his genius for organization. With the tactical skill of a guerilla general, he planned four robberies that rocked the Metropolitan Police Force off kilter. A daylight raid on a bullion shipment: six masked men in an assault timed to the second. The loot of a pay-roll destined for eight thousand men in an automobile factory. Raids that sent members of Parliament scurrying into the House to demand action. Then, at the most spectacular moment in his career, Sullivan pulled out.

Flanked by two of the shrewdest criminal lawyers in London, Sullivan called a press conference in the restaurant of a West End hotel. Burnt brown by the Riviera sun, restrained in Savile Row lounge suit, he announced his retirement from crime. The reporters of five national dailies turned in stories that were given more space than that given to a political parley at top-level. During the last four years, Sullivan had been interrogated by the police seven times, twice arrested, charged and acquitted. A sensation-hungry public gave his exploits the same hysterical approval that they gave to the romances of film stars. Sullivan accepted arrests with bland protestations of a new-found virtue. With those who really knew him, he had the reputation of being ruthless, clever and, within the Code, completely dependable. His name had become the symbol of hoodlum success from the Elephant and Castle to Hoxton.

If Greg could make it worth while for Sullivan to help, he could do it.

It was nearly ten. He had had nothing to eat since the previous night. The Humber was still parked outside the library. He passed the man at the desk with a friendly nod and went out to the street. The square was already filling with Embassy cars. Few uniformed police bothered to investigate a square where nine out of ten vehicles had diplomatic privilege. He put on the chauffeur's cap and uniform coat and turned the Humber down Brook Street. He drank coffee in a small Italian café, chewing the stale salami sandwich and staring into the fly-specked glass in front of him. Leaving a coin on the counter, he went out to the car. At the top of South Molton Street, he turned into a garage and checked the Humber in for a week, leaving a false name and address. The coat and hat, he left under the seat. When they came to move it, he thought, they'd have fun with the putty and mercury.

He walked the four hundred yards back to the library, his nose in a newspaper. In a deep leather chair in the Reference Room, he smoked a half-dozen cigarettes, trying to work out a schedule. It wouldn't be too difficult to get in touch with Sullivan. The guy was listed in the phone book under his business address. DANIEL SULLIVAN, SCRAP METAL DEALER. And he had to do something about Judith. By now, she'd be half-crazy. Her phone would be tapped but there would be time for a few words with safety.

Not until five did it grow really dark. He had to keep off the streets as much as possible till then. If he managed to get hold of Sullivan, he'd fix a meeting somewhere safe. Here in the library, if it was before six. He looked round the room. Maybe he'd better put this place to more practical use. He had to have both coat and hat. The police knew the colour of the suit he was wearing, that he had left the stormcoat behind in the cottage. The accent was on trust in the library. Hands Across The Sea. Books, films, records—all were lent on trust. There was no admission in the atmosphere of a cruder approach to human relations. Hats, coats and briefcases were littered round the rooms at the whim of their owners. Most of these kept their property realistically near them.

He strolled back down to the drinking fountain. There was a plan on the wall showing the layout of the building. He saw that the top floor was used by a staff of Americans. Research librarians, lecturers, photographers. At the top of the marble stairway was a swing door that he pushed open. The floor had been converted into sound-proof offices. In front of him was an empty reception desk with an intercom speaker. An air-conditioning unit purred air through the floor at the right degree of humidity. Under a portrait of President Eisenhower, half-a-dozen men's coats and hats hung on pegs. Keeping an eye on the office doors, he tried on the coats. A dark blue cashmere fitted him and he turned it inside out so that the lining showed. It seemed more prudent in case he met the owner on the stairs. He took a hat at random and went back down the staircase. The man at the desk was talking to a girl. Greg went down the steps to the street. Once outside, he donned hat and coat and walked briskly north.

Wherever he phoned Judith from, the police would be there in minutes. They'd be searching the neighbourhood. Using the Park Lane entrance, he ducked down into the subway at Marble Arch. He bought a ticket for Highbury. In the train, he sat near the door. At Highbury, he stayed close to a group of people on the escalator, handing his ticket to the busy collector. Both ticket booths were busy. Across the hall, one of the five phone booths was unoccupied. He slipped into it, taking off his hat and coat. As far as he could tell, he had been unobserved.

Sullivan's number answered immediately. A girl with a cold asked his business. Under pressure, she said that Mr. Sullivan would not be at his office till the next day. Greg left the name of a man known to both Sullivan and himself and rang off.

Talking to Judith would be far trickier. There was a limit to the time in which police were able to trace a call. He had no intention of lingering, however, and kept a foot in the door. The Henley dialling tone sounded almost immediately. Judith would have taken the children in to school. He saw her now, moving around in the small timbered house with its grass to the river, polishing her possessions. The monk's table they'd bought from a farmhouse deep in Somerset, the Queen Anne tallboy that had been her mother's, the small French table, the things whose permanence she cherished.

When Diana had been born, buying the house had been part of the pattern of security that Judith demanded. It was not just a home but an assurance of a life that would be the same next week, next year and so on till hell froze. She'd had a difficult time with the baby. He remembered a night of frantic phone calls to a sweating doctor. The cool competence of the district nurse and the thin bleat of the second girl.

He'd sat at Judith's side afterwards, pity bringing him nearer to her than he'd been those past months. Solemnly, he told her that things for them were going to be different. First he would buy a house and put it in her name. They had four thousand pounds and her mother's furniture. He'd get a job—there were plenty of opportunities for a man like himself. The life that had terrified her, steeling her against every person he brought to the house, all that was over. Because he believed what he said, Judith believed it. Damp with weakness, her hand found his. Ten days afterwards, he was back in business with Sloane, deep in the details of some new score. Rather than face the fights that left them sick with frustration, he invented an occupation that accounted for his absences. Not until his arrest had he found out that Judith had never accepted his glib tales of deals in surplus war material. Her coolness he attributed to his offhand portrayal of a husband.

Each month, he paid in enough money to her bank to cover the mortgage charges and household expenses, feeling vaguely righteous. When he went down to Henley at weekends, there was a wall of resentment between them that the children were beginning to sense. One morning, at breakfast, the frustration of two people wanting the impossible from one another had exploded in a slanging match that ended in hostile silence.

He'd gone back to London and met the Nicholson woman. Judith took his arrest at first with a sort of Spartan loyalty that irritated him. After a month, she saw him at the court.

"This is the way *you* wanted it, Greg." She avoided looking at him, choosing the words she had to use in front of the police jailer. "You've never cared about me or the girls. Only yourself. For years, you've been telling me to accept life as it is. That's what I'm *going* to do. I don't want another penny of your money, Greg. And if you have any feeling at all, forget all about us."

He hadn't seen her after his conviction. Her letters, written to Wandsworth, were mostly about money or the house. There were two more payments to complete purchase. He'd left enough cash with his lawyer to cover this but Judith refused to meet the man. Nevertheless, as far as Greg was concerned, nothing had happened that money wouldn't straighten out. Twenty-eight thousand pounds. Everything Judith wanted, a life she and the children could share, all could be made possible with money. He didn't doubt that his own longings for security were not permanent and practical.

He heard Judith say "Hello!" with her deep voice and lilting vowels.

He spoke rapidly. "It's Greg. This phone is tapped, Judith. The police will be here in minutes. I'm all right and you're not to worry. Just keep in touch with Mary." There was no answer. "Judith! Can you hear me?"

He waited seconds till she answered. "I don't care *what* happens to you," she said distinctly. "After what this has done to us, I'd give you up to the police myself." The phone went dead.

He looked round the booking hall. Nobody was paying any attention. He had to avoid leaving a description that helped the police still further. He jumped on a bus, not putting on his hat or topcoat till it was moving. At Golders Green he got off and bought an afternoon paper in front of the station.

HUNT NARROWS FOR ESCAPED CONVICT

read the headline. There was a fairly accurate account of the search in the mews. Rosa Pacelli was described as "aged twenty-three, domestic servant." Gregory was known to be wearing a grey sports suit. His physical appearance was given again but there was no photograph.

He could see Judith's nostrils curve as she read her paper. He made for the public lavatory but swerved when he saw the two uniformed policemen. They rocked on their heels, watching a man who was opposite the bus queue. Rapping a pair of spoons on his elbows and thighs, he was capering in the gutter. Pompously, the pair moved towards him.

Greg ducked through the traffic, avoiding the pedestrian crossing. The detours round foot-slogging cops were nerve wracking but at least you could recognise the police. You could be on top of a plain clothes man before the hard, nervous eye and watchful mien tripped a danger signal in your brain. The women were even worse. There were hundreds of them out in plain clothes. Matronly women with shopping bags—young ones with roll-ons and swinging behinds. All carried warrant cards in their purses. Worst of all was the black Squad car that slid up in front of you. Always in front, for two men had already been dropped to cover the rear. The big outstretched hand—"Just a minute. May I have a word with you?"

There was a cinema in front of him. White stone with a black canopy. Massive staircases climbed to a world of fantasy presided over by " usherettes " in yachting trousers. There was a café that served a Quick Business Man's Lunch. He took a seat at the window and ate sausages as he stared at the flakes of snow that had started to drift by the window. It was a matter of time, he thought, before the police in England used the television service as they did in the States. Then, a man on the run could be any place where a television set was operating. Shooting a line, maybe, about who he was and what he did. Out of nowhere, his picture would come on the screen.

" If you have any information about this man . . ."

The menu was in a leather holder covered with celluloid. He took the celluloid and cut it into two strips, nine inches long, two wide. He paid his bill, went downstairs and bought a ticket for the show. He was no longer worried where he slept that night. Sloane might be. He dozed till it was dark outside.

It was nearly six. The snow had turned to a dirty mush in the streets. Southbound buses and underground trains would be empty but it no longer mattered about shillings. He flagged a cab and directed the driver to Manchester Square.

Sloane lived in an old-fashioned mansion block off Marylebone Road. A gloomy building with respectable tenants, vast flats and a hand-rope lift. Greg walked north, his collar up against the flakes that drifted into his neck like cold moths. He moved briskly, ready to run with the first person who spoke to him. The neighbourhood was popular with cruise cars.

Off George Street was a pub and a huddle of shops. In a pet store, he bought a three-pound sack of sand to put in the bottom of a mythical bird cage. A case-opener in a hardware store. Sloane's routine never varied at night unless he was working. He took his meal at the Pastoria Hotel and went back to his flat when he felt like it. From the booth at the corner, Greg called Sloane's number. There was no reply.

Under the entrance to the block was a flight of steps that led down to the porter's flat. A light showed there. A few homeward-bound pedestrians paid him no heed as he went up the steps to the entrance. A coal fire burned in an open grate in the hall. Beside it, a wicker chair where a ginger cat slept on a newspaper. A stately board had the roll of tenants inscribed in gold. A wide staircase with faded green carpet curved to the right of the lift. He went up, treading close to the wall to avoid creaking boards.

Sloane's flat was one of two on the second floor. It was a dark heavy door with brightly polished brass. Over a Chubb mortise lock was a Yale-type safety. He moved quietly to the well of the stairway. There was no sound from above or below. Taking one of the strips of celluloid, he bent at the bottom of the door and pushed the strip sideways through the crack. Slowly, he lifted it to the level of the mortise lock. It passed the keyhole. He pulled up further. Where it hit the projecting tongue of the Yale, he stopped. It was typical. Over the years, Sloane had become as knowledgeable about locks as anyone. But he still fitted an ordinary Yale on his door and went out without using the mortise.

He had the celluloid strip in his hand, when the door behind him opened. A women, dressed for the street, was fastening two mortise locks on her own door. He rammed the celluloid into his pocket and raised his hat.

"Would you know if Mr. Sloane is in? I had an appointment with him . . ."

She spoke with a tasty accent, parting with her words reluctantly as if their utterance gave her incredible pleasure. "I really don't know. Mr. Sloane keeps very peculiar hours." She smiled. "Uncertain hours. Have you tried the porter?"

He gave her the thanks due a brilliant suggestion and followed her downstairs. She waited for a cab and he went down the steps to the porter's flat, standing motionless outside the door till he heard the cab drive off.

At Sloane's door again, he ran the celluloid strip down from the top. When it hit the cup on the inside, he drew it back fractionally then pushed. Following the curve of the tongue, the resilient strip forced back the spring. The tongue was now held free of the cup. He put his weight on the door. It opened.

He closed it behind him. The manoeuvre had taken slightly longer than would have done a key. The woodwork was undamaged, the paint unscratched. There was no way of telling that anyone had opened the door.

The hall was large with a fireplace with a radiator in it, a French rug on the floor, hunting prints on the walls. The drawing room was on Greg's right. The two bedrooms were in front of him, separated by the bathroom. At the top of the short corridor was the kitchen. From the dark drawing room he took a look at the street below. He had plenty of time to prepare but as insurance he fastened the safety chain on the door.

He drew the heavy, lined curtains in Sloane's bedroom. He resented this comfort this big man lived in. Carpets, beds, chairs—all had been chosen with care. Sloane learned well. There was a clothes closet that ran the length of an inside wall, with sliding doors. He pulled and stood looking at the array of hanging suits. Sloane outweighed him by fifty pounds and was three inches taller. Nevertheless, his clothes could be worn at a pinch. He chose a dark-blue herringbone and found three white silk shirts in a pile. In the drawers at the end were a grey tie, socks and some black shoes. He carried them to the bathroom. The topcoat from the library, he'd keep. It was of no help to the police.

He went through every piece of furniture in the room thoroughly. Under a pile of handkerchiefs, he found three passports. British, Australian and Irish. All bore different names and Sloane's picture. He put them in his pocket. A couple of bankbooks in the drawer showed that Sloane had a balance of over five thousand pounds. If it hadn't been for me, the bum wouldn't have had a nickel, Greg remembered.

Taking the one evening sock in his hand, he closed the bedroom door behind him. In the hall, he emptied the cage sand into the sock and tied the end with a piece of string. This he left on a table in the hall. He had to find sheets now. There was a stack of them in an airing cupboard off the kitchen. He chose one of the coarsest, doubled it and punched holes down the edges with a meat skewer. It was warm in the flat. He took off his jacket, padding round the flat in his stockinged feet. There wasn't a loose penny in the place but he hadn't expected to find money. The thin gold cigarette case and cigar cutter that had been in Sloane's dressing table were in Greg's pocket.

Fifty times, he'd watched as the other put away the tools they used. Over the years, they'd collected a burglary outfit as complete as a crooked locksmith could make it. There was a five feet high refrigerator in the kitchen. Greg pulled it away from the wall and unfastened the inspection plate at the back. On top of the meter was a canvas fishing-tackle bag. He unzipped it. Wrapped in soft, old, polishing leather were a hundred skeleton keys. Keys that controlled all but the most expensive mortise locks made. For these, they cut specially from the blanks. There were hotel pass-keys. Relics of the idle days when Greg checked in at one of the West End hostelries, grabbed a cuttlefish bone impression of the chambermaid's pass-key as she did his room and checked out the next day. From the impression, Sloane made a key that they hoarded until it was needed. There were safe keys, picklocks, forceps for turning a key that was on the inside of a door, strips of mica ready-cut to size. He refastened the bag and put it with his clothes.

He went back to the drawing room, taking the chain off the door as he passed. The room was red, warm and inviting. A low trolley was set with scotch, gin and sherry. A dozen great golden chrysanthemums nodded in a vase. Over the fireplace was a Toulouse-Lautrec original. Sloane had not missed a trick for his comfort. Television, a radio-player with bookshelf space, an imposing cigar cabinet.

This morning, thought Greg, the big man had been stinking in a soft bed while Greg was dropping into the night with the law at the door downstairs.

He switched on the television, setting the dial at Channel 7. No picture showed on the screen, but the speaker crackled with the monotone instructions of a radio-cab despatcher. In the past, these and the salty comments of the drivers over the two-way circuit had earned him money. Names, addresses, and destinations came over the air. Sometimes, idle eavesdropping had given them a lead on someone already known to them by name. Occasionally, there would be the high-frequency police broadcasts to be picked up. He spun the dial now with no result.

When the tall gilt clock on the mantelpiece chimed ten, he switched the light off and drew back the curtains. Back in the kitchen, he found the main switch and cut off all light and power from the flat. For the next hour, he sat in darkness at the drawing room window.

Shortly after eleven, a car stopped outside. He could recognize Sloane's Ford but the angle was too acute to see Sloane leave the car. Greg waited behind the front door, the sand-filled sock swinging in his hand. There were footsteps then a key was pushed in the keyhole. As the door opened, Greg stepped backwards and sideways. In the half-light from the landing, Sloane was fumbling with the light switch in his hall. Holding the sock by the top, Greg swung in an arc that finished high over the big man's ear. He made no sound. As Sloane's knees collapsed, Greg swung again, this time striking at the base of Sloane's neck.

The half-cry from the landing turned Greg's head. A girl was standing there, her mouth round in her effort to scream. He straddled Sloane's unconscious body, grabbed her by the wrist and pulled her into the flat. He took Sloane's keys from the floor, refastened the mortise on the inside and put the chain on. Grabbing Sloane, he ripped off his jacket and trousers then sprinted to the kitchen and threw the switch on again. The lights went on. In the hall, the girl was slumped in a chair, shaking with laughter.

Hysteria. She could wait. Spreading the doubled sheet on the floor, he rolled Sloane over on it, face down. He tied the man's limp hands behind his back, using silk ties from the clothes closet. He fastened the big man's ankles, then joined both sets of knots. Taking the edges of the sheet, he pulled them up behind Sloane's back. They barely met. He threaded more ties through the holes that he'd made and fastened the ties securely. When he had done, he had Sloane's bulk in an efficient strait jacket. He turned Sloane on his back and went to the bathroom. The pitch of the girl's laugh was rising. As he passed her, he slapped twice with the flat of his hand on her cheek. She bent her head, shoulders still heaving but quiet.

In the bathroom, he soaked a cloth in cold water and wrapped it on Sloane's face like a barber's towel, lifting the stuff round the nostrils to let the man breathe. Though the bastard would be better dead, he thought.

For the first time, he took a good look at the girl. She was twenty-five, possibly, but he had never seen her before. It wasn't unusual since he knew none of Sloane's girls. He pulled her clinging hands from her face. His grip had left a weal on her wrist. She looked at it blankly and started to moan.

He brought his face down close to hers. The eyeblack had run on her cheeks and her nose dripped. "Listen," he said, savagely. "Do as you're told and you're all right. This is between me and him. You've elected yourself in on the deal and if you open your yap, I'll kill you. D'you understand?"

She nodded dumbly, massaging her wrist. " Help me pull him into the bedroom," he ordered. He took the cloth from Sloane's face, slapping it round the big man's mouth. There was a wide strip of plaster on Sloane's forehead. He bent at the other's body, trying to lift. Encased as he was, Sloane offered no purchase at Greg's end.

" Lift!" he snarled. One of the girl's heels had broken. She stumbled, trying to get her hands under Sloane's feet. Greg pushed her aside. Getting down on his knees, he turned Sloane over sideways, rolling him into the bedroom.

Sloane stirred as they dragged him on to one of the beds. His eyes flickered then closed. Greg came round to the head of the bed and pulled down Sloane's eyelid. " Come on, dasher!" he said. " Open 'em up." He was gloating. " This is one visit you didn't expect. Rat!" he said suddenly. " Coppering rat!"

Sloane's dark face was cautious. His big shoulders writhed under the sheet as he struggled to free himself. It was seconds before he understood what had happened to him. Pursing his lips, he spat in Greg's face.

Greg wiped the spittle. Dirt from the floor and cupboards streaked his face and shirt. His trousers were torn at the knee. He backhanded Sloane carefully across the mouth. "*I'm* going to finish this, Sloane," he gasped.

Flat on his back, the big man's eyes were intent on the girl. She had been standing passively at the end of the bed. Now she ran for the door, shrieking, " Police!"

He leaped the bed and caught her arm as she went through the door to the hall. Struggling, she bent her head and bit his left thumb. As her teeth closed on the old scar, he shivered with pain. He crooked his right arm and put it round her throat increasing the pressure till she fell on the floor. He prodded her upright.

" That's all, brother!" His breath came in gasps. The bite had drawn blood from the scar. He shoved her in front of him to the bathroom. Taking the key from the door, he sent her staggering inside.

" You've got five minutes to do whatever you want in there. The window's forty feet from the ground. If you break it, I'll put you through it. Get busy."

He folded a second sheet like the first. When the girl came out, he escorted her into the bedroom. When he had them both on the bed tied back to back, he stuffed a handkerchief in Sloane's mouth and went to sleep in the other bed.

The girl's crying woke him in the morning. The pair of them were awake. The eiderdown had slipped to the floor. He replaced it, untying the handkerchief from Sloane's mouth. He went to the kitchen. It was six-thirty and still dark outside. He yawned, searching for tea. When he found three cups, he made toast and carried the tray back to the bedroom.

The girl's eyes were swollen, her hair snarled. Sloane was a mask of defiance. " Why don't you be a man?" he croaked. " She's got no part in this rat-race!"

" She hasn't?" Greg held his left hand up for Sloane to see. " This time, it's me giving the orders, Sloane. Don't worry about my etiquette. This isn't a parlour game." He untied the girl.

She sat up unsteadily, making vague passes at her hair. " Never mind that," Greg said. " *He* probably thinks you're beautiful. Feed him this tea if he wants it. You can listen to me." He grinned at her. " We've no secrets now. Just one happy family." Snug in Sloane's camel-hair robe, he carried his own tea to the window.

The girl sat up on the bed, cradling Sloane's head in her lap, holding the cup to his mouth. " Wounded hero," Greg said sardonically. As the thought struck him, he pointed at the girl. " I suppose you know my name?" She nodded. He put his cup down and crossed the room swiftly. " Who?" he demanded, standing over her. " Who?"

She flinched, unwilling to meet his look. " The man who . . . the man who . . ."

" The man who *what?*" He was shouting.

" I saw your photograph," she faltered. " That scar . . ." She looked down at his thumb.

" You're a liar," he said flatly. " That rat on the bed told you. OK. I'm the man who broke out of jail. And I've got news for you—whatever trouble I'm in, I'm taking care that your boy-friend is in it, too."

Sloane twisted his mouth free of the cup. " Why don't you forget it? The kid knows what she's read, that's all. She'll forget it, too, won't you, Rosemary?"

Rosemary! A bitch who bedded with Sloane and sank her filthy teeth in your hand. He went back to the window and brooded over the dark street. When he spoke again, his voice was quiet and relaxed.

"*You* made me do this, Sloane. I'd kill you if I thought I could get away with it. You're a rat like the rest. But there are a couple of things you'd better know before you get any more bright ideas. I've got your three passports." Sloane's head swivelled to his clothes closet; "There's a jail term in every one. Another thing, there's a statement by me that goes to the law the moment I'm pinched. In it, I've stuck every single thing we've done together, Sloane. They can't do any more to me—not after ten years, they can't."

Sloane licked his dry lips. As he moved his mouth, the front teeth bobbled ludicrously on their plate. "What do you want from me, then, Greg?"

He sat on the end of the bed. "You're a no-good rat. I wouldn't trust you an inch. If I get the help I need from somebody else, I want *nothing* from you." He pulled Sloane's car keys from the pocket of the robe and swung them from his finger. "I'm taking your car for a while. When I come back, I'll let you know if there's anything for you to do."

Sloane sneezed and the mucus dribbled from his nostrils. The girl wiped it away with her handkerchief. He shook his head impatiently. "You're going to let Rosemary go, aren't you, Greg? She's got people. They're going to be wondering."

"Too bad." Greg picked up the sheet. "Judith was wondering, remember? She'll stay here. Flat on your face," he ordered. The girl hesitated.

"Do it!" said Sloane. His voice was tired. "Greg . . ."

He pulled the sheet up round the girl's shoulders, knotting it in the small of her back and at her knees. Then he rolled her over. She made no sound but the tears brimmed over her lids, coursing down to her neck.

"What?" he asked Sloane.

The big man made a motion with his head, like a tortoise in its shell. Here it came, thought Greg. Sloane's bounce was gone. He was ready for a plea under the Old Pals Act.

Then "Nothing," said Sloane. He wet his lips again. "Take this thing off for a couple of minutes, Greg. My hands have gone dead."

Greg stood looking down at him for a while. Without answering, he went into the bathroom and changed into the blue suit. There had been a wallet in the clothes he had stripped from Sloane the night before. In it, he found two five pound notes and a one. He checked the pockets of the grey suit he had discarded. There was a crumpled piece of paper, Bridget Selkirk's address. Without knowing why, he tucked it into his jacket and went back to the bedroom.

Sloane and the girl lay side by side, immobile. The man's dark eyes flickered. " You bastard," he said. " You bastard!"

Greg came to the bedside. " Sure. It's tough medicine to take, isn't it? You'll get used to it." He lifted the sodden necktie from the floor. Avoiding the biting mouth, he shoved the gag into Sloane's face and knotted it tight.

He took careful stock of himself in the mirror. The looseness of the big suit was not apparent under the topcoat. He snapped the brim of the hat. Picking up the bag of skeleton keys he closed the door to the bedroom and left the flat. The porter was cleaning the hall as Greg reached the foot of the stairway. As they passed, the porter was sour with the morning's suspicion. He ignored Greg's nod.

Sloane's car was fifteen yards up the street. It was nearly ten and the pavements were dry. A cold wind searched out the aches in his body. He hurried to the booth on the corner and called Sullivan's number.

The same girl answered. No, she didn't know if Mr. Sullivan was in the office.

He was there, thought Greg. Everyone who knew the man had the same story. Sullivan as a legitimate citizen was the same ball of fire. He ran his team of scrap metal buyers with the identical flair and organization he had used on his Heavy Mob.

" Find out, will you?" Greg asked the girl. " It's important." Once more he gave the name of the man who was known to Sullivan. He could see the porter standing at the top of his steps, sniffing the day. Maybe he'd best say something to the guy, Greg thought. Block any call he might make at Sloane's apartment. Then he decided against. Milk, he seemed to remember, was left at the back door. There was no reason for the man to go near Sloane. Anything Greg said might boomerang, create suspicion in the man's mind. Better left well alone. Greg would be back some time in the afternoon. Tough tiddy if the two in the bedroom weren't comfortable.

He could hear the girl's voice at the other end of the line, making enquiry. Then silence, as she cut him out of the circuit. If he could get results from Sullivan, he'd forget Sloane. One thing was sure—now that the big guy knew the position, he'd do what he could to keep Greg on the run. He was there if Greg needed him. Inspecting the teeth marks on his thumb, Greg remembered something would have to be done about turning the pair of them loose.

Suddenly a hoarse cockney voice came on the wire. "Who's this?"

"It's a friend of George's. George Bendel." Hating the need, he gave the great man the deference due. "I'd like to see you, if that's possible."

"A friend of George Bendel's? So what? What's your name?"

"Can't it wait?" asked Greg. "It's about 'the other,' I want to see you." It was the catchall phrase of the thief. Used to refer to a matter best left unvoiced at the moment.

There was a pause. "Yeh, I get you. Are you coming here?"

"Can you make it the Admiralty Arch—off Trafalgar Square. I'll be parked in a black Ford. This year's."

"I can't do it before two," answered Sullivan. "Any good to you?"

"Two," he said. Trying to keep the fear from his voice, he asked. "You're going to be there?"

"I'll be there," said the other.

Two. That meant nearly four hours to kill. No sense in fronting that porter again unless he had to. When he went back to the flat, it must be for the last time. He had to free the pair himself. If he rang the porter or the flat opposite, it would mean the cops being called in. Neither he or Sloane needed cops enquiring into the circumstances of the tie-up. He would be safe enough in the Ford. Now that he had spoken to Sullivan, he felt better. The change of clothes and few pounds in his pocket gave him new confidence.

He left the booth and crossed the street to the Ford. There was no sign of the porter. Unlocking the car, he threw the bag of skeleton keys in the back. You never knew. Wheeling into the southbound traffic, he kept the speed of the car down. Giving way to anything on wheels, taking no chance of an accident.

Halfway down Park Lane, he passed the sleek black Jaguar, sliding through a gap in the block and accelerating north. He watched the car disappear in the driving mirror. The Squad, he thought. High on their list of stolen cars would be the Humber. He hoped they got fat on it. Unless they had a definite lead, the cruise cars were harmless if you were mobile. It was impossible for the cops to recognize anyone at the wheel of a car that they weren't looking for.

The petrol gauge on the dash showed the tank nearly full. He turned through Saint James' Park, past Scotland Yard on his left and over the bridge. With his eye always on the mirror, he drove aimlessly through South London for a couple of hours. In a Croydon department store, he bought a meal. Going back to the car, he bought the day's batch of newpsapers. He scanned every page. There was no mention of the escape.

Maybe no more, he thought. More important things had crowded him off the pages. For what it was worth. But every cop in the town would be still be eating, drinking and sleeping Paul Gregory. The police didn't forget a man who owed them ten years. Most of the time, they remembered when the man himself had forgotten.

He knew the concern with which his type of break was treated by the Yard, the Prison Commission. They had the public ever in mind. What Greg had done was a nose thumbed at retribution—an encouragement to every practising thief in the city—a criticism of their security measures.

He drove back to the West End, climbing the rise to Wandsworth Common. The expanse of sere grass and tangled brush was made uglier by the prefabs that cluttered its edges. Women in slippers and curling pins slutted to lines of dingy washing. On the other side of the road, the jail sprawled to the railway tracks. A group of warders, muffled against the east wind, were leaving the wicket in the Main Gate as he passed.

He sent the Ford slightly faster till the yellow and red brick fronts of the gloomy houses replaced the high jail walls. Somehow, he had expected to see the spot where he had climbed, marked with some official recognition of his feat. Then he remembered that the prison authorities would read only the signs he had left.

Since the raid on Sloane's flat, Greg had started to discount his partner's share in the escape. From start to finish, Greg reasoned, he'd made his own luck. With the memory of the big man, hog-tied and helpless on his own bed, it was easy to go back to the comforting picture of Sloane as he always had been. Now, no longer reliable, maybe but at least predictable once more. A chump whose muscle had gone to his head.

It was ten minutes to two when he tucked the Ford into an empty space behind the Admiralty Arch. He had no idea which way Sullivan would come. Whether he'd arrive on foot, by cab or by car. Greg was sure that he would recognize him. Too many times, that thin face with the odd brooding eyes had stared at him from some newspaper or other. Sullivan on his way to court. Sullivan in a night club. Sullivan perched on a pile of scrap he had sold to the Belgian Government. From being camera-shy, success had turned the man into a lens hog.

A troop of cavalry trotted up from the Horse Guards Parade in the direction of Buckingham Palace. Chinstraps gleaming, cloaks flapping, the troopers paraded their pageantry to a knot of sightseers on the gravelled walk.

He watched from the car, smug with the feeling of impending freedom. Real freedom with the need to duck and dive gone. It didn't matter *how* he left—flat on his face in the bilge, in a coal barge—any way as long as he had his money with him. With Sullivan, he needed to make a deal that would be worth the man's while. Sullivan had more money than he could ever have. Greg had to flatter the man—play to the big, big wheel who was able to fix everything. Whose word in the underworld was law.

He had the feeling that Sullivan would arrive at the rendezvous knowing as much about him as was necessary. The twenty-eight grand was no secret, anyhow. Since his arrest and conviction, the secret of the unrecovered loot remained a challenging enigma to every thief in the town. In spite of the newspaper accounts of an abortive police search at Henley, the boys still tried.

While he had been held waiting trial in Brixton Prison, a pair of naïve spivs had been picked up rapping half-heartedly on Judith's door. The local police rounded up the suburban screwsmen and pinned " Loitering with intent " raps on them.

Sullivan still had an organization. To swing it in behind Greg was going to cost money. How much, Greg didn't know. He was ready to offer three thousand pounds for a guaranteed landing somewhere and a passport in any name.

The clock on the dash showed two o'clock. He climbed out of the car, pulling up the collar of his coat. For a moment, he leaned against the radiator, the warmth easing his aching ribs. In front of him, the traffic between Trafalgar Square and the palace was thick. Behind the arch, the Mall widened on both sides, leaving parking space for forty or fifty cars. There was no one in sight that he recognized. He hoped Sullivan wasn't going to be late. What he had to say was going to take time. He didn't want to leave that flat for too long. At the back of his mind, doubt was growing about the girl. Maybe she did have people who would worry. Who might even know that she had been with Sloane the night before.

He walked up as far as Trafalgar Square. At the foot of the Column, the hungry pigeons strutted round the fountains in search of food. The wind carried the spray high in the air, wetting the square to the steps of Canada House.

He looked sourly at the big stone building. There was one bunch of people who would be glad to see the back of him. Her Majesty's representatives of Canada in England. The interviews came back to him. The smooth-faced man with rimless glasses and a Canadian Legion button in his lapel.

" You're not helping to give the people over here much of an impression of us, Gregory. Maybe the best thing that could happen to you would be to leave England. Why not give it a thought?"

That, they could say again. And for his money, they could keep England. He had long since outworn his welcome. It had been a long time since that first dawn arrival. Clean shaven, eager, in a freshly-pressed battledress with lieutenant's pips on the shoulder straps. A hero, he recalled with vague self-pity. A hero on a bedding-roll, staring fascinated at the balloon barrage that hung high above Liverpool. The army had taught him a lot. How to get righteous over something you managed to take by force. To kill or be killed. To understand that law was merely a matter of expediency. At the end of it all, the army slapped your back and told you to forget it now. The war, soldier, was over.

Turning in his tracks, he walked back to the car. As he approached, a grey Buick weaved from the traffic line and parked at the side of the Ford. He recognized the driver: it was Sullivan. In the back of the Buick, two other men were propped in the corners. One he did not know. The other was George Bendel. Sullivan raised a grey gloved hand and pointed at the Ford. Greg opened the door. The two men followed and sat in the back.

In the driver's seat, he turned so that he half-faced them. Sullivan was dressed like a casting director's conception of a prominent gangster. Black topcoat with a clove red carnation in his buttonhole, a pearl grey hat. Bendel's swarthy gypsy face made a half-grin of recognition.

" You Gregory?" Sullivan's query had a note of respect.

A thief's acknowledgement of a gesture of defiance by one of his own kind.

Greg nodded. " You guessed?"

" Giving George's name helped," said Sullivan. Bendel nodded. Both men were leaning far back in the car so that they were hidden by the rear pillars.

Greg felt that he was expected to speak. He shrugged. " What I had in mind was for you, Sullivan. But George is all right. We've known one another long enough. I don't worry about George." He hoped that the strain in his laugh was imaginary. Sloane had been all right. Cameron had been all right. The whole goddam bunch of them were till they had reason to sell you out. Honour among thieves. A crack with as much truth in it as any other bogus claim for solidarity in the underworld. Sullivan had to be different to the rest. He had helped frame the Code. He would live by it.

" Well—you know my position—the spot I'm in," he said suddenly. " The sort of help I need. And I need it the worst way." The memory of the money in the vault gave his smile confidence. " I've got a proposition, Sullivan."

The other man's small eyes were unwinking. His head moved slowly from side to side. " Not for me, you haven't, mate."

Greg had no concern. When Sullivan heard the offer, he would show a little more interest. " You don't know what I'm going to say," he said with a grin.

" That's right," said Sullivan. " I don't. And I don't want to. You're too warm for me, mate. Much too warm."

Bendel broke in eagerly. " When did you leave Sloane's place, Greg?"

Uncertain of the right answer, he groped for the words. He didn't know the implications. Nobody could know that he had been at Sloane's flat unless either Sloane or the girl had reached a phone. He tried hard to remember whether he had locked the bedroom door. How Bendel and Sullivan knew didn't really matter. It wasn't likely that Sloane would be of concern to either of them. And this was a personal argument between Sloane and himself. That they would respect.

" Why?" he asked. " I left this morning." He spoke easily, striving for the key to the strange reserve he felt in the others. " This is Sloane's car, as it happens."

Sullivan showed his teeth. " I know it is. And if I was you, the sooner I dumped it the better I'd like it."

In the back of the car, both men kept their eyes on the passing traffic. In the Buick, the third man had moved to the wheel. Exhaust smoke hung at the back of the big car. The man had the motor running.

" I still don't get it," Greg said pleasantly. " Is there something I'm missing?"

" Sloane's dead," said Sullivan.

Greg swung violently in his seat, his elbow catching the horn button. A couple of pedestrians looked curiously at the car. " What do you mean, dead?" he repeated.

" Tell him," said Sullivan.

" The woman who cleans found him," said Bendel. " Eleven o'clock this morning. Him and a girl tied up on a bed. His false teeth rammed halfway down his throat. He was dead before they got him to hospital."

Greg bent his head or he felt he would vomit. The blue stuff of his trousers was against his mouth. It was Sloane's car. He was wearing Sloane's clothes. Somehow, he had to amend the admission he'd made.

" I never knew . . ." he started, stalling for time.

" This cleaner let herself in with her key. Did it every day." Bendel seemed to relish the recital. " She phoned the law and Sloane died unconscious. Didn't say a word."

Greg grabbed at the implicit allegiance. " The rat's in his place," he said. He waited for the comforting slap on the shoulder, the declaration of loyalty. Neither man moved.

" That girl give your description," Bendel continued. " Plus the fact is she's told the cops that you broke into the flat, slugged Sloane and threatened to kill them both. Then you took his clothes and the car. That's what she said."

Greg wiped the back of his glove round his face. " All right. All right—what are you here for?" He looked up quickly. " How is it that you know all this?"

Sullivan pulled the stalk of his flower deeper, then brushed his coat. " I got no love for the law, Gregory. What I hear, Sloane was your partner." He clapped his hands together. " That's your business, mate. I got hold of George after you phoned. It wasn't hard to work out who you were."

" You was on the one o'clock news, Greg. And the number of his car," Bendel spoke sombrely.

Somehow Greg found words in a rush of explanation. Sloane's treachery—Cameron and the police—striving to show that Sloane's death was deserved and his own innocence.

Sullivan's eyes were unchanged. " I got a duty to people like you, mate." There was an incongruous note of sincerity in his voice. " But it don't go as far as murder."

The man wasn't making sense. " Murder?" The word didn't even sound right. " I tied the guy up. If he choked on his teeth, what's that got to do with murder?"

Sullivan had the door at the back half-opened. " If you use violence doing a felony, mate, and somebody dies, that's murder, ain't it?"

As Sullivan straightened his back, Bendel thumbed at the catch on the door, like a dog anticipating its master's whim. " Hold it," Sullivan said to him, and leaned his arms on the back of the driving seat. Some of his polish went with his earnestness. " There ain't much to say, mate, is there?" He shook his head. " I've always taken care of a good thief. I'm on your side. But there's nothing would suit them better than to get me mixed up in something like this. They'd throw the key away and all the straightening irons in the world wouldn't get me out." He thumped his fist into the fabric of the seat. " I still dunno why they haven't picked you up in this lot . . . Leave it where it is, mate. You'll be better off. You got money. That's a help."

Greg moved his head in agreement. It seemed senseless to try to explain. Minutes before he had been offering Sullivan three thousand pounds. " Yes. I'm all right," he said.

For years, Sullivan had taken himself seriously as arbiter of crime in the Metropolitan area. The plums in the business were brought for his inspection. If you were lucky, you were with Sullivan and made your scores with a sense of security in his direction. If things went against you, there'd be a good lawyer in court. Not only well-paid, but competent, and ready to pull every card in the deck to avoid a conviction. There'd be someone ready to stand bail. A weekly dole to your wife, if you had one, and an envelope waiting for you when you came out.

Quietly determined men visited bars, gambling clubs and cafés. Anywhere that the boys patronized. They carried the " list " with them. " Joe's in trouble. I'll put you down for a tenner, all right?" At the top of each list, whether he knew the man or not, Sullivan's name would probably figure. DANNY SULLIVAN in sprawling, Third Grade handwriting. He had a dozen tearaways ready to smash his disapproval wherever he felt necessary. Ready to razor a man to squealing surrender whenever Sullivan decided the Code had been violated. Even if it meant paying the victim to avoid a prosecution for "Grievous Bodily Harm", Sullivan punished in the only fashion he recognized. The same stringent pattern of behaviour made his office the end of a pilgrimage for men on the run and those who were recently out of jail. Even in the suburbs, obscure thieves nursed their troubles with the inner conviction that Sullivan would take care of things, if only they could get to him.

Sullivan wore his responsibility heavily. "You got money," he repeated approvingly. "Listen—d'y' know Liverpool at all?"

"I've been there," said Greg. Six to a cabin complete with plated plumbing fixtures. The silent boat drills at dawn on a slippery deck. His company—red-necked wheat farmers from Saskatchewan, ill at ease playing soldiers. Big quiet men from the lumber camps with French Canuck names and old, sweet songs. Sixth ship back in a convoy three miles long.

"Yeh, I've been there," he said again.

Sullivan studied the loom of the car rug. He looked up suddenly, his decision made. He scribbled a name and address on paper and gave it to Greg. "See this geezer. I'll give him a ring to expect you. He's solid. And as long as you can pay, he'll help. He owes me a favour." He took his right glove off. He gave Greg's hand a hearty clasp. "Good luck, mate. Best thing for you to do is to remember you'll be on your own. There ain't nobody going to be on your side when it comes to doing anything much. You got to do what you can, the best way you know."

Bendel behind Sullivan, the two men climbed from the Ford and got into the Buick. They were driven away without looking back.

While they had been there, Greg's numbed brain had been incapable of registering more than the basic facts. Sloane was dead. And he was wanted for murder. In the ashtrays at the back of the Ford, the two men's cigarettes were still smouldering. Reminders that Sullivan and Bendel belonged to a different world now. They had vanished at speed along the Mall, being driven God knows where, and to them the mention of murder would mean no more than a proprietorial interest in his plight. That half-arsed big shot with his crap about his duty to help,

Greg thought bitterly. A self-appointed Devil's Advocate. That pair of jerks had come to the meeting, prepared to run at the first sign of danger. Like people who go to a jail to visit a prisoner. Soaking up the dramatic values, smugly certain that at the end of twenty minutes they could walk through the gate.

You're on your own, the great man had said. As if he had been imparting some magical talisman—a formula that would screen Greg from trouble as soon as he recognized it. Well, he knew he was on his own. In a jungle, he was on his own. And he'd defend himself the best way he could.

There were too many things to think about. Their order didn't matter. He'd offered Sullivan three grand. Right now, he'd take that three grand in ready against the loot in the vault. He couldn't be sure that Sloane *had* died without talking. Whatever they said on the air or printed in the papers was what they wanted you to believe. Sloane might well have told the police everything. That store basement could be stiff with cops who were waiting for him to arrive.

Till today, it hadn't mattered too much if he'd been picked up before he had got at his money. They'd have thrown him back into jail and he'd have lost, maybe, six months' remission of sentence. But at the end of it all—if it had to be done—that money would have been there waiting. Still—even six years ahead—the answer to his problems. Now, freedom meant more than the money. It meant going on living.

Murder. The word didn't make sense when you thought of it like this. He'd tied Sloane up. There'd been an accident and the big rat was dead. But that wasn't murder. The events of the night crowded his brain, reviving memories of trials he had read. The macabre jailhouse gossip about people who had been topped.

In this country, they didn't miss a trick in a prosecution for a capital offence. From the moment they started to use the ominous formula: "*The police are anxious to interview Paul Gregory, who may be able to assist them in their enquiries.*"

From that point, there was no let-up. It was an impersonal process with the end fixed by law. The jury had nothing to do with excuse or explanation. If you'd done what the statute said was murder, they found you guilty on the facts. And the sentence was mandatory. There was no provision for copping a plea.

The significance was deadly. You killed a man and they hanged you. The girl's evidence would ruin him in any court. He had quarrelled with Sloane—she knew that. He'd broken into the flat, robbed the guy and used violence. Sloane had died as the direct result. The intention didn't matter. The ingredients the law required were all there.

He shook himself out of his apathy. He had to defend himself the best way he could. Going to Liverpool was out. He could forget that with the rest of Sullivan's play to the gallery. He had no money. He was uncertain about Bendel—how far he could stand up to pressure, if needs be.

Methodically, he started to wipe the wheel, handles and dash of the car free from possible fingerprints. As he remembered, he hadn't taken off his gloves but the precaution was necessary. If it ever came to the worst, he must swear that he'd never seen Sloane's car. The clothes he was wearing would have to go. The girl would be able to give a description of them to the police, down to his underpants if necessary. He picked up the canvas bag of skeleton keys from the floor of the car. This, he thought, hefting it in his hands, was the best way out of his immediate troubles. The thirteen pounds in his pocket was better than nothing but only just. Even the need of a place to sleep that night was more urgent now. There was nobody he could go to—burglary alone could provide him with shelter. It had to be done skilfully. Not a sign left for some needle-nosed cop on his beat to investigate.

It had to be a new kind of job. A complete reversal of everything he had gone after before. A house full of people—or even temporarily unoccupied—was no good to him. What he needed was a place that had been left empty. Somewhere he could hole up in safety.

He locked the doors of the Ford and walked quickly away from the car. He headed in the direction of Trafalgar Square. There was a gravel bin on the side of the Mall. As he passed, he dropped Sloane's car-keys into it. He walked close to the people next to him, trying to appear as if he belonged there. He crossed Northumberland Avenue, patting the head of a small boy whose mother smiled approval. Outside the News Theatre, he bought a ticket and went to the back. It was one place safe, off the streets and a refuge to think.

EIGHT

He sat at the end of the row, the bag of keys between his feet. The cinema was full. Through a smoke haze, Walt Disney animals capered on the screen. The man next to Greg sat back, leaning to laugh, lost in the simple comedy. He wiped his eyes. Jutting across the seat-arm, his elbow dug into Greg's body.

Greg jerked, smothering the fear that leaped inside him. Unless he controlled himself, he was gone, he thought. Any sort of outburst in public—the wrong word—an argument—might mean the police. It happened. A man on the run, and the most innocent of movements became fraught with danger. Without a lead, the police still had no more than a description to go on. Well, and a picture. But they had to have a lead. They could send squad cars roaring round all night but they didn't know where to begin. That was the important thing—not to give them a lead. By now, the car had probably been found. He underestimated none of them. Maybe, they'd built up a picture of his movements over the past three days that was reasonably accurate. Nevertheless, they neither knew where he was nor where he would be that night. Nor did he.

He shrugged deep in his seat, closing his eyes. The key to Bishop's flat was still in his pocket. A temptation. He knew the way into the block and Sloane was dead. Still, he had no idea how Sloane had found the place. There could be some receipt, an agreement, even. The cops would have spent all day going over the dead man's flat. If a paper were there, they wouldn't miss it. Half a dozen cops could be up there, sitting in the dark, waiting.

It would have been easier had he known if Bridget Selkirk had recognized him—knew who he was. Just how far her distaste for scandal would carry her. Somehow, with her, he'd had the impression that she would listen if he talked. The need to talk—to explain—grew stronger as the time passed. What did you do, ring up someone you scarcely knew and invite them to listen to your version of a killing! People reacted strangely—uncharacteristically—to murder.

There he went again. Those three words kept spinning into his brain to be received with astonishment. Dead man: murder. Things like this happened to other people—not to yourself. Either they gave you no chance to explain or there was no one to listen. Sloane was dead. He was glad Sloane was dead but he hadn't meant to kill the guy.

The tinkling music in the cinema died abruptly. The screen went blank and the house lights brightened. Two girls moved up the aisles, carrying trays of ices and candy. The man in the seat next to him leaned across, the laughter still frozen on his face. He beckoned the girl with a thin hand wealed with blue veins. He looked like some old-fashioned solicitor's clerk. One who should be sitting like an old crow, surrounded by deed boxes covered with dust.

The man held a chocolate-covered ice with genteel fingers. He clacked his teeth as he spoke conversationally to Greg.

"These things are still very good value, I find."

Greg pointed to his ear, unwilling to trust his accent unless necessary. The man nodded sympathy. As the house lights dimmed, Greg slipped from his seat and found the lavatory.

He shut two doors behind him with relief and locked himself in one of the stalls. It had to be after four by now. There were only minutes before it would be dark outside. More and more, he was the hunted animal, shunning the day, lulled by the dark.

Judith seldom listened to the news broadcasts. Even so, he thought, there'd be a dozen people ready to call in with the news. All the friends who had pursued her since her marriage with wagging heads. Now, they would be really justified!

That wouldn't be, any more, he realized with a strange sense of relief. Whatever happened, he and Judith were through. If he ever made it out of here, Judith wouldn't join him nor would he ask her. Despite the relief, there was sadness for the things that might have been. For those, he was always sad—it was their only value for him. The kids would be better off without him, anyway. He'd never been much more than the man with a present in his pocket. The impatient provider of entertainment, trying to buy his way ahead of Judith's control of the girls. As a father, he'd been lousy. Maybe it was because he had never wanted kids. Never, if it came to that, wanted marriage. It had been the only way that he might have Judith. From the very first day, he'd hated the responsibility, the implicit loss of individuality. Fear had driven Judith to what she called "a sensible talk". A talk that degenerated into a bitter argument, with the desire to wound uppermost in both of them.

" Women," he'd said, " are born to possess. Men resent being possessed. It's as simple as that, Judith. No good telling me what other men do—I know it. From your point of view I'm a shit and I can't or won't do anything about it."

And that's the way it was—if you didn't conform, you were a shit. There were thirty million dutiful husbands and fathers in the country to prove it. What women disliked to accept was your determination to stay as you were. Or if they accepted, they resented at the same time, which is what Judith had done.

The first time he had been arrested, shock and the relief at his acquittal had brought them close. There had been a time when Judith demanded less and he gave more. Then the resentment flared. " Love!" she'd said, sad in her personal defeat, " you haven't the first idea what the word means, Greg!"

He'd touched her hair, warming her with his denial and knowing she was right.

He left the cinema by a side exit, into the short twilight of a London winter. The narrow street descended steeply to the river. It was cold, still. Stamping his feet in a doorway, a newspaper seller offered Greg the still damp pulp. He took the paper, pushing it under his arm. In front, the wind off the river whipped dust and litter at the base of the Hungerford Footbridge. He climbed up, his own and footsteps of someone ahead of him echoing along the wooden floors. Over his head, the lamps threw brief circles of light on the dirty steps. There was a bin at the top, used for sand. He looked both ways. He could see no further ahead than the next lamp, but the other man's footsteps were gone. He took off his coat and hat, making them into a bundle that he filled with sand. Knotting the sleeves, he heaved the bundle over the side of the bridge. Faint, he could hear the splash as the coat hit the water. Pulling himself up on the balustrade, he peered down at the oily river. The bundle had sunk.

High over Westminster Bridge, the lighted dial of Big Ben showed a quarter past five. Near it, facing the clean sweep of the County Hall, the sombre outline of New Scotland Yard. Never either closed, full or empty. Shift after shift of police. Shirt-sleeved and sweating, running topcoated through corridors, out on an assignment. Hundreds of the bastards backed by every technical device on the market. The Flying Squad, the Fraud Squad, the Murder Squad. But he still had the initiative.

All his life, he'd succeeded in hating the people who stood between him and his need. It had been a constant pattern. As long as he could remember, there'd been someone to hate. Some tangible target for the frustration that grew with the years. The police were no exception. Out of the army and a thief, he centred an uncompromising hatred on the men who sought to catch him.

Times, to prove a point, he made play with the law of averages. " Cops," he said, " get no halos with their warrant cards. Look—", he argued, "—take a hundred cops, judges, bakers—book publishers. You're bound to get a percentage of 'em crooked. That's the fallibility of human nature. Let's not argue the percentage. Just say a man's not necessarily straight because he's a cop."

Secretly, he credited none with virtue. In face of undeniable proof, his hatred for the man was constant. Though it was the calling rather than the man.

On both sides of the river, office blocks were shutting down for the night. Here and there, a late worker's light hung in the darkness, seemingly defying the law of gravity. On the north side of the river, drivers of a hundred cars jockeyed for position. Every single one of them knew where he was going, he thought.

Hearing footsteps, he jumped down from the side and walked towards the south side of the river. Twenty yards ahead, a man carrying a briefcase was coming in Greg's direction. As they passed, the man eyed him curiously, saying goodnight with the false civility of those who meet in lonely places.

Wearing no hat or coat was bound to draw attention to himself. That was why the man had looked. He had to buy some sort of covering immediately. At the far side of the bridge, he looked at the newspaper under a lamp. It was on the front page. Couched in the careful language of a press trained to avoid any statement that might seem a pre-judgement.

There was a brief account of the police being called to Sloane's flat by the cleaner. A man and a woman had been found on a bed, trussed in sheets. The man had died, subsequently, on his way to the hospital. Death appeared to have been caused by the victim's false teeth becoming lodged in his throat. The police were anxious to interview Paul Gregory whom they believed might be able to assist their enquiries.

He balled the paper and threw it to the river. Picking up the bag of keys, he went down the steps. To his left, the traffic ramps of Waterloo Station climbed above the squalid streets. In front of the brilliantly-lit Airways Terminal, the bays were filled with buses ready to leave for the airport. He could read the destinations on the illuminated signs—ROME, BARCELONA, STOCKHOLM, GENEVA.

He cut through the bombed-out desolation, over to a street market where street traders and cheap stores wrangled for custom. In one, he bought a cheap raincoat and nondescript hat for five pounds. Buttoning the flimsy stuff across his chest, he walked back to the footbridge, keeping to the silent side streets. On the other side of the river, he climbed through the Adelphi, across the Strand and past the National Gallery. Turning right, he took a narrow street mounting to Leicester Square.

At the Central Reference Library, he went in. A large room lined with shelves had a dozen or more tables. A girl at a desk gave him the back issues of *The Times* for the last month. He carried them to an empty seat and switched on the reading lamp.

What he wanted was a house or flat that had been left furnished but unoccupied. Not a place big enough for servants to be there while the owners were away—or a house with the kind of valuables that would make certain surveillance by the police. He ran his gloved finger down the Social Column, rejecting the addresses that he knew to be hopeless. The great squares in Belgravia, Mayfair and Chelsea. As he finished with each newspaper, he folded it neatly and added it to the stack at his elbow. Nobody paid him heed. The other readers were intent on their own tasks. A hundred times in the past, he had been in this room, using its shelves to determine some fact that made a successful burglary. Here, he had found information on a man's lineage, hobbies, business interest and family.

Finished, he carried the papers back to the issuing desk and asked for the voters' list. He had two names and addresses on the slip of paper in his hand.

Mr. and Mrs. Sholto Mackinnon, 153 South Street, Mayfair.

Miss Raphael, 28a Prince's Gate, S.W.7.

Both families had announcements in the social columns, asking for mail to be forwarded to addresses in Italy and Madeira.

The voters' list was invaluable. In every public library was the list for its borough. Here were not only the names of the householders but those of anyone permanently resident in the house at the time of the census. Prince's Gate and South Street were both in the City of Westminster. He scanned the printed list with attention. Both addresses were dealt with fully.

South Street

151 ********
152 ********
153 Mackinnon, Sholto John
Mackinnon, Margaret
Floyd, Anna Jane
Soper, Christine

Prince's Gate

27 *******
28 *******
28a Raphael, Selma Deborah
Mintz, Hannah

Carrying his pencil between his teeth, he went back to the shelves behind him. Sholto Mackinnon was listed in *Burke's Landed Gentry*, *The Directory of Directors* and *Who's Who*. He was fifty-seven years old, married, with one son in Kenya aged thirty. Directorships in two firms of jute spinners were mentioned. Almost certainly, the other two names were of servants.

The Raphael woman was single. Mintz would be either a friend or servant in all probability. There was no reference to Miss Raphael in any of the appropriate books.

As a final check, he searched the telephone book for both names, raking the numbers. Pulling down the brim of his hat, he walked down the steps to the street. In front of him was the portico to the Pastoria Hotel. Through the half-drawn curtains in the restaurant, he could see the waiters setting their tables. Sloane's had been the one by the end, a niche in the elegant world to which he had aspired.

Ducking into the criss-cross of intersecting streets between Coventry Street and Regent Street, he walked north. The main thoroughfares were still bright with window displays. Already the crowds of suburb dwellers had gone, leaving the district to the theatre-goers, the whores, the early drunks who stumbled from club to pub and back. This was the edge of Soho. The most elderly and cheapest of the city's seven thousand hookers patrolled their beat from Shaftesbury Avenue to Coventry Street. A radio blared from a penny arcade where a group of G.I.'s, their clothes sharply creased, lolled against the front, pay-happy. It was nothing but an ambitious Skid Row, with a plain-clothes man in every other doorway and a neighbourhood to be avoided.

At Maddox Street he cut across Regent Street, leaving Savile Row and its ornate police station on his left. In C Division, there were a dozen detectives who knew him by sight. At the top of the steps in Lansdowne Row was an empty telephone booth. He called the house in Prince's Gate. Immediately, a woman with a thick German accent answered. " Wrong number," he said and rang off.

He let the Mackinnon's number ring for five minutes without any response. He pressed the button and the coppers clattered into the box beneath. He dialled O and spoke to the girl.

" Operator—I've been ringing this number without getting any reply. As far as I know, there should be someone there."

You could never tell. There could be a faulty connection. He'd done it before. An unanswered phone might mean someone in the bath, or too lazy to answer.

The girl was brisk and efficient. " What number are you speaking from?" He told her. " Give it a special check," he asked. " The name is Mackinnon."

" Insert three pennies, please, and I'll try to connect you."

He could hear the phone ringing at the other end. Then again with a slightly different note as the girl changed the line. " I'm sorry," she said, " but there's no reply."

He took a look at himself in the mirror. The swellings over his ears had completely subsided. Those on his cheekbones still remained, narrowing his eyes. He had to be doubly careful from now on. Mayfair at night, even as early as this, was the hottest district in London. A Mecca for thieves, and the people who lived there were burglar-conscious to a man. Police patrols were frequent. Cruise cars had a habit of parking without lights on one of the more fashionable streets. Scrutinizing the passing cars and pedestrians. A known thief with a couple of convictions was asking for trouble to be abroad in the area without excuse. The ambiguous charge, " Loitering with intent to commit a felony ", gave an arrest-hungry cop scope for fantasy.

It was no more than four hundred yards to South Street. He would have little time to waste, looking at windows and doors. Much depended on the type of house it was. He couldn't remember. He'd have to make a trial walk past the door to give him an idea of the locks he would have to deal with. The next time he must be prepared to go straight up the steps with at least the right type of key ready.

He propped the door of the booth open so that the light would not come on. Kneeling on the floor, he detached a dozen or so of the sort of key he might need. Beautifully tooled Hobbs and Chubb blanks that Sloane had cut to the basic patterns of most types of the maker's locks. A skeleton key was a perfect instrument in the right hands. All locks fell into prescribed patterns. In the mortise locks, the variations were limited. The business end of a key might look bewildering to reproduce, with angles showing a dozen or more points that appeared likely to function. Yet, always, the pattern could be reduced to a few basic edges that lifted the levers in the locks. An expert like Sloane could look at a lock and make two keys. One would fit. Greg was less skilled but, given the time, he knew that there were few doors that he couldn't beat with the bag in his hand.

A man fumbling at a lock on a front door meant nothing to the casual passer-by. Provided it was being done with the right amount of casualness. This was one time a dog on a leash would have given him the appropriate touch of innocence. The most suspicious of cops passed a man with a dog without turning his head.

As soon as possible, he had to do something about his appearance. Maybe plastic surgery. There were a dozen surgeons in Paris and Rome, able and willing to cut the flesh from your finger pads and graft on new skin from your back. Old-timers would tell you it couldn't be done. That the prints always grew in. He'd seen a couple of the results. Smooth pink flesh without a line. They could take your prints from a hand like that, feed the card into their identifying machine from here to eternity. And never have a hope of identifying you from it. Once he got out of the country, he'd get his fingers done—a new nose, maybe—and alter his hair line. Then he'd forget about cops for as long as he lived. All he had to find was the money. With time, he could devise some method of getting to the vault. Once he was out of England, when the chance of a pinch was impossible. Tonight, he was screwing for a bed. The next time he used the tools it would be for something worth while. Without money he could do nothing. Even that was difficult. There wasn't a buyer in the country he could trust. Trying to peddle jewellery legitimately made as much sense as knocking on the Main Gate of Wandsworth Prison. The cops were no fools.

They might sense that by now he was really on the run—forced to burglary in order to gain food and shelter. Unless they thought that already he'd managed to get at his money. His assumption had to be that they knew of the vault. At least, for the time, he had to plan that they knew. One good deal, even for three or four thousand, would get him out of the country with luck. Provide enough cash to satisfy the guy up in Liverpool or someone like him. And leave Greg with loot that could be peddled with safety abroad. Already, he had accepted his future as it would now have to be. A thief, if he ever succeeded in leaving England to continue to be one.

He came out of the telephone booth, stepping briskly down to the bottom of Curzon Street. Above all, he had to give the appearance of knowing exactly where he was going. He reached the beginning of South Street without incident. One-five-three was at the far end on the other side. He crossed over, avoiding the lighted entrance to an apartment block where a group of porters and chauffeurs was gossiping.

Since the night of the break, he'd kept the crêpe-soled shoes he was wearing. He trod without sound, making himself as inconspicuous as possible. The odd numbers were his side of the street, now. The houses were crowded together in box-pleated elegance. Georgian mansions; modern ones, pretentious with oversize windows; stately town houses, last-ditch strongholds of ducal families. One-five-three was two houses from the end.

He slackened his pace as he came to the Mackinnon residence. It was old, three storeys high and had a basement area and six steps leading up to the front door. The door was sheltered by a shallow porch. He put one foot on the bottom step and bent at his shoe-lace. There was nobody on his side of the street nearer than fifty yards away. Straightening his back, he walked up the steps and had a look at the door. Lights from the basements each side of him made it possible to distinguish the locks. Two were mortise, fairly new and, by the brass surround, made by Hobbs. It was too dark to see whether there was dirt in either keyhole. Scratchmarks on the bright, polished metal looked as though both locks were in frequent use. Above them was a Yale.

Putting both hands on the door, he leaned, testing the pressure at lock level. All three seemed to be on. The pedestrian who had been behind had now drawn level. At the same time, a car turned the corner on to South Street, its lights silhouetting him against the cream-coloured door. He went through the motions of raising his hat to someone inside and pulling the door shut after him. The car drove on. At the bottom of the steps, he fell in behind the pedestrian, a woman, clicking her way home in a hurry.

From the size of the keyhole, the keys he needed were about half an inch long in the wards. Neither lock had looked particularly difficult—standard models of reasonable security. Dropped or raised E's were the most common pattern used on the type. He had a dozen of them in the bag that had been cut from Hobbs blanks. He turned up South Audley Street, looking for a place where he might open the canvas bag unobserved. North, were the gown shops and florists, their show-windows pastel-shaded glows. The lights of the cars and cabs that were passing made him conspicuous. He walked away from the stores to the church. In the shadow of the great studded door, he unzipped the canvas bag. Without a light of any kind, he had to grope with naked fingers, feeling the shapes of the keys. He found four and a strip of celluloid. He put his gloves on again and rubbed the smooth surfaces of the metal and celluloid with his fingers, obliterating all trace of a print.

You handled tools with bare hands—put your gloves on then dropped something, maybe without noticing it. Hours later, the cops appeared at your house, with big grins and a warrant for your arrest. It was the dropped letter or driving permit—the handkerchief with a laundry mark—that were the hazards. As damaging as a signed confession. Many guys went out on a score with pockets that had been emptied of all but money. Even their car keys were left on top of the sun visor or under a floor-mat.

He patted the pockets of Sloane's suit. There wasn't a thing to drop that was identifiable except two slips of paper. The addresses of the two houses he'd got from the library and that of Bridget Selkirk. Bridget's was in the book, anyway. He crumpled the slips in his hand and dropped them through a grating in the gutter.

The four keys and celluloid strip went deep in his left-hand coat pocket. Carrying the canvas bag in his right hand, he started back towards South Street, following the wall of the churchyard. Head down, he looked neither to right nor to left—a man who knew exactly where he was going and was in a hurry to get there. The tall blank line of bricks ended in a door, deep in the thickness of the wall.

As Greg passed, somebody spoke.

"Just a minute!" A uniformed constable stepped from the shadowed doorway, shaking his arms free from his cape. He faced Greg, blocking the pavement.

Greg waited. For a second, they eyed one another warily in the half-light.

"Do you live near here—sir?"

He's not sure, thought Greg quickly. It's a casual, routine enquiry. Both men moved easily but with calculation. The constable seeking to jockey Greg into the light from the street lamp ahead. Greg to avoid it.

"Yes, I do, officer." "*Constable!*" he thought. *Officer was wrong.* Pushing the words to the front of his mouth, he tried for an English accent. "I'm going home to Curzon Street, as it happens." He let the enquiry sound in his voice.

It was the constable who stood in the light after all. He was young with a fresh face, pleasant as he smiled his apology. He eased the chinstrap of his helmet. "We have to do this, you know, sir. I suppose you've come from somewhere near here?"

Start, route and finish were already in Greg's mind with a story to account for them. He'd been to the American Embassy and was on his way home. "Yes—from Grosvenor Square. Is there something wrong?" He tried to gauge the angle from the darkened doorway in the wall to the shadow of the church. It would be just possible for the cop to have seen him kneeling at the bag.

"No—just doing a job, sir." The constable took a step nearer. The light from the lamp finished at his feet. His eyes did not leave Greg, taking in the cheap mackintosh, the shoes, the bag. "I expect you've got something on you to prove your identity—a letter or something of the kind, sir?"

Greg made a bluff of searching his pockets, shifting his feet to bring him round to the constable's left. "I don't think I have . . . perhaps you'd better tell me what this is all about."

The young cop was still unsure of himself. Obviously uncertain how to apply theoretical tactics learned on a training course. He cleared his throat self-consciously. "Would you mind just opening that bag?" He raised a finger, pointing at the bag of keys in Greg's right hand.

Delay would be fatal. Greg took half a step forward into the light as if putting the bag on the pavement to open it. Then lifting it, he swung the dead weight of metal at the constable's unprotected jaw-line.

In the brief moment before the man ducked, Greg read recognition in his eyes. The impact caught the constable flush on the bridge of the nose. He fell forward to his knees, clutching at his face. The bag swinging in his hand, Greg ran.

Thirty yards away, he heard the piercing probe of the police whistle. There was no time to look round. Hugging the wall, he sprinted towards South Street. Two men came in his direction, walking hurriedly. Side-stepping, he managed to avoid a collision. They stood irresolute as the whistle shrilled again.

" Burglars! " gasped Greg pointing in the direction he was running. " Stop thieves! " he shouted.

A cruising cab slowed and the two men jumped on the running board, yelling for Greg to join them. He shook his head. " Police! " he called and sprinted off again. The men on the running board gave the driver some excited instructions. The cab raced off. As Greg ran, he heard their shouts drifting back. Nearing the entrance to South Street he slowed to a walk.

There was no sound of following footsteps. The whistle had stilled. That meant the cop was probably at a police box. The direct line to the Yard could send a half-a-dozen cruise cars converging on the area within minutes. He'd seen it happen. Somebody called in an alarm that was being broadcast from the control room at the Yard simultaneously with its reception. If the radio cars were in the vicinity, they could be at the address before the caller had replaced the receiver.

South Street was quiet. Lower down, the porters and chauffers stood looking curiously in the direction of the whistle. In the two basement areas, the lights had been extinguished. One-five-three stood locked in silence. He ran up the steps, keys and celluloid ready in his hands. He put the bag on the floor near the base of the door. For a second, he tried desperately to fill his lungs. Breathing hurt where Sloane had booted his ribs. Suddenly his mouth filled with the bitterness of bile and he coughed, spitting. He bent at the locks. The mortises came first. Once turned off, they allowed the door more play at the level of the Yale. He needed this for speed. The looser the door, the quicker he might spring the Yale. He pushed back his hat, the sweat on the cheap band needled his head as if it were pinned with red ants. He put the first key into the top mortise. The wards were too long—it wouldn't go into the keyhole. The second passed the keyhole but the bore of the shank was wrong. The third key fitted snugly. At twelve o'clock, the key stopped. He could feel the levers half-turned. There wasn't enough lift. Holding his left fore-finger under the shank, he lifted slightly, turning the key. There was a click as the tongue of the lock freed from the socket. With a little more manipulation, the same key turned off the second lock. He licked his lips. Only the Yale left, now.

A car turned slowly into South Street, travelling close to the kerb, moving towards him. He flattened himself against the side of the doorway, standing immobile as the car went past. He stood there for a minute in case another car followed. There was none. But at the other end of the street, a pattern of criss-crossed flashlights was working up in his direction.

Both hands flat on the door, he pushed till the pent-up breath left his body with a rush. He worked the celluloid into the crack in the door then brought it down to the Yale. He pulled it back a quarter inch then pushed hard. He could feel the edge of the strip tear. He was working too quickly. He had misjudged the level of the socket and torn the celluloid on its side. He took a glance over his shoulder. The flashlights were appreciably nearer. The police seemed to be concentrating on the basement areas. Had he waited in one of them, by now, he'd be in a police car, on his way to Cannon Row to be charged with murder.

There wasn't time to trim the celluloid. He reversed it and tried again, feverishly weighing patience against the approaching flashlights. He felt the strip go home in the socket. He pulled on the letter box, pushing the celluloid. Soundlessly, the door opened. The dark hall was refuge. He closed the door quietly. On his face on the floor boards, he waited. The police were nearer. He could hear them as they shouted casually to one another across the street. He groped for the bag of keys at his side. His hands made frantic circles then he remembered: the bag was where he had left it on the steps outside.

It was too late to do anything. He'd go out the back if they came to the door. There'd been no time to re-fasten the mortise locks. The door was held on the Yale. He could feel a short burglar chain over his hand. Reaching up, he fastened it. He squatted at the letter box. Outside, the bag sat on the white steps like some voiceless hound-dog. The cops couldn't miss it. They were immediately outside now. Briefly the lights flashed, sending a silver sliver through the letter box. Then it passed. No steps outside, nothing. He heard the voices as they neared the end of the street. Cautiously, he raised the flap in the letter box. The steps outside showed and the street for a dozen yards on each side. There was no movement out there. They had gone by, using their flashlights on the locks of the door, the beam missing the bag on the ground.

Gently, he turned the handle of the Yale lock, pulling the door open a fraction. Flat on his belly, he pushed his arm through the crack, grabbed the bag and pulled it in after him.

NINE

He lay where he was for a long time, shaking. Indifferent to everything but the security of the silent house. After a while he was able to distinguish the contours of the side stairway leading to a half-landing. There, through a chink in the curtains of the long window, he could see a strip of light. He climbed laboriously up. The window gave on a short garden ending in a high wall topped with old-fashioned, revolving spikework. He pulled the curtains slightly apart. It was impossible to be overlooked. Now he could make out the parquetry of the hall and a red runner that went to a door at the back.

Where he had lain, a few letters were scattered around. Standing at the window, he ripped one or two of them open. They were bills. The date of posting showed that they had been delivered two weeks before. Not even a woman to come in daily to look at the place, he thought. Nobody. Otherwise, the letters would have been picked up. He had taken his gloves off. No longer did it matter if he scrawled his name on the mirrors, printed ribaldry in soap as some of the boy burglars did, or left his fingerprints on each piece of furniture in the house. By the time the Mackinnons returned from Italy, he'd be out of the country or dead. Dead.

In England, they tried you and hanged you right smartly for murder. Took about as much time as they used in other countries to grow tired of asking you questions. In spite of his refusal to accept the word murder, the macabre rigmarole of the court persisted in his head. The sentence of the court upon you is that you be taken from this place to a lawful prison and thence to a place of execution and that you there suffer death by hanging and that your body be afterwards buried within the precincts of the prison in which you shall have been confined before your execution.

Deliberately, he willed himself to think of nothing but bed. It couldn't be much more than eight o'clock. He couldn't risk a light, not even with drawn curtains, but he hadn't heard a clock chime. Because there'd been nobody to wind them, he realized with satisfaction. Carrying the bag of keys with him he mounted the stairway slowly. This house had a normal feel about it. There were no sudden sounds, no unexplained clatters, no ominous atmosphere.

On the second storey, the landing fanned to three bedrooms and two bathrooms. The first bedroom he entered had blankets folded at the foot of a bed and the pillows were without cases. Remembering, he took the keys from his mackintosh pocket and went down to the hall. He locked both mortises from the inside, thumbed up the catch on the Yale so that the key could not be turned, and fastened the short length of chain. Not yet content, he rammed home the one stout bolt at the bottom of the door. He rubbed his hands down the front of his coat, ridding himself of the dust from the bolt. With or without keys, anyone trying to get in would have a time.

The door at the rear of the hall masked a staircase that led to the basement. In the corner of the large modern kitchen, he was able to make out a tall refrigerator. The kitchen windows were heavily barred. The door leading to the area, bolted and barred. At the back was another door to the garden. He unbolted this, leaving the key in the lock. Should the worst happen, this would be his line of retreat.

Back in the bedroom, he pulled his clothes off, letting the garments stay where they fell. Then he got into the bed and rolled himself in the blankets. His side still ached, making him cough. He buried his face in the pillow, stifling the sound. There had been no time to look at the lay-out of the house. Until there was, he had to be careful about any noise that could be heard next door. He lay in the darkness, staring at the curtains, listening to the occasional footsteps of the passers-by. Each passing car brought the urge to tip-toe to the window, expecting to see the car parked at the kerb, its lights extinguished, the occupants waiting. After a while, he slept.

He awoke to the sound of a tolling bell. For a second, he was back in the jail. Relieved, without knowing why, by the thought of the effortless day ahead. All his imperative needs would be met, after a fashion. He'd be fed, watered and sheltered. In a minute, Griffiths would crash open his cell door, there'd be hot tasteless tea and skilly. Then he'd sew sacks in the shop and come back to his cell. He'd do that today, tomorrow and for the next six years and eight months. Only this wasn't the querulous summons of the jailhouse bell, but a deeper tone with a doleful import.

The church, he remembered and rolled over on his back. He sat up. It was cold and, shivering, he pulled the blankets round his shoulders. He took a look at the room he was in. There was another bed at his side. Soft tinted blankets were piled neatly there. Both bedspreads were rich in Italian damask. Hogarth prints decorated walls papered with heavy, embossed flowers. The emerald carpet stretched from wall to wall. Yawning, he dragged himself from the bed, trailing the blanket behind. He pulled a few drawers here and there. They were empty. A guest-room, he decided.

The three bedrooms were separated by bathrooms. The Mackinnons slept in the centre room where framed photographs of a man and a woman stood on the tables beside the Chippendale beds. The closets were filled with clothes, faint with the insistence of good scent. He went through the bathroom. In the square tub, water had dripped unchecked, leaving a rust stain on the enamel. There was a shower stall in the corner, beside it some spring chest-developers, attached to the wall. Scales, a full-length mirror and dressing table opposed a cabinet. He touched a switch and waited. There was a faint gurgle as an immersion heater went to work in the tank. He switched off. First, he'd have to see where the water outlet was. Then decide if it was safe to take a bath. The last bedroom belonged to the son in Kenya. It was a horsey room with a post horn on the red walls, pictures of a young man playing polo, jumping fences, place names and dates on the frames.

He opened the giant Norman *armoire*. A dozen good suits hung on a rail. Shoes, underwear, ties and, in boxes, hats. Without wasting time, he tried on the clothes. Apart from a little looseness under the arms, they were a reasonable fit.

With three or four hundred burglaries behind him, he had never before spent an unauthorized night in someone's home. There was a strange feeling. At times, like a child who climbs stairs in the dark, at others, the sense of complete ownership that the man in Shiel's book, " The Purple Plague ", must have had. The only survivor in a city struck by a disaster that he had escaped. The secrets of a city, its riches, his alone but no-one to share them with.

In the bathroom cabinets were stores of soap, new toothbrushes in their plastic containers, banded boxes of toothpowder. The unconsidered trivia of a wealthy household. He found towels in a linen cupboard and went back to the basement. Sooner or later, he had to explore the house from top to bottom. Ensure that it held no secret to bitch him later. Once done, he would make up his mind which rooms to use. The Mackinnon home would be a base from which he would operate, he had decided. There was a completely fresh wardrobe for him upstairs. He'd seen books, radios, a television set. With the shutting of the front door by the Mackinnons, one-five-three South Street had been erased from the minds of the neighbours. The family was away, the house securely locked up. It was his, to do as he liked with so long as he obeyed the basic principles—not to be seen, entering or leaving or in the house. And to make no betraying noise.

He could stay holed up for the day. Leave after dark, using one or both mortises on the front door but not the Yale. A chance pedestrian, a cop, even, seeing him return would be faced with a presentable man using his front door keys. If anyone bothered to look. He was smiling to himself as he crossed the hall. With the new confidence, his brain took a better grasp of his problems. It was too bad that he didn't know where the Mackinnons garaged their cars. Otherwise he could have used one. A car would have been invaluable now.

Hunger reminded him that it had been a long time since he had eaten. In the well-equipped kitchen, the store cupboards were stocked with canned and preserved foods. There were cheese, eggs, in the refrigerator, butter. He could see neither bread, milk, meat nor fresh vegetables. But he could bring back enough to last for a few days if necessary.

He looked through the barred windows into the area. Stone steps mounted to an iron gate in the railings at street level. Two dustbins, lids off and empty, stood by the kitchen door. He could just see where the drainage system emptied under a grating in the middle of the area flags. The area was a tiny yard, twelve feet lower than the road, between the steps to the front door and those of the house on the left. Only someone passing directly overhead could see or hear water emptying into the sump. The bath was safe enough to use. The lavatory might be difficult. An emptying cistern had repercussions all over the place. The people next door might hear. It might be safer all round to bail the bathwater into the john. He had plenty of time.

He put his ear against the kitchen party wall. Very faintly, he heard the noise of somebody moving around. Good solid walls, he told himself. If he watched his step, he might stay here days. It would be seven weeks yet, according to the announcement in *The Times*, before the Mackinnons returned. There was an electric kettle that he filled. Tea and sugar and a tin of condensed milk were in the store cupboard. He boiled an egg and ate rye biscuits with it, washing and drying the utensils from force of habit.

In the bathroom, one of Mackinnon's razors was in its case. In a tub filled with steaming water, Greg eased the aches from his body. The swelling on his ribs had gone down, but when he pressed the casing a pain cut deep at his lungs. It would be great if they'd punctured, he thought. He'd have to get to a doctor, some time. He thought briefly but pleasurably of Sloane. That was it—it wasn't that he wouldn't have killed the big bastard, he just hadn't tried. How could an accident be murder. After the stubble was scraped from his neck, he felt better.

In the son's bedroom, he took time choosing his outfit. He had no idea what hour it was. He'd have to look round for a watch—or set one of the clocks by the radio. The dark grey flannel suit would be inconspicuous at night. Black brogue shoes. He could buy thin rubber soles and heels and stick them on the shoes. A white shirt and navy-blue silk knitted tie. A pair of Mackinnon's cuff buttons were plain gold and platinum. Approving, Greg threaded them through the buttonholes. The dark green hat and brown tweed overcoat would give him a switch of appearance that the cops could not expect.

Tentatively, he tried pads of cotton in his mouth, over his gums. They looked obvious and he spat them out. If only he could be sure that Sloane hadn't talked . . . that leg splint was the best possible distraction for a suspicious cop. Suddenly, he remembered Bridget Selkirk. Instinctively, he felt that if he could determine the right approach, Bridget would be someone he might rely on. But one good score and he need rely on no one. There'd be enough ready money to take care of Sullivan's man up in Liverpool and a pocket of loot to buy time once he was abroad. He wouldn't trust the trains to make the trip north. Better to hire a limousine and chauffeur and drive. You had to decide which was best—to be one of the crowd, jammed railway coaches with chummy characters nosing out your business, the terminals lousy with cops, or putting yourself in expensive conspicuousness. The cops might figure you both ways but they could never tell what you were going to do.

" You will remember, gentlemen, that the real secret of tactical success is the retention of initiative. Be content to let the enemy worry about *what* you're going to do, if the b . . . . . . want to. *But keep the initiative!*"

The lecturer had been some old dug-out colonel with red staff trimmings and the face of a goat. He had little to say but all of it made sense, even now it made sense.

He carried the top coat and hat down to the hall and left them on the table. He spent the next hour slicing the mackintosh and Sloane's suit to strips with a razor blade. He fed them into the lavatory bowl, sluicing them down with buckets of water from the bath tub. The crêpe-soled shoes, he left. He'd ditch those at night when he went out.

He had no idea where he would start operations. Jobs worth three or four grand were not found, walking round the streets, knocking on doors. Nor yet by telephoning the addresses of the publicized rich. Good scores generally came by patient investigation, the use of planning and imagination, reliable information. He had no time and nothing to investigate. The lists of prospective jobs had been destroyed when the Nicholson woman appeared. It was to have been the last job of all time for him. Keys, equipment, the goodwill of the business, everything had gone to Sloane then. Now, there wasn't even one of the touts to feed him information for twenty per cent of the take. Sullivan had been right—he was completely on his own.

He spent the rest of the morning prowling around the house, searching with no attempt at concealment. At least it made him forget this need that he felt to watch the street. Ransacking closets and drawers required an effort that claimed all his senses but one. Always his ears were ready for some danger signal.

The stockings and underclothes piled on Mrs. Mackinnon's blue bedroom carpet. Handling a bag of lavender, his fingers probed the incongruous hardness of its interior. He opened the bag. The bright, slender key could only belong to a safe. In the adjoining bathroom, he discovered the hinged mirror. It swung back to show the port-hole face of a wall safe. He opened it. Save for a few documents and one hundred dollars, American, the safe was empty. He pocketed the five twenty-dollar bills. That figured—you didn't leave jewellery in an unoccupied house, not if you wanted the insurance company to pay out against loss. Sticking the dollars away out of sight was typical. It was still an offence for a British subject to possess unauthorized dollars. A crazy restriction that turned people like Mackinnon into lawbreakers, for a lousy thirty quid.

He riffed through the rest of Mrs. Mackinnon's clothes with appreciation. There were suits by Hardy Amies and Lachasse. Revillon's spring furs. Her mink would probably be in storage—not that he'd have been able to do anything about it without a buyer. Funny, the way you became able to handle the intimate clothing of a woman you'd never met and feel precisely nothing. Divorcing your mind from every significance but the economic one. Burglars seemed to acquire a professional detachment towards belongings—something like a doctor examining a woman's body.

He closed the door on the shambles in the master bedroom. The son's room would be best for sleeping. There was everything he needed, to hand. Downstairs, the first-floor drawing room was cocooned in dust sheets. He lifted the corner of one. The tall china cabinet glittered with gilt, blazed with enamel. Touching the rich dark wood, he remembered Judith. She could have had a room like this, he thought bitterly. If only she'd . . . The inability to point his resentment added to its intensity.

He crept round the room, fingering the cut-crystal, the weave of the tapestry on the wall, the warm smoothness to the silver boxes. It wasn't only Judith: Christ, *he'd* wanted a room like this! Some of the graciousness of life. The chance to live like a gentleman and some of those four goddamned freedoms they were so busy talking about a few years ago. Whatever chances you had, you made on your own. He'd learnt the hard way, he reflected.

What did they do for you in this man's world! What had *his* parents ever done for him! Educated him, they'd say. Sure. School after school with the sons of the very rich. The "sons of gentlefolk" as the prospectuses said. Making sure every instinct was channelled into an unthinking acceptance of the things that money bought.

Graduation Day and the Dean of Men. ". . . and to each and every one of you, I say this:"—the gown had been proudly lifted over the skinny shoulders. "This school has done its part in preparing you for the places in society which are yours by birth, tradition and education. Yours is the heritage of gentlemen. And I am minded to recall to you the definition of a gentlemen that we like in this school. A gentleman is a gentle man. You will do well to remember that."

Sure. A gentle man in a household as expectant as a maternity ward!

A family that waited for you to be brilliant, successful or intelligent. Anything but gentle. Then came the carefully engineered job on the grain exchange. Customer's man with a salary at which a truck driver would have belched disgust.

And his father. " Mr. Donaldson tells me that you are dissatisfied, Paul. I'm completely unable to say why, if it's true. You've got a career ahead of you that most men of your age would give an eye for. Five years with Donaldson and you'll know the grain-broking business. Be ready for a seat on the floor." The martyred smile. " You see, Paul, your mother and I have made some sacrifice for your education. We want you to obtain the benefit." The man-to-man look. " It hasn't always been easy, son."

You bet it hadn't! It had been easier waving goodbye to the hero off to the wars. ". . . and a commission in the Toronto Scottish. Such a *good* regiment with officers of his own class, thank God! "

Then peace. The frantic, bewildered cables enquiring what had come over him. He couldn't be serious about staying on in England, looking for a job! Marry by all means. No doubt Judith was the sort of girl they had always wished for him! But bring her home! Donaldson had his old job waiting for him.

The cables had dwindled to curt polite notes from his father, tearful wails from his mother. His first arrest had fixed the whole thing. The rambling old house out at York Mills no longer had an heir. With Biblical bitterness, his father had cut both Greg and the arrest from his consciousness.

The flap in the front door clicked. He stood where he was, tensed. Craning, he managed to see the head of a man through the window, going down the steps. He watched as the man climbed the next set of steps and pushed something through the mail box. Greg picked the printed paper from the floor. SUPPORT THE UNITED NATIONS. He crumpled it in his hand and went back to young Mackinnon's room. Switching on the bedside radio, he muffled the set to a minimum. He had no newspaper to check the B.B.C. programmes. But sooner or later, there'd be a time signal. He listened to the music without hearing it. When it had ended, he waited for the staccato pips. The announcer broke in with a bland voice, completely without personality.

"This is the B.B.C. Home Service. Before the one o'clock news, here is a police message. Will anyone who may have been in the vicinity of Gillam Mansions, Gillam Street, W.1, on the evening of Wednesday, the fourteenth, where a fatality occurred, please get in touch with New Scotland Yard, telephone Whitehall one-two, one-two. I will repeat the message : will anyone . . ."

That was the address of Sloane's flat! *Fatality*, they called it, now! He was sure that nobody had seen him go in. There was no one on the street. But that woman he'd seen on the landing—the one who lived opposite Sloane—surely the police would have interviewed her already . . .

He could picture the room at the Yard. Plain deal table and a guy with a pipe—the Assistant-Commissioner's Office, maybe, with a dozen thief catchers trying to look honest in their frames—men blocking every exit open to him, sensing each excuse that he might hope to offer in court, seeking to meet it. They had the girl, the porter, the woman who lived opposite, his fingerprints. That wasn't enough. Now they wanted someone to swear that he'd seen Greg go into the block. Swear anything as long as it hitched the knot securely behind his ear.

He set the clock in the bedroom and went down to the library. There was a deep bucket seat behind the desk. He switched on two of the bars in the electric fire and sat down. The announcement meant little. Take a pack of hounds: you know where a fox runs, trail him till you see his brush vanish over a hedge. But when he breaks trail, the hounds lose the scent. After last night, all the police could do was sniff the breeze. After a while, they'd go back to the old runs, cover the familiar ground. Finally, they'd just wait. That was it. The waiting game. More than imagination, even, a good cop had to be ready to wait.

He pulled open the drawers of the writing desk, rummaging through the jumbled papers. Letters, bills, insurance cards in the names of the two maids and, pinned to them, a couple of country addresses. On the same slip of paper, someone had scribbled "Till the twenty-eighth". That was two weeks or more before the Mackinnon's return. Obviously, the maids had been given a holiday till the twenty-eighth. They'd come back to open the house. If he needed it, he had almost two weeks clear in the place.

There was an album of photographs in the bottom drawer. A Cotswold manor-house with the Mackinnon family under an oak on the lawn. The son on a pony. A lake with rushes spearing its edge and three swans, sailing.

If he had a place in the country . . . somewhere to disappear till the heat of this thing cooled off. Not an inn or an hotel, linked to London by people coming and going. But a house buried remote from police, gossip and danger. It would have to be someone who would accept him for what he was. There could be no evasion. Whoever sheltered him had to think of his safety as theirs—to know that this was a guy on the run for murder they were harbouring. The impossibility of the thought discouraged him. If your friends, your wife, wouldn't do it . . . Without reason, he kept thinking of Bridget Selkirk. The way she lived, her strong defiance of what she was required to do by convention, her loyalty. If he could sit her down in that chair across the room. He was past lying about anything—he'd tell her as much of himself as she wanted to know. If you could convince a woman that she was needed. Desperately needed. Innate pity sometimes over-ruled all other consideration. Only he'd never have the chance to convince her.

He dozed in the heat of the fire. When he awakened, the street lamps slitted patterns through the Venetian blinds at the window. The room was stuffy. He kicked off the switch and went upstairs and washed. It was senseless to go off halfcock on some burglary that would undo all that he had won so hazardously. It was safe enough here for the time being. Tomorrow was another day. Maybe by then, his brain would be able to plan again. One of the ready-made scores of bygone days might present itself, forgotten and now ready to take. Values were different now. What had been too dangerous then might be feasible. He would climb, creep and break wherever the reward justified it. But there had to be just one job. One good score, that's all he needed.

Unconsciously, he was flexing his thumb where the girl had bitten on the scar. He wouldn't be taken. If they were going to kill him, it might as well be with a fight.

It was a quarter to six. Once more, the interior of one-five-three South Street held a silent protection he was unwilling to leave. But there was bread, meat, milk to get. More importantly, a flash-light. That he had to have. Cabs cruised up and down outside, all day long. There'd be no difficulty finding one quickly. After last night, the less time he spent on the street, the better. Most of the big stores would be shut by now. But in places like Soho and Earl's Court, there were little shops that stayed open late. Earl's Court was better than Soho. Anywhere away from the West End. On the Earl's Court Road, an English accent was almost an exception. Four thousand foreigners lived in a quarter-mile square. Poles, Frenchmen, Negroes, Eurasians, Canadians and Americans.

He put on the brown tweed coat and green velour hat. Leaving the catch of the Yale up, he locked the front door behind him with the mortise key from the bag. The rest of the keys he left in the house. He went down the steps to the street with an odd sense of venture. The night was at once a menace and a promise. Turning sharp left, he walked briskly towards Bond Street. A cab slowed.

" Earl's Court Road," he told the driver, muffling his face with a cigarette.

The driver took his cab through Belgravia, avoiding the Knightsbridge traffic. They passed the end of Lowndes Square where the lights of Cameron's club showed discreet yet distinctive.

At the junction of Earl's Court and Old Brompton Roads, Greg tapped on the window. The cab stopped. He paid off the driver and walked two hundred yards to the stores flanking the underground station. Workers poured from the lighted entrance, crowding the pavements, queuing like bell-wethered sheep for their newspapers. He crossed to the post office and turned down a side street, cutting through to Hogarth Place.

In a small delicatessen, a bald man wearing a monocle was slicing ham behind the counter. The store was heady with spice. Notices, appeals for charity, were printed in Polish and hung against the wall. In the corner, a stuffed white eagle glared glassily from a stand. The store was empty.

He considered the stacked shelves. Bread, he needed. Milk. There was a chicken on a tray, already cooked. String beans from the deep-freeze, some Polish sausage. Pumpernickel. It had been years since he had tasted the damp, nutty bread. A carton of cream. The store cupboard at home held racks of canned fruit. *At home*, he reflected. Why not—the dark friendly house on South Street held a security that he could never find in Henley.

Fingertips pressed together, the Pole waited for Greg to fill his order. " Chez? " he asked suddenly, spitting the consonants.

Greg shook his head. " I have cheese. That's the lot. Give me a bag to carry the stuff in, will you? "

He watched as the Pole snapped the paper bag with delicate fingers. Then he saw that the man had no more than fingers. Thumbs on each hand were missing. Christ, he thought. The Poles here were a strange bunch. Completely alien in thought and custom. Doggedly grafting a piece of their own country on to England. Most of the army-in-exile had taken British citizenship. He'd met colonels pressing pants, cavalry captains behind bars. Those Poles who had been soldiers or in some way connected with the one-time government clung to ancient memories, refusing to accept history. Like this man with his stuffed bird, the symbol of Old Poland. The man's thumbs were gone, God knows how. Most of these guys had a story that made his own something from a kindergarten reader.

He still had a fiver and two one pound notes. Best to break the big bill. Often there was trouble in changing a fiver. He pulled the black-and-white paper from his pocket and laid it on the counter.

The Pole nodded as he added the cost of the groceries. He pushed a pen at Greg, asking for a name and address on the back of the note.

" Is custom," he smiled.

" Sure."

Greg took the pen, bending over the counter to write. Here was another crazy thing, this business of writing your name and address on the back of a fiver. Anything satisfied them. The information was never challenged, yet in some way the manoeuvre satisfied the Englishman's love of a formality. He was scribbling a fictitious name and address when the door to the street opened behind him. Without turning his head, he sensed the newcomer's interest in him.

Suddenly an arm reached out, the hand grabbing his shoulder.

" Gotcha! " said a voice.

Greg spun sideways, knocking a tray of salami to the counter. The five pound note drifted to the feet of the Pole.

" Gotcha, Greg! " The newcomer's tanned face crinkled in a grin. He wore his clothes with a raffish air and was hatless, showing a head of startling white hair.

The Pole was making change at the register. To get time to think, Greg reached across, picking the sausage from the counter, putting it back on the tray.

" S'truth, Greg, it must be a bloody year since I seen yer. Where've you bin? " It was a strong Australian accent, thickened with drink.

Greg looked at the man steadily. Jack Anstell was a friend of Cameron's, for one thing. An ex-partner of the British Columbian. A con-man who'd stayed on in Europe when the bottom of his racket seemed to have dropped out Over the last ten years, he'd made a good living, riding the boats. The professional fourth at a bridge table, his finger routine with a deck of cards was the best in the country. He had a line of gab that kept middle-aged women dissatisfied with their husbands and he drank like a sink.

" I've been around, Jack," Greg answered quietly. As far as he knew, Anstell was no copper. But none of the others had been. That stuff was out. *Nobody* got the benefit of the doubt, now. He watched the Australian warily, impelled to know what the man was thinking, unwilling to hear it. Anstell had to know what the score was. The guy spent his nights in Cameron's bar. And there couldn't be a single grafter in London by now who didn't know about Greg's sentence and Sloane's death.

He pocketed the change, nodding goodnight to the Pole. Anstell seemed to have forgotten whatever he had intended buying. He followed Greg to the door. The whisky made his breath powerful. " Blimey, Greg," he said heartily, " you're the first of the mob I've run into." He shut the door after them. " I just got back from Jamaica today." Putting an arm round Greg's shoulder, he squeezed roughly. " How yer *doing*, pal? "

Under the street lamps, the Australian's tan had a greenish tinge. His eyes were boiled and shining. Half-boozed already, thought Greg. And before the night was over, Anstell would be stewed to the balls. Jamaica! That might account for it—there was no reason why Anstell should know what had been happening in England. It wouldn't be long before he did. Greg wondered what sort of story Cameron would blow down his friend's ear. *Jamaica!* He had a surge of rancour as he thought of Anstell's liberty to leave a place like the Indies.

" I'm all right, Jack," he said shortly. He shifted the bag of groceries uncertainly from one hand to another. This was a dark side street but he was uneasy in the other man's presence. The feeling of anonymity was gone and Anstell responsible for it. " I got to go, Jack," he said suddenly. " I'll see you around. Maybe I'll look in at Cameron's later." He turned to leave.

The Australian blocked his way, rocking slightly on his heels. His teeth were white against his face as he hiccoughed. " Let's go up there together. The evening's on me. Where's a cab?" He peered into the gloom.

"I'll have to take this stuff home first," Somehow, he had to shake the Australian speedily. "I'll see you up there, Jack."

Anstell put his head on one side, his hand on Greg's sleeve. "You live down at Henley," he said cunningly. "You're not bloody well going home. You've got a girl lives round here." Once more, he hiccoughed. "Get her to ring a friend. We'll make a night of it. Spend some of that dirty sucker money." He planted himself squarely in Greg's path. With drunken effort, he strained at seriousness. "Now *there's* a place for you, Greg, Jamaica! Not one good burglar on the island and the bloody place lousy with jewellery. All those Americans over in Montego for the winter. You'd make a fortune, Greg. The cops ain't looking for people like you. They're watching the niggers stealing off the clothes-lines."

"Tell me about it later," soothed Greg. "I'll meet you up in Cameron's, okay?' He kept his voice reasonable, friendly.

The good humour left the Australian's face. He moved his shoulders combatively. "You don't want to be like that, chum. I'm asking you to have a drink. What's the matter, I stink or something?"

It was dark—he could kick the guy in the balls and run. And leave someone else who was hostile. Another to add to the wall of stony, indifferent faces. With a couple of drinks in him, Anstell was a troublemaker. Poison unless he was handled carefully. Greg had seen him, drunk. Rapping around blindly with his cane because someone had asked him to take a place on a bus queue. With liquor in him, Anstell would make a scene on the steps of the Central Criminal Courts, if he felt like it.

"I'll have a drink with you, Jack," he said slowly. "Only I'll have to make a phone call first."

The Australian linked his arm in Greg's. "*That's* my boy. Let's get a cab." They walked towards the Earl's Court Road.

Greg was thinking quickly. It wasn't leaving Ansell that worried him but the scene. Once the Australian went into his shouting act, anything might happen. The police could arrive.

The pair crossed the street to the Underground entrance. The phone booths were on the other side of the barrier. "I'll slip through and phone," said Greg. He put the bag of groceries at the Australian's feet. "Keep your eye on those for me."

The hell with it—the phone booths were out of sight of the

barrier. He'd slip down to the tracks and catch the first train in any direction. Anywhere, to get this menace off his back.

Anstell bent down for the groceries, swaying. "Jesus!" he coughed. "This weather kills me, Greg. Over at Montego Bay yesterday, it was seventy-eight in the shade. I need my head examining, coming back to this bleeding cold." He walked to the barrier with Greg nodding at the ticket collector. "Going to phone," he said. Breathing liquor into Greg's face, he was arch. "Let *me* talk to her, chum. The old man hasn't lost his speed. Brisbane's original lover, that's me. I'll tell her to get a friend."

In the booth, Greg blocked the phone from the other with his body. He dialled the number of the booth. The high insistent bip of the engaged signal sounded immediately. He turned, handing the phone for the Australian to hear. "Engaged, I'll talk to her later."

"Do it from Cameron's," said Anstell. Still carrying the bag, he led the way up the street.

"Don't make it Cameron's, Jack. If the girl's going to join us, I don't want to be on show."

The Australian nodded heavily. "I get yer. Where, then?"

Any pub in London, a cop could walk into the bar. Maybe for no more than a free beer. Then, he'd be finished. The clubs where he was a member would be even more dangerous. Elegant rat-races where he would be safe for as long as it took some police informer to reach a phone. For a moment, he reconsidered taking Anstell down a side-street and letting him have it.

"I got it!" Anstell flagged down a passing cab. "Beauchamp Place," he directed the driver. "The Balearic Club. It's at the end." As the cab wheeled south, he patted Greg's knee. "Safe as in Brixton Prison, you'll be. Your wife'll never know you've been there. Empty, it is, always." Struck with a drunk's sudden melancholy, he repeated. "Empty. I-don't-bloody-well-know why."

These days were becoming a rushing horror of cab after cab. Escaping from something to reach somewhere to escape from. Now this lush with his patting and slapping. Like his buddy, Cameron. The same false comradeship that was part of the conman's approach. After a few drinks, Anstell would be chasing the first girl he saw. There was bound to be a lavatory, a room at the back of the club—he could slip out while the Australian had his nose buried in a glass.

The cab was making speed along the Old Brompton Road, past the bottom of Queen's Gate. Events seemed to be forcing him to return to the very districts where he was hotter than a firecracker. The sooner he was back in South Street, the better. If he'd been sober, Anstell would have taken the hint. If not, Greg could have laid it on the line: " Look, Jack. I'm on the run. Leave me out." But with the head of steam the Australian was carrying, there would be the all-for-one, one-for-all, routine. A drunk con-man, helping *his* buddy escape from justice.

He leaned back in the cab, watching the doors of the stores lest they had some memory of danger for him. He couldn't remember a club on Beauchamp Place. But there were hundreds of them in London, dozens in the Chelsea-Knightsbridge area. He'd have one drink, then out. If Anstell wanted to make a scene then, let him. At least it would be off the street.

The driver slowed, watching the numbers. When he had made the circuit twice, he pulled over to the kerb and opened the glass partition behind him.

" What was that name again?"

" The Balearic Club. Whatsamatter—I thought you said you knew it!" Anstell's temper was deteriorating.

" I didn't," the driver answered shortly. " I got no time to remember every one of 'em. Beauchamp Place, you said. You got it." He swivelled round in his seat. For the first time, they had a glimpse of the flattened nose that spread under the man's small corduroy cap. " Yus," he repeated to Anstell. " You got it."

For a second, the Australian forgot him. " That club's been here a bloody year. Ever since Morry Fisher opened it. Half these bleeders," he complained, " ought to be off the roads. It's a f . . . . . waste of time, telling 'em where you want to go."

Morry Fisher! Another swell. One-time race-track tout, still runaround man for the Australian mob. A willing wearer of Sloane's mantle and a friend of his.

The resentment grew in the cab driver's face as Greg watched. This could be it, thought Greg. He must have been crazy to get in a cab with Anstell. To walk a step on the street with him.

Murder, he thought. That's what the cops wanted him for—not any more for a jailbreak. Yet calmly he was considering walking into a club with this drunken trouble-maker. Out of the dark street into a lighted room. Could be that this was all an act. Maybe Anstell had known from the start—was walking him into a reception committee of Sloane's friends. The police, even. There was no possibility, left, so wild that he could afford to ignore it.

This time, the cab-driver pushed the glass right back so that he could lean his face into the aperture. He twisted his big shoulders round, puffing a little.

" This is the end of your ride, mate," he said to Anstell. " And you can forget the tip—if you'd thought of one—just pay what's on the meter."

Hurriedly, Greg fumbled for change. " He doesn't know what he's saying, driver," he began.

Anstell cut him short, staring earnestly into Greg's face. " Here, hold it! Didn't you hear what this balls-aching bastard said to us, Greg?" He slapped both palms on his knees. " The end of our ride, the man says, Greg."

Greg jerked his arm free. The very thing he had feared looked like happening. He shoved some change at the driver. " C'm'on take this."

The man ignored him. " You got a lot to say for yourself, mate," he said to Anstell, heavily. " I ain't so sure I oughtn't to teach you a lesson."

Anstell's mind struggled with the implications, his reactions slowed by the liquor. Then, before Greg could stop him, he had the door of the cab open and was through it. Staggering, he wrestled with his topcoat, trying to get it off. " Get off that bleeding seat," he yelled at the driver. "You Pommie bastard! We'll see just how good you are!"

Already the noise of the Australian had attracted the attention of some people across the street. They stopped, staring curiously as the Australian lurched dangerously near the kerb. Further down, Greg could see what looked like the shape of a helmet in a shop doorway. He slammed the cab door shut. " Get moving," he yelled at the driver. " This can cost you your licence!"

For a second, the driver was irresolute. Then, changing his gears, he put his cab in motion. The shouts followed them round the corner. The partition was still open. The driver spoke over his shoulder, squaring his frustrated pugnacity.

" Licence or no licence," he said heavily, " I don't need to take that kind of abuse from anybody. I don't care *'oo* he is!"

The cab followed the back of Harrods into Hans Crescent, the chauffeur seemingly steering by instinct towards the West End. The silent house on South Street was a cupboard on the stairs. A place for Greg to creep with the sudden pain in his side. The hurt allowed no recognition of anything but its growing agony.

He rapped on the glass with his knuckles. " I'm sick," he gasped. " Get me back to South Street as quick as you can!"

The wet on his face and neck was cold. He leaned forward, forcing his head between his knees. Once more, the driver pulled his cab to a halt. Turning, he took a good look at Greg. " Outside, mate, if you're going to spew. I gotta clean this cab myself. A nice winning turn," he remarked sarcastically. " A coupla drunks."

There was no will to explain. Just the need to be left alone. If they'd leave him alone for a minute, he'd be all right. He'd be able to breathe properly—break this ring round his chest. Dimly, he knew that if he collapsed on the street it was his finish. This was it, he thought. The lowest point of human resistance. With an effort, he got his head up. On the floor, the groceries had spilled over his hat.

" Just—get—me—home." He struggled the words out.

The driver bent his head lower, staring into the back of the cab, then he whistled. " 'Ere—" he said, " I'm taking you to the 'orspittle, mate." He slammed into first gear. The cab went round the bend as though on rails, heading for Saint George's Hospital.

In the back, Greg wiped his face, hands and neck, striving to concentrate, to avert this disaster. " No hospital," he said distinctly. " Heart trouble. Boots!"

They passed the casualty entrance to the hospital, filtering into the traffic that sped down the slope to Piccadilly. " I got yer," the driver nodded. " Boots, Piccadilly Circus." His rancour was gone. He spun the cab through the gaps in the traffic lines, impatiently using his horn button. " Sure you're all right, mate?" he asked over his shoulder.

Though the pain had gone for the moment, Greg had no answer to give. He shut his eyes, willing himself to work this thing out properly. Boots—the only drug store that was open night and day in London. The midnight rendezvous of the drug-addicts, filling their twenty-four hour Home Office prescriptions with the first minute of the new day.

The cab made the circle of the brilliant Circus and stopped in front of the chemist's. Like an automaton, he opened the door and felt his way to the pavement. In a jumping field of coloured neon signs, a clock showed a quarter past nine. The lights worried his eyes. Holding the side of the cab, he spoke to the man.

" Wait. I'll make it all right for you. Only be a minute."

The driver nodded. Like a sleepwalker, Greg went through the door into the shop. Right and left were cosmetic counters. Trays stacked with patent medicines and hot water bottles stretched to a light at the end of the store where a girl waited curiously. White-coated, she watched as he lowered himself into a cane-bottomed chair. He knew this was crazy. Outside was the Hub of the Empire, the glittering heart of the city. Every foot of the pavement out there crawled with hands that were ready to grab. And he couldn't help himself.

He raised his head, realizing the girl was waiting for him to speak. Licking his lips, he made the strained English accent grotesque.

" I had a dizzy spell. Can you give me something to take? I've not far to get home."

Her uniform was white and her face pleasant with brown eyes and hair. Compassion, he thought suddenly. All the stinking ills of the body in front of her every day, she could still feel pity. He faced her like a dog with a broken paw, watching its master.

She took a clinical thermometer from the tunic pocket, whipping the mercury to the end. " You don't look at all well." She pushed the thermometer into his mouth. " Do you have these attacks often? Have you seen a doctor about them?"

He shook his head, already alarmed by the questions. She took the thermometer from his mouth, looked at it then put it on the counter beside him. " I'll mix you something to take," she said quickly. " You've — a slight temperature."

Now he mistrusted anyone who left him, to return later. She was out of sight behind the counter. He listened for the sound of the lowered voice. *Police? There's a man here who looks like the escaped convict! Yes, the man you are looking for.*

But there was only the clink of glass upon glass as she prepared the draft. Above his head was a tray of adhesive tape, bandages and gauze. Reaching, he pocketed a roll of tape and the thermometer.

The girl came round to him, stirring the mixture as she walked. " Drink this," she ordered. " It'll do you good. I'd go straight back to bed if I were you and get somebody to call your doctor."

He nodded, draining the brown, evil-smelling mixture till the rough dregs gritted on his teeth. As he walked slowly to the door, he sensed her appraisal. The cab-driver looked up, opening the back for Greg.

" You look a bit better, now, mate. Give me a bit of a turn, back there, you did." His flat nose twisted as he smiled. " 'Ere," he said pleasantly. " I know your face, don't I? Can't place you though."

He sat on the edge of the seat in the back. I can't run, he realized. There's *nothing* I can do. Wearily, he raised a hand. The cab moved off. " Yes," said the driver. " I've got a good memory for faces, I 'ave. On the films, ain't yer?" Greg made no answer.

He paid off the cab at the bottom of South Street. When its light had disappeared, he walked up to the house. There was nobody on the quiet street to watch as he fumbled like a drunk at the front door. He fastened everything that could be closed, behind him and sat in the dark for a while. The draft had cleared the spinning discs from in front of his eyes. He took his breath in shallow gulps and the pain was less. Thirst took him to the kitchen. As he crossed to the sink, the bright enamel of the refrigerator winked in the half-light. He remembered. The groceries he had left the house to buy were on the floor of the cab where he'd left them.

Pulling himself up the banisters, he sat on the edge of the bath, feeling for the switch. He ran a bath as hot as his body would stand it. Then he lowered himself into it till the water lapped underneath his armpits. You couldn't go on like this without a let-up, he reasoned. Nobody could. There was no respite. Events were no longer a challenge but a demand that he could not meet. But he *had* to have the will to go on. This cracked rib or whatever it was, was that big copper's legacy. Sloane reaching out, adding his mite to ensure Greg's capture. He moved gratefully in the hot water, soaking the warmth into his aching side. To screw Sloane was worthwhile in itself. With fresh determination, he stood in the bath, drying his body thoroughly. In the dark, he couldn't see his skin where the pain was but the swelling was slight. Carefully, he taped his side with the adhesive. When he was done, the skin was stretched stiff but the spot stood the probe of his fingers without too much hurt.

Tonight had been a close one. The obvious place for a man on the run to hide was a hospital. The police knew it. Every hospital had close links with the cops. Had he passed out on the street, there'd have been a couple of cops by his bed, waiting for him to come to.

Naked, he groped his way to the bedroom. He stretched up to pull down the window, grimacing. Shut it again, first thing in the morning, he impressed on his memory. A milkman, the people in the house opposite, might notice a thing like that. There were the clean, fine sheets that he'd found, on the bed. He was still thirsty and fought the impulse to go back to the bathroom for water.

I'll count a hundred, then go, he told himself. It was his bedroom at home. He lay still with the weight of the snow shifting on the roof over his head. He waited for the sound of his father's car as it swished on the driveway. I'll count a hundred, he said, then he'll come. He turned on his good side and slept in exhaustion.

TEN

He awoke to the strange hush of a Sunday morning. The adhesive tape on his side had ridged slightly but still held. As long as he kept his breathing shallow, there was no pain. The thin thermometer was on the table beside him. He put it under his tongue and went to the window to take the reading, 99. He pushed the window up. The fever was gone. It was nine o'clock. He had slept nearly eleven hours and was rested.

There had been little traffic to mark the powdered snow on the pavements beneath. With the realization of Sunday, he remembered. Just a week ago since he'd crawled through his cell window. Since that first success, everything he'd touched had gone sour on him. He sat on the edge of the bath and lit a cigarette. He had eaten little in twenty-four hours and knew this was bad. Fitness was safety. He needed not only rest but good food.

Downstairs, he scratched up a meal and ate it standing. Now and then he went to the party wall and listened. There was the faint sound of a radio playing. Another day to kill, he thought. Nine hours in the friendly gloom of this house and then what.

It was hopeless to think of pulling a job in his condition. There could be a wall to climb—a window to be dropped from. And this pain in his side, ready to pounce, crippling him into capture. He didn't even know where to start. The night had done nothing for his memory of delayed scores. Channel 7, perhaps. There was a set downstairs. If he sat in front of it long enough, may be there'd be a name from the past—the kicker his imagination needed.

He shook his head. A sick guy on the lam with a bag of keys, waiting for some cab dispatcher to bail him out of trouble. No. There had to be some other way. It was time that he needed. Leisure to plan. And London was no place to do it in. This house was innocent of all menace but it was still in Mayfair. Sooner or later, he had to leave it. Either for food or for loot. Last night had shown the danger of the simplest move that he made. Suppose, instead of that lush, it had been some off-duty cop buying his groceries. He could have tumbled Greg from behind, slid unobserved to the street. Greg would have walked out to a reception committee of twenty of the bastards.

As long as he stayed in England, the passing days helped him more than they did the police. If he could manage to hole up somewhere and get this rib fixed, get himself in really good shape mentally, as well, there'd be other assignments for the cops. As time went by, with no sign of him, no lead to follow, they *had* to assume that he'd managed to leave the country. The routine HOLD at the port would be on. The warrant for his arrest still active. Being under cover could never mean that the chase was called off. But it would cool off.

He was still hungry and found a can of corned beef in the kitchen store-cupboard. He grilled slabs of it, eating them between cheese crackers. There was relief in his decision to postpone the burglary. He took stock of what he could offer Sullivan's man up in Liverpool. It was little enough. Three hundred dollars, American, Sloane's gold cigarette case—there was no engraving—it would fetch fifty, perhaps. A few other bits of gold that had been around. A hundred pounds' worth at the outside. He had a picture of himself up in Liverpool. Sullivan's man would know all about him, for sure. The Golden Boy—the Twenty-eight Thousand Touch Wonder—arriving with a lousy century and a tale to offer. The guy would be a sucker to do anything but slam the door in Greg's face. The best way, that left Greg a stranger in a town that was a port and full of coppers—the worst way, it could mean complete failure.

It was a matter of time again. If he could borrow a little, he could work out some scheme in hiding. Maybe knock over a place that was near to his bolt-hole. He'd make no move on it till he was sure of his escape route. A guarded phone call to the guy in Liverpool perhaps. Find out the sort of money the man wanted then make the one good score and goodbye.

It was cold downstairs and he went up to the library. With its big heater and deep leather chair, it was the most comfortable place to sit. He leafed through an encyclopaedia, hoping to find something from which he might diagnose the pain, remedy it. All that he read about ribs was prosy and useless. He closed the book. The tape seemed to help. If the hurt grew no worse, he'd get by. Later, there would be the chance to get some sort of plaster if he needed it. Make a shield that would hold the rib-casing firm. Cracked or broken, a rib was a bone. Bones healed, free of movement. A plaster cast should not be impossible. With luck, he might even get to a doctor. The word tripped a danger signal in his mind. That cab-driver from the previous night—any time he might remember where he had seen Greg's face and screech round to the Yard with the information. The cops would know Greg was in London, the clothes he was wearing, that he was a sick man. That girl at Boots would be pestered with cops asking how he had looked, what injury had been treated. Every doctor in the country could be circulated with his description. It was possible. Anything was possible if they wanted a guy for murder.

The question of clothes worried him and he went upstairs to change them. Imagination was a boomerang. You followed a line of thought and were struck with the result. He took a brown suit from young Mackinnon's wardrobe and switched the topcoat for a belted country coat. He went back once more to the library. When you lived outside the law, you ditched most conventional standards of behaviour for the Code of the underworld. The bull-shit code that so few thieves honoured.

Sloane, he remembered. Delivery boy and bouncer for the con-men. The guy who'd made a fortune on Greg's back. To him, the Code had meant nothing. A man who would spring his friend from jail then shake him down for the money he'd gone to jail for! Cameron and Anstell. Both with the con-man's acceptance of any other kind of thief that was the Gentile's for the Jew. Coloured by some intense inner superiority. Superior! Cameron, who'd find you a bed then send the cops round to arrest you in it. Honour among thieves.

The only people that Greg had the right to call on were those who were meant to be on his side. The thieves, the grafters. He should have been helped by those who shared his hatred of the police. Only their hatred was a thing of the mouth. Like their drunken sentimentality.

" Poor old Gregory," he heard them saying. " A good thief and one of our own."

He was never one of the bastards. There was none of them that he trusted. Sullivan, maybe. At least Sullivan had put it on the line. " You're too warm for me—you're on your own." But always you needed somebody, surely. The fine brave defiance of a man, a good score behind him and no fear of the law was great. But always, there was someone to carry the ball in the rush.

He pulled out the album of photographs from the drawer. For a long time, he stared at the sunlit fields, the mellowed old manor-house, the peace of the water and trees. Suddenly, he dragged the telephone book to him. OK. He'd tried the thieves. He could do no worse with the Square Johns.

Bridget Selkirk's address was listed as Cadogan Gardens. He knew the tall brown houses, replicas of the Mackinnon's home. There'd been something she'd said that night at the flat—something about her father and mother. He tried remembering if she had said that she lived with them. Most of the great town houses of the Cadogan Estate were now flats. She could quite easily be living alone. A check of the voters' list would tell him.

The phone was in front of him. Why not—if you left your house for a couple of months, you did one of two things. Either you called the exchange and asked to have your phone disconnected for the time you were away, or you left it as it was. There'd be maids here in a few days, with calls to take, shopping to order. He picked up the instrument. He dialled the Westminster Public Library. The number rang and was answered. Waiting to be connected with the Reference Room, he knew this was a step that could never be retraced.

The girl gave him the information he wanted. 340 Cadogan Gardens was three flats. Number 3, according to the voters' list, had one occupant. Bridget Selkirk. He wrote name and address on the pad before him. As he concentrated, the pile of cigarette stubs grew in the ash-tray in front of him. A hunch was one thing—you had to use your head at the same time. He could have tested Bridget Selkirk's scruples with safety if she had never seen him before. There was a classical thieves' gambit that covered the case.

A bunch of grafters might need a stranger who came with a reputation of performance and solidity. To be cut in on a deal where the mob's safety might depend on how the newcomer would stand up to the cops. A couple of the mob, unknown to the man, picked up the recruit on the street. They carried warrant cards and posed as detectives. He'd been seen with well-known thieves, they told the newcomer. Threatened an arrest on a trumped-up charge unless he produced whatever information he had of his partners. They always left the guy with a number to ring at the Yard. The recruit had three choices. He told the questioners what he knew of the mob—he told them nothing, nor did he report the incident to his partners.

Or he came back to the mob with a faithful account of what happened. The last was the only version acceptable.

There was no way that the play could be used as it stood. Nobody to pose as a cop and the girl knew him. But there was still a precaution he could take that would sound her out. He'd need a car for a few hours. That was essential. There was enough mercury in that clinical thermometer to bridge any ignition lock. This time, he would get an eye-dropper. He packed his few valuables in his inside pockets. The best of the skeleton keys, he distributed in his top-coat. He'd carry no bag—once was enough. He shut the front door behind him with a sense of regret. Could be, he would never come back.

It was a cold night. The stars in the sky were small guttering candles. He was finding it easy to walk. His strapped side gave him no pain at all. The keys clanked and he wrapped them anew in a couple of handkerchiefs. At the bottom of Mount Street was a small chemist's shop with old-fashioned bottles of coloured water in the window. It was shut, but a bell at the side had a sign above it.

RING FOR PRESCRIPTIONS

An elderly man, in slippers, opened the door to him. He smiled with the diffidence of the old who still earn a living. " Good evening."

" I need some amyl-nitrite phials," said Greg.

The old man moved ahead with irritating slowness, muttering to himself as he switched on the lights and searched the drawers.

" And an eye-dropper," Greg added.

" Here's the eye-dropper, sir." The man smiled again, nervously. " We usually supply amyl-nitrite on prescription."

" I've got one." He made a show of searching his pockets. " At least, I had one. Is it essential? My mother gets all her drugs here."

" No, sir. It's our own rule. Youngsters get hold of it . . ."

" The name's Hill," Greg broke in. " Fifty-two Farm Street. This is an emergency and I've no time to waste. I'll send the maid round with the prescription."

The old man's fingers shook as he made up the package. " If you wouldn't mind, sir."

" Yes, all right," Greg broke in, impatiently, " I'll see that it's done." He paid the man and walked down Carlos Place. Amyl-nitrite, the heart restorative that his mother had used when asthma strangled her breathing. The memory had been a godsend. A phial, broken in a handkerchief and inhaled would revive a dead donkey. He turned west to the park. The safest place to find the car that he needed was a garage. He knew twenty mews in south-west London with lock-up garages, cottages over them. Often, the people who lived there knew neither the cars nor their owners.

He waited at the bus stop outside Grosvenor House. Cameron, he thought suddenly. Cameron's car would be perfect. The club was shut on Sunday. In the winter, Cameron's routine was invariable. He came back, after shutting his club on Saturday night, and parked the car where it stayed till Monday. Sunday, he spent at home, playing canasta.

Greg held up a hand, stopping the bus that barrelled down Park Lane. On top, there was an empty seat at the back. He took a ticket to Kensington High Street, then walked south. He kept to the back streets, using the dark squares and gloomy terraces as cover. Across Cromwell Road with its hopeless hotels and shabby rooming houses to the back of the Gloucester Road underground station. He called Cameron from a street booth.

The con man answered immediately, his voice bland with comfort. "Hello—yeah?" Greg kept quiet. "Hello?" said Cameron again with a touch of impatience. Then the phone buzzed as he broke the connection. A smooth article, Greg thought bitterly. Cameron was no fool. There'd be a bolt on his door till Greg was arrested. Maybe he had asked for protection from the police. If he had, he would have gotten it. The cops took good care of their own.

Cresswell Mews jack-knifed from the Old Brompton Road to Fulham Road. A cobbled thoroughfare where the tubbed plants of the affluent faced the dirty milk bottles outside the unconverted cottages. At the top end, there were four lock-up garages flanking a yard where the municipality stored their garbage trucks. Single-storeyed, brick-built, the garages were just that—there was no accommodation above them. Cameron kept his car in the last.

He walked down the mews swiftly, then back. Two lamps, hung from the walls, were the sole lighting for a hundred yards. His footsteps rang on the cobbled stones and he moved to the side, near the house fronts. There was less chance of being seen from either end. He'd have to get rubber shoes or soles from somewhere. It was impossible to move around like a Brigade of Guards. The double doors on Cameron's garage opened outwards, one Yale lock holding them at shoulder level. He stood with his back to the doors, testing the strength of the lock. One of the doors was held by bolts, top and bottom. He took the strip of celluloid, working it into the cup of the lock. Then a light in the house opposite shone suddenly, throwing the pattern of the ornamental grille-work on the stones at his feet. He stood still as the curtains were drawn. A red sports car parked in front of the door screened him from most of the house but he waited. Inside, a man called to a woman and then there was silence. It was broken only by the occasional click of a passing pedestrian at the ends of the mews.

He pushed and the badly hung door grated open. He pulled it after him and struck a match. There was a switch on the wall by the door. He stood on the fender of the Austin, fastening a rag to the naked bulb in the ceiling. He thumbed the switch. There was enough light to work by. He tried the doors of the car. They were open and the keys hung in the ignition lock. This was a break. The first car he'd stolen would be put down to him with a certainty by the police. If two went in a week, both with the mercury technique, they'd draw the obvious conclusion and have another lead on his movements. He turned the key and saw the needle on the petrol gauge hover half-way on the dial. He opened the hung doors, lifting them to avoid the scraping. Not that noise mattered. The Austin was too heavy to roll out—he'd have to use the motor. If they heard, the people in the house opposite would be too late to see anything but a car driven away. But there'd be no reason for them to suspect. As the thought hit, he closed the garage doors again. The switched number plates were always certain confusion, even if the car were reported stolen. It was hours before the vehicle was on the list put out by the Yard, printed and circulated. Till then, the mobile units relied on the details given over the police network. Type, make and year were given but the operative clue was the registration number. At night, the rear lights of an absconding car showed nothing but the licence tag.

Finding a wrench, he unfastened the plates from the Austin. He slipped out to the mews and stood motionless at the door of the house. One ear at the mail box, he could hear the noise of crockery being handled. The smell of cooking drifted from the hall. He bent by the sports car, unscrewing the bolts that held the plates, then went back to the garage. It took only minutes to complete the change. He tossed the wrench down. Cameron's car would scarcely be missed—if it was, he'd left a mess for the cops that would take some unravelling.

He backed the Austin to the mews, closed both doors and drove up to the Old Brompton Road. That this was the right thing he was doing was no longer a hunch but an insistent certainty. The car handled well. Like its owner, he thought, big, smooth and sleek. Touches of Cameron showed in the blue and white hounds' tooth seat covers, the nameplate let into the dash. That could be fixed, he thought savagely. It wouldn't be hard to leave the car a wreck.

He cut over on the Fulham Road, watchful of the passing traffic. A hundred yards to his right, behind the cliff face of Cranmer Court, was the Chelsea Police Station. It was an active police area where the boys were bright and wasted no opportunities. He turned left then forked at Cadogan Gardens. Changing down, he scanned the numbers as he drove. The street was a dark spot in the patchwork Chelsea lighting. Tall houses of mellowed red brick led to the endless squares, crescents and places of the Cadogan Estate.

Three-four-seven was in the middle, facing the flat, forbidding door of a convent. He parked beyond the house and lit a cigarette. There were a few people on the street, wrapped against the cold. Most of them hurried into the church ahead. Thirty yards behind him, a cellarman was unlocking the padlock of the pub lavatory, ready for the night's trade.

He closed the door of the car quietly and walked back to the house. There was the usual basement area, now in darkness, and broad black-and-white steps to the front door. He tried the door with the flat of his hand. It was shut, fastening on a simple spring lock. Enough light leaked through the fanlight to make the names on the brass plate legible.

Flat 1 MISS BRIDGET SELKIRK
Flat 2 COMMANDER HORSEFALL R.N.
Flat 3 MRS. D. PURSEY

Hers would probably be the flat on the first floor but it was no certainty. From where he stood, he could step on to the sill of an open window. The curtains were back and the room in darkness. These converted houses were turned into large flats. The drawn curtains meant nothing. Bridget could be in a room at the back if this was her flat.

OK, he thought. Let's see how *she* played! He went back to the car and drove through the quiet streets to Sloane Square. A couple of booths were tucked away at the back of the Royal Court Hotel. He called Bridget Selkirk's number.

The phone rang for a full minute before a girl's voice answered.

" Miss Selkirk?" he asked softly.

" Yes." The voice had the resigned acceptance of one whose phone rings too often. " Who's that?"

" Philip Drury," he said. " I don't know if you remember . . ."

" I remember the voice," she said quickly. She said no more.

Some of the earlier certainty had gone. He struggled to choose the right words. He could still back out. Hang up, dump the car and go back to the house on South Street. But tomorrow would be no different. Just a day later in a city that held increasing danger for him.

" Hello? Are you still there?" Her voice seemed to have dropped. To have become conspiratorial, matching his own.

He found the words in a rush, aware of their brashness, trying to impart some of the urgency that he felt. " I've got to see you. Are you alone?"

This time, the silence was of her making. At last, she said: " Why? Why do you have to see me?"

How did you say it—because you mean safety to me! Because of the need for someone who'd listen! Someone who'd accept the truth and reject condemnation with a rebel's defiance of law!

" I think you know why," he said. " If you don't—say so and forget that I called."

He heard the intake of breath but could never know the emotion that prompted it. " Where are you?" she said quietly.

He lied. " In a booth opposite the Albert Hall."

" Then you'd better come here," she said hesitantly. " If you think it's all right." When he made no answer, she added, " the address is in the book."

" That's out," he said definitely. " The park's shut and I can't wander round. Before I come there, I have to talk to you. It'll take you ten minutes by cab from where you are. I'll wait twenty." He opened the door with his foot. " The front entrance of the Albert Hall."

He gave her no chance for a decision but spun the dial once and went to the car. It took him three minutes to turn the Austin into the end of Cadogan Gardens. He parked at the end of Moore Street. Crouched in the back seat, he had a clear view of the front door of the house. This should tell, he thought.

Not one single word had been spoken that could not be innocuous in another context. But he was certain that Bridget knew. This was the crucial moment. If she was calling the police, right now, they'd do one or both of two things. There'd be a car at her flat within minutes—she'd be told to wait—and the area round the Albert Hall would be covered. If she kept away from the phone and the cops, it meant that, at worst, she would have no hand in his arrest.

He sat, still crouched, as footsteps rang on the pavement. A man crossed in front of the car and went into the church. The lights had gone on in the pub on the corner. The door of the house opened. For a second, she stood in the lighted doorway. Her long hair was without a hat—tied as it had been before, behind her ears. She wore a dark, belted coat. She came down the steps and turned right, towards him. As she passed, he sank lower in the back. As soon as she'd gone, he backed the Austin and drove after her. He was unsure whether she would use her car, if she had one. She'd talked of driving up from the country but that could mean anything.

There was a cab on the stand opposite Nell Gwynne House. She drove off in it. He followed. There was no sign of a cop and the station was no more than a couple of hundred yards from her home. So far, so good. The cab led him up the slope of Prince's Gate, stopping on the corner of Knightsbridge. He parked behind and watched as she walked to the main entrance of the Albert Hall. There was a concert. The portico and exits were lit and the short driveways jammed with ticket-holders. Outside the iron railings, she walked to the end of the block, looking across at the locked park. Keeping her in his view all the time, he passed twice. She ignored the car, searching the crowds that hurried into the hall. For fifteen minutes, he watched. Once, quickening step, she followed a man who came from the shadows. As the man turned, she retraced her steps, brushing her hair back with a gesture Greg remembered. The last of the concert-goers was in.

She glanced at the watch on her wrist and started to walk towards Kensington. She had spoken to nobody. There were no dubious cars, parked or cruising. Just the girl, walking with long strides, scanning the traffic as if in search of a cab.

He put the Austin in gear. Abreast of her, he pulled to the kerb and opened the door. She turned her head quickly. Then, without fuss, she took the seat next to him. He drove off, an eye on the mirror above his head. For a minute, neither of them spoke. She was rummaging in her purse. She found a cigarette case. In the flame of the lighter, her eyes were serious. She watched him.

" Paul Gregory," she said suddenly.

He made no reply, glad of the need to drive. He turned the Austin up Church Street, climbing the hill.

" Did you kill that man?" There was neither fear nor condemnation in the words. Just simple enquiry. He shook his head. " But you're Paul Gregory—the man who escaped from prison?" He nodded. She lapsed into silence, as if uncertain, now, what to say.

There was warmth in her presence—a friendliness that increased his need of her. Despite her brief uncertainty, she showed no anxiety. He was impressed by her coolness. He turned off Church Street, climbing the incline to the top of Campden Hill. Presently, they were high over Kensington. Below, wound the tree-lined avenues of Holland Park. Beyond, the bright hanging lights that led to Shepherd's Bush and the west country. In the dead end of Airlie Gardens, he braked the car to a halt. Turning in his seat, so that he faced her, he lit a cigarette. It was quiet in the short street—the tick of the clock on the dash unnaturally loud. Twice, he dragged the tobacco smoke deep in his lungs before he trusted the words that came, unsought. " I was in Sloane Square when I phoned you," he said suddenly. " Not the Albert Hall. I followed you from the moment you left your house." He pulled out the ash-tray roughly, resenting his weakness, unsure of his intention.

Her face made a lighter patch in the deep coat collar. " But why?" She made no attempt to disguise the puzzlement in her voice. He shrugged, turning again to his hands for relief, touching the fabric of the seat covers. " The police," she said with decision. " Well. If you thought I'd do that, why did you phone in the first place?" She caught her breath, letting him know her exasperation. " I knew who you were," she said quietly, " that night at the club."

The memory was fresh. He saw himself struggle to his feet as she came to the table. His fear of denouncement must have shown on his face. And she'd known. Recognized his fear with the vicious curiosity of a cat toying with a maimed bird. But *Bonne chance!*, she'd said. And raised her glass. That, too, belonged to the memory. Always, there was this bleak insistence on the worst in others. The bitter acceptance of an intended betrayal. He knew his own fear but the shame was new and unwelcome.

" There's a lot you've got to know about me." The worst, he thought savagely. And the hell with you if the telling displeases. " It'll take time, but you've got to know. It's important to me."

Her body swivelled in the darkness, touching his as she moved in her seat. " Will you tell me why it should be *me?*"

At another time, the words could have been an affront—an excuse to attack, indifferent to consequences. His father's voice was remembered, heavy with reason. " It maybe satisfies you to cut off your nose to spite your face, Paul. But don't expect applause for doing it."

He lifted his hand then let it drop. " I dunno. Because there's nobody else, maybe. I started out on this thing tonight "—his hand took in the car and her presence in it—" with a lot of smart angles in mind. You were a woman. I thought you'd been pushed around. Not the way I have—but there'd be some way I could use your defiance. I guess that was it. I wanted to use you."

He waited for her voice but she gave him no help. Suddenly, she reached to the light in the roof and switched it on. Instinctively, he shielded his face, dropping his arm as she made no further move but met his fear with understanding.

" What was that for, exactly?" he asked, forcing the smile that must always cover alarm.

" To see," she said, putting her hand to the roof again. " I wanted to see your face. You're not a liar, are you?"

Though the car was in darkness, he shut his eyes. As if to hide what she'd read there. A face wasn't to be trusted. Not his face. Maybe he *was* a liar. A fine, new-style liar who kidded to himself. " If I am," he said slowly, " it's because I don't know where truth starts or finishes. But you've got to believe this, Bridget—I'll tell you the truth as I see it." The use of her name came, unexpectedly. " To start with," he went on, " everything you've read in the newspapers is probably true. With one exception. I didn't kill Sloane, if they say so. I'm a thief—I've been a thief for years. I meant to tell you this, with a difference. I thought I could *handle* you." He harboured the word with its memory of Cameron. " Cameron," he said suddenly.

" The man at the club?"

" This is his car," he said heavily. " I stole it tonight."

Her voice betrayed no concern. " What do people call you—your wife—your friends?"

" Greg," he said sombrely. " That's what my friends call me."

" Have you ever had one?" she asked. " A friend, I mean?"

" A million. This guy was one." He pushed a finger at the nameplate on the dash. " He found me a bed, that night at the club. Sent the police round, a couple of hours afterwards." He laughed, shortly. " I was supposed to be in the arms of his waitress." On an impulse, he started the motor and ran the car down the slope. Five hundred yards away, he parked again. " It's the staying still," he explained. " I can't take it." Her silence was an enigma of which he was weary. " Look—this is a lot of crap," he said. He released the handbrake. " Everything about me is wrong for anyone like you. Dead wrong. And we're wasting time. I guess the right thing to say is that I'm sorry I rang you. I'm not. A guy in a spot like mine can't afford to be sorry for anything." He touched the starter. " I'll drop you anywhere in reason, Bridget." The helplessness in his voice irritated him. He jibed at himself—Big deal! Any gesture requiring sincerity is beyond you!

He felt her arm move, saw the strong red-tipped fingers in the light of the dash. She switched off the motor. "Suppose you listen to me, for a change, Greg. Before you become impossibly heroic. *And* stupid. I'd have helped you that night at the club—if I'd known how. In Norman's flat, possibly, if I'd known then." She took a cigarette, worrying it with her lighter. "We're not so far apart as you may think. For as long as I can remember, there's been one thing that mattered to me. Really mattered. Being the sort of person you evidently don't believe in. A friend to somebody." He started to say something. She shushed him to silence. " If you feel about a thing like that strongly enough, you don't worry about conflict with laws—moral issues." She made a sound of impatience, flicking her ash to the floor. " Could anything sound more pompous—drearier—the way I'm saying it! In any case, I haven't made much of a hit. But I'm a stubborn girl. Probably as stubborn as you are, Mr. Gregory. So I go on looking for the chance."

He narrowed his eyes in the darkness, as if to read the vague shape of her face. Unselfishness was something that belonged to a woman—if you accepted its existence. If this was the truth she was telling, it might explain so much that he didn't understand. A loyalty that kept her free of scorn for a man's troubled spirit, for instance. Obliging her to endure the farce of engagement to a homosexual.

As though she had sensed his doubt, she continued. " Say that its because of something inside of me that operates like reciprocity or whatever the word is. If I do this for somebody, perhaps I can hope for someone equally determined, objective, when the time comes. When *I* need help. *That's* why I came to meet you tonight. For no other reason. That's something you'll have to accept, cynic or not."

He moved his head nervously. Wanting to believe, he backed from this girl's sincerity like a hound from a crackling fire. Even in a woman, unselfishness was bound up in self-interest. " This is a cock-eyed business," he began, then let his breath go, sure for the moment of her intentions. " I think I trust you more than I've ever trusted anyone. I've got to," he said simply.

" Then give me your hand," she said. " This isn't Boy Scout stuff. Your position is so dreadful to me that I can't even begin thinking about it. I don't *know* what there is I could do to help, Greg. But I'll try."

Groping, he found her hand, the sense of comradeship robbing the gesture of ridicule. " *I'll* try," he told her, only dimly aware what he meant.

She turned away, shrugging deep into her coat. " That's settled, then," she said with composure. " Where are we going to be able to talk? Have you a room or something?"

She listened as he told her briefly of the house on South Street, the days and nights that had gone. He omitted nothing, eased in the telling. He could hear her fingernail tapping against her teeth.

" You can't go back there," she decided. " That's obvious. How you could sleep, I don't know. One of the maids could have returned unexpectedly—some relative of the people could have arrived. What about Norman's flat?" she asked. " He's still in Spain and I have a key somewhere."

" Sloane—the guy who's dead—took it." He jibbed at the word fiancé. " There'd be an agreement between him and your friend. The police might have found it."

" Then that leaves Cadogan Gardens," she said. " You'll have to come there."

He made a half-hearted attempt at protest that she stopped. " Before we go any farther, forget all about Sir Galahad. I'm twenty-one and perfectly aware of what I'm letting myself in for if I'm caught. There are a dozen judges in the family, who'll roll in their graves. My father and mother believe the worst about me already. The main thing is—will it be safe for you to come to the flat?"

"Do you live alone?" he asked.

"Yes. There's a woman who comes every day to clean. I can easily put her off. Say that I'm going down to the country or something. You'll have to tell me about things, Greg. It's all new to me. The police. Everything."

The fresh security gave edge to his voice. "My job's to get off the streets and keep off. I'll have to get rid of this car. I'll wreck it."

"Does that make sense?" she asked. "Suppose someone sees us walking away. Just leaving it. Why bother? You'd probably be doing this man a favour, anyway. Just mean a new car for him."

He started the motor. "You're right. I'll dump it somewhere north of the park. Somewhere quiet."

They dropped down the slope to Notting Hill Gate then filtered into the squares of Bayswater. He parked in the long forecourt of Oxford Terrace. With a cloth from the cubby-hole, he started wiping the surfaces of the car's interior. "Fingerprints," he explained. The street lamps were enough to show her face in detail. She was following his movements with an interest he found flattering.

She fished in her purse for a flapjack. As she looked in the mirror, she moved her mouth, touching the stick to her lips. With the intimacy of the movement, he was aware of her desirability as a woman. He turned away, lest his face showed the thought and alarmed her.

There were people passing near, on the pavement, but screened by the shrubbery, they were out of sight. The houses in front of them were silent. They left the car, closing the doors behind carefully. He fastened the master lock and dropped the keys down a grating.

On the pavement, they walked towards the Edgware Road, looking for a cab. Then her hand crooked under his elbow. He looked down. She gave him a friendly smile, hair swinging. "It's common," she said, "but it looks respectable."

ELEVEN

In the cab, both were content to be silent. He could not help comparing this girl with Judith. His wife's love of her home, and all that it stood for, was fiercely protective. There had been a time when she would have helped him, even in a jam like this. Now, she would fight him instinctively as a threat to her life with the children. But this girl defied instincts—or maybe it was that with her, they worked in a different way. Bridget Selkirk's need to protect was as strong as Judith's, and as determined.

He lit a cigarette impatiently, sick of the search for motives. When fear makes a muddled mess of your own thinking, there's no room for a hopeless analysis of others, he told himself.

They were nearing Sloane Square. Bridget searched her purse for change. He made no attempt to stop her. Nothing mattered now but acceptance of whatever she offered.

" I'm glad it was me you phoned," she said quietly. " And nobody else."

He made no answer but tapped on the glass division in front of him. The cab pulled to the kerb at the bottom of Sloane Street. " Pay him off here," he said. " Go ahead—I'll tell you why in a minute."

She nodded. As she stood by the cab, Greg turned his back, looking in a shop window. They crossed the street, towards Cadogan Gardens. Once more, she found his arm in friendly pressure. " Why did we do that?" she asked curiously. " There was nobody following. The police can't even guess that we know one another." She lengthened her stride to match his.

" Cab-drivers remember faces—and addresses. Take a look some time. Notice the way they'll never drive off till you've opened your door. The lot of them are would-be police informers. Frustrated coppers," he said bitterly. " That guy could quite easily see a picture of me some place. If we'd gone to the house, God knows where it could end."

They rounded the end of Draycott Place. There were still few people about. Cold and the forbidding emptiness of a London Sunday made the street a gauntlet that pedestrians ran unwillingly. Bridget pushed her hair free of her coat collar, pulling the cloth round her neck.

" Don't you find it terrible to live like that? Hunted—always having to remember things like cab-drivers and police? I don't mean now but before."

For years, he had never thought of it. The cautious look and ready ears—the extra-sensory acknowledgement of danger—had become part of his life. A crowded bar where the shape of a neck sent you back on your tracks—the mechanical voice from a police loudspeaker—the blast of a doorbell when your table was covered with loot. All these had been accepted as hazards that belonged to a life outside the law. But it had never been terrible till now.

" It wasn't so good at times," he answered.

" I'm not being critical. It's a bit late to preach—not that I'd allow myself to! I imagine that you've always done exactly as you intended, anyway, from the beginning. You're afraid now, but that's because everyone's against you. You must have started all this with your eyes wide open." She made a question of the words.

" I did." Had he known how, this was no time to explain. He hurried her on.

As they passed the door of the church, the verger shuffled out, viewing the night with suspicion. The sound of the creaking door, as he closed it, carried after them in the cold air. The empty church, with its smell of stale incense, pulled his mind back to Wandsworth.

The dreary chapel there, its curtained stalls for the men under sentence of death, flanking the altar. The English had always been blind to the refinements of their cruelty. For centuries, they had found excuses for flogging men with metal-tipped whips, dropping them through a hatch with ropes round their necks. They produced high-sounding phrases and a macabre ceremony to cover what they loved—due process of law.

With the entry of a condemned man into Wandsworth Prison, a prurient preoccupation with F block affected both screws and cons. F Block—the fiction applied to the painted walls leading to the administration offices—blank, save for the door that led to the condemned cells. You knew that someone was in there. The word came from Reception, the Part Worn Stores. The guy's clothing had been drawn—an ordinary jail uniform but with tapes on the flies instead of buttons, shoes without laces, cloth buttons on the jacket. Under sentence of death, a man's life became important to the state. Two screws never left him, night and day, till he went through a hole in the floor at their feet.

Chaplain, doctor and Governor. Variously intent on saving the man's soul, keeping him alive till the day of execution, breaking his neck. The condemned man moved in the jail, unseen but heard. Exercised where none might see him. " Three clear Sundays," after the weird wording of the law, a strange respite between days of sentence and execution. Three Sundays when the words of the morning services took on new meaning for the shuffling mass of convicts, impelling their attention, adding sincerity to the Amens that boomed in reply to a prayer for mercy.

He shivered slightly, standing flat against the wall as Bridget opened her front door. She led the way through a carpeted hall where some letters were strewn on a chest. Stairs, dull red in the soft light, reached to the other two flats. She opened another door on her left. He followed her in, bolting the door behind him.

It was a tiny hall with a rug on the dark boards. There was a shooting-stick, some field-glasses, a coat on the tallboy. She took off her street clothes, shaking her hair free then stood at the mirror. Through the glass, she smiled.

" Are you nervous?"

" Scared, not nervous," he answered. The pain had started again in his side. It seemed to return with the night. He threw his coat on top of hers and inspected the door. The burglar-proof lock was of a make that lived up to its claim, the heavy bolt an inch in diameter. He followed her voice to the room at the front of the house. She was drawing the curtains he had seen from the steps.

The room was big, with the extravagance of space that belonged to another age. There was a stone-coloured carpet, blue velvet curtains and old unmatched furniture. An ottoman next a cut-down Welsh dresser. On the dresser were thirty or forty books, a lamp and a picture of Norman Bishop. A sad-eyed red setter plumed its tail in greeting as it walked towards him. Bridget pulled the cord of the curtain, settling the folds with her hands.

" That's Rusty," she said. " A mass of affectation and quite useless against burglars." She smiled at him.

With the shutting of her front door, her cool competence

seemed to have warmed, the friendliness become less clinical. It was as if he had known her a very long time and was returning to a place where he was welcome.

"Do you like dogs?" she asked.

"Sure. But any I've had ended by belonging to somebody else," he said, pulling the setter's ears. The dog got between him and the fire, pushing its head on his knee.

The pleated skirt of the thin woollen dress swung as she walked to the dresser. She opened the cupboard. "I can offer you gin, brandy, Pernod . . ."

The setter pawed at Greg's side and he flinched.

"Are you hurt?" she asked quickly.

He settled the dog, holding its legs. "I'll live. A souvenir from one of the friends you were talking about."

She carried the tray of drink to the table at his side. "Help yourself while I get you something to eat. When *did* you last eat?"

"A year ago," he grinned. He poured a large glass of the brandy. He was catching something of her mood. For the first time since his escape, at ease. In this room he felt neither interloper nor on sufferance.

She moved among her possessions, showing the delicately-blown Chinese sampan, with its exquisite tiny figures—the walnut table, its marquetry silk to the touch, old Bristol china from her home. Every piece had a history that she told diffidently but with affection. When she smiled, he thought, it was with pleasure and for no other reason. Hers was a face that smiled infrequently. Seeing her here, she might have been some country cousin of the girl who had said *Bonne chance!*, that night at Cameron's place.

He found his voice suddenly. "Bridget!"

She came from the kitchen to the door, incongruous with the white oven cloth against the blue of her dress.

"What made you come tonight? Really made you come?" Jealous of her composure, he sought to disrupt it.

She hesitated for a moment. "My mother would say it's because I'm always attracted to the wrong type of man—God knows what she'd say about you." She shook her head. "I've given you the real reason. You're a bad cause. That's always better for me than a good one."

She set a tray that he took on his lap. He ate the hot food greedily. When he was through, she sat in the chair opposite, the dog at her feet. Unprompted, he talked of the house that his grandfather had built. A rambling home, remote among the pine, larch and maple—a forgotten corner of the Humber Valley where his father counted dwindling dividend checks, investing them in his son's future. Of the Dieppe Raid and a hospital bed where he awakened to the first real meaning of fear. Peace and the realization that normal moral values no longer mattered to him. Of his start as a burglar, the twenty-eight thousand pounds and his hopes for a life with Judith.

Unconsciously, his voice was low as he told the humiliating truths, as if it were a plea for her acceptance. Chain-smoking, she listened to him, the setter's head cradled on her feet.

When he was done, her voice was curious. " What about your wife, she must be out of her mind with anxiety."

The pain in his side was sharp again and he sat upright. " She is. She's wondering how long it will be before the cops get me. And for her, it can't be too soon. Once, I phoned. The line was tapped but she managed to let me know exactly what she felt." He moved his shoulder, dismissing the memory. " We're through."

" But the children," she persisted. " Surely . . ."

He broke in. " The kids are better off without me. Maybe it's expedient to reason like that but Judith's right. They're all better off without me. Kids soon forget."

" Just like that, you say it," she said, wonderingly. " As if parents meant nothing to a child."

" Did mine?" he asked. " Did yours?"

She made no answer. He looked at the clock. It was after midnight. Through the door on his left was her bedroom. There was no sign of another. Since that moment in the car, there had been no mention of where he would sleep. She carried the tray to the kitchen, coming back with an armful of blankets, sheets.

" This is your bed." She pulled on the straight-backed ottoman, opening it to a single bed. " No one's complained about it to date. I'm going to take Rusty out for his walk—the bathroom's over there." She nodded at her bedroom door.

He heard the bolt unfastened, the front door closed. On the impulse, he cut the light in the sitting room, going to the window. He watched the street from behind the curtains. She was walking slowly towards Cadogan Square. The setter followed, nosing the wall.

He went through the intimacy of her bedroom to a bathroom

where a glass-topped table showed a litter of scent, powder and nail varnish.

A bath would strip the tape from his side. He took off his shirt, plunging his head into the bowl of water. Pulling his trousers up, he sat on the edge of the bath, scrubbing his feet and legs. He turned to see Bridget in the doorway. She had a towel in her hand.

She walked forward quickly, bending at his side. Her hair was straight and smooth, smelling faintly of her scent. " What *is* it?" she asked. " A bullet?"

He swung his feet to the bath mat, taking the towel from her hand. " Sloane's footprint. If it wasn't for this feeling of passing out, it would be nothing. I'm scared it could happen on the street." He told her of the night before. The visit to Boots. " I can't take a chance on a doctor now."

Her face was sober as she straightened. " I'm getting frightened—out of my depth. I'm managing to remember that you have to be hid and that's as far as my mind takes me. It's a blank after that. What *does* happen, Greg?"

He spat paste and water into the bowl, scrubbing his mouth with the towel. Turning, he took one of her hands between his. " I don't know. To me, the police are all-important—but to them, I'm only one of a dozen men who are badly wanted. If I can last—if I can last just a few weeks, I'll be over the hump."

" But what happens then," she persisted. Taking her hand away, she draped the bath mat on the edge of the tub.

" Just a few weeks," he said uncertainly. " They'll have forgotten about me. The cops can't make a country like this leak-proof. They couldn't even do it during the war. This guy in Liverpool will fix me up. All I've got to do is find the money."

She picked a loose cigarette from the table and he held a match to it. " How much would it cost? Perhaps I could give—lend you the money . . ."

" Not this kind of money, you couldn't," he smiled. " I'll have to find it, the only way I know how. It isn't impossible. All I need is out there." He jerked his head to the hall where his coat lay heavy with keys.

She leaned her long back against the mirror, watching him again. Her silences were making him nervous again. He picked at the tape on his side, avoiding her scrutiny.

" My home's in Radnorshire," she said suddenly. " A place called Coedmawr. Have you ever been to Wales?" He shook his head. " It's a wild country. Two miles from our lodge gate, you'll find fields where people pass once, perhaps, twice, in a year. A shepherd or farmer. There are woods and mountain streams, little else up there. Do you think you'd feel safe down there—in a place like that?"

He shrugged. " A stable out of London sounds good to me now. But I know how I am. There'll be people to meet, questions to answer. In a day, I'll be wanting to move again."

" There'd be no one to meet. There's a sheep farm on our land that's been empty for years. Even the track that leads to it is lost in a spinney, now. It would give you time. That's what you said you needed."

" That's what I said I needed," he repeated. It had been a strange thing that she'd said before—thank God that he'd phoned her and not someone else. There had *been* no one else. But she'd said it as if certain that with her he was safe. He believed her.

" We'll drive down tomorrow," she decided. " There'll be all sorts of things that you'll need. This farm is primitive—just four stone walls on the side of a mountain. No light—water from a well." When she frowned, her brows were a straight line above her eyes. " It's the only place I can think of."

" You're the boss." He hesitated. " Maybe I'd better hit the sack."

" A sleeping bag," she said suddenly. " Some sort of stove and food. I'll make a list in the morning." She turned to the basin. " Goodnight, Greg."

It was dismissal. He moved awkwardly, searching for words that would express what he felt. " I want you to know . . ." he started. " Ah, the hell with it. There's nothing I can say that would be right. Goodnight and thanks, Bridget."

" Goodnight," she said again. " We're going to pull this off."

In the room at the front, he switched off the light and got into bed. Deep in the soft blankets, he lay listening to the faint sound of the traffic on the King's Road. Cold air drifted through the window. Beside him, the dog moved closer for warmth. A long while after, it seemed, he heard the door to her room closed quietly.

He woke gladly from a dream where he ran endlessly, the voices of his pursuers always close behind. It was six by the lantern clock on the dresser. He pulled the blankets round his bare body and sat up. Then he remembered—in a few hours, he'd be on his way out of London. During the night, the setter had moved to a blanket by the wall. Now it yawned, stretching, stiff-legged as it followed Greg to the kitchen.

He found tea, milk and sugar and stood by the stove, warming himself at the gas. The dog moved its ears, whining, and Greg heard Bridget's voice. Outside her door, he called to her.

" Are you making delicious tea?" Her voice was blurred with sleep.

" Uhuh. It's still dark and snowing outside. Six-fifteen if your clock's right."

" It is," she called. " May I have some tea, too?"

He busied himself, taking pleasure in finding the tray, a cloth to cover it. " Room service," he said outside her door.

" Bring it in, yours, too. We can talk."

The room was pearl grey in the light from above her head. She turned lazily in her bed, sitting up, shivering. He put the tray at her side and threw her a sweater. Draping it round her bare shoulders, she tied the sleeves under her chin. Her hair was still coiled at her neck and without lipstick, her mouth was younger, tenderer.

She nodded approval at the tray. " My *dear*, how elegant! You couldn't have seen the pint mug in the kitchen. That's what I usually have in the morning."

The setter jumped, landing on the bed beside her. Averting her face from the dog's eager head, she said: " Norman was always jealous of Rusty. Can you imagine a man being jealous of a dog! Or Norman being jealous of me," she added. She broke off, reaching for her cup. " I forgot. You don't know Norman."

" There was a newspaper cutting in the flat. I read it." This was dangerous ground and he sought to avoid it. " I guess it should have explained something or other . . ."

" And didn't," she said. " Well, before you appeared, Norman was my most ambitious effort as a Girl Guide. And it fell flat on its face. When he pushed off to Spain without saying a word, I knew the best thing for me to do was to give up. In fact, that night we met at the club, I'd decided to do just that. The evening was supposed to be a celebration." She put her tea down, curling deep in her bedding.

Self-consciously, he followed the curve of her body under the blankets, avoiding her eye when he realized she was watching him. " How far is this place we're going to—and where do you have your car?"

"In the garage, with the battery on charge. They open at eight. Coedmawr? Eight or nine hours driving. The A40 passes the house." She peered along the bed, scrutinizing his clothes. "Those things are useless. You need a thick sweater, gumboots. Would one of those army surplus stores be any good, do you think? There's one in Charing Cross."

He rapped a cigarette from the pack and lit it. "Nine's for the boots. Waterproof trousers, a windcheater. I'll give you some money when you get up."

She poured herself another cup of tea. "That can wait." She turned the palm of her hand up, stretching it towards him. "Cigarette, please." She savoured the smoke before she went on. "If—*when* all this is over, will you promise me something?"

He had a quick recognition of a staked claim. Here it came, he thought, with her no different from the rest. To every woman's help there were strings. They could be slender, but always they were there. "Both my arms and one eye you can have," he promised solemnly.

She sat up, her chin on her knees, better to see him. "It could mean more to you than that, what I have in mind. Never come back to this country, that's first."

He nodded. "That would be unlikely in any case. What next?"

Taking her time, she searched for an ash tray. "If you found a job . . ." she hunched a shoulder. "Wherever you go for the rest of your life, you're going to remember all this—" she moved her hand. "The police won't forget."

He got to his feet, walking the carpet from door to door. "Your approach is oblique but the gimmick's the same. As soon as a woman has a personal interest in a man, she wants to make him over. Go straight. Put behind you all this wasted life. Work out your salvation and all the rest of the crap." He stopped his pacing, looking down at her. "I'm the ne'er-do-well son, waiting in the library to be kicked off decently to the colonies—with you as the maiden aunt, creeping in with a bag of sovereigns and some tearful advice." He made a sound of exasperation. "It won't work. I'm a thief, Bridget. Wherever I go, France, Cuba, Morocco, I'll need money. I know one way to get it. What sort of job do you think I'd get as a foreigner without papers? No experience?"

He sat down again on the end of her bed, reasoning. "Look —I'm trying to be more honest with you than I've ever been."

The warmth of her body was disturbing. He sought her eyes. "Once I stole enough to be able to say I'd forget being a thief. They beat me for the loot. There won't be a second time. There's another thing," he nodded, confirming the certainty. "They're never going to put me on trial for murder, Bridget."

She threw her half-smoked cigarette into the empty cup. "It's your life," she said quietly. "I'm selfish enough to want you to keep it. And I *am* being selfish," she repeated. "If you get away, keep away, I'm always going to be able to remember that it was because of me." Her voice became sure—convincing. "And when you go, I never want to see or hear of you again."

He sat for a moment, killing the bitter words that were ready. The hell with her reason for helping, as long as she helped. This woman was a head-case. For the rest, you couldn't lose what you never had. Knowing he lied to himself, he assured her. "You won't hear of me."

Her smile was unexpected. "Now you look like Rusty when he's been whipped for something he didn't do! You're hardly gallant, Mr. Gregory. 'As soon as a women has a personal interest in a man'!" she quoted. "My interest in you is mostly impersonal. I like you. Oddly enough, for myself, I wouldn't want you to change. Certainly not for a moral reason. But I'm not the least bit in love with you, as the saying has it."

He started to speak but she stopped him, covering his hand with hers. "No—you listen to me, now. As long as we both know what we're doing and why, we've got a chance. You need help desperately. That's your reason. Mine's not so obvious, apparently. Because everyone's against you, Greg, I'm on your side. It's no deeper than that—or as deep, perhaps."

He shrugged. "I'm in my place—neatly and at the hand of an expert. It's seven. What happens now?"

"I'm getting up, to start with." Once again, the competence was strong in her tone. "There are all sorts of things to do. Ring the A.A. and get a report on the roads from here to South Wales—phone my woman and put her off. Make yourself some breakfast while I'm gone. Don't worry about me—I never eat it."

Still struggling to hide an aggrievement that lingered, he took the tray from the table. In his own room, he made the bed awkwardly. He kept the lights off though it was still dark outside. The dog at his side, he sat by the fire till she came to her door. She was dressed for the street. " The bathroom's yours." She moved round, straightening cushions. " I should have a bath and not worry about the tape. I can get some more. It'll be your last chance of a bath for a long while."

" What about your people," he said curiously. " Aren't they going to wonder, you turning up unexpectedly?"

She pulled on her gloves and checked the seams of her stockings. " I doubt it. Nobody's surprised at anything I do. I'm bad style in the county—paint my nails and live alone in London. The worst kind of whore."

He grinned back at her. Once again, she lifted the hem of this strange reserve, letting him feel her comradeship. Her odd clinical manner seemed to be turned on like a brake, he thought, a safety-valve.

" Don't answer the phone or the door while I'm gone," she warned. " Everything will be in the car when I come back. I'll be as quick as I can. You'll hear me sound the horn once. Come straight out. Watch for the Commander, upstairs. He's a dirty old man and nosey. He'd be delighted to see a man leaving my flat at ten in the morning. You can bring Rusty and I'll wait for you round the corner, Moore Street."

It was difficult to see her expression in the darkened room but he sensed her encouragement. He raised a hand and she turned. The dog following her to the door, nosing till Greg called him away. The front door slammed. He watched at the window till the swirling snow hid her.

For a long time, he sat by the fire, facing the window. The dog seemed to share his uncertainty, nuzzling his hand. His fear was back, he thought. And only because she had gone. He wanted to know every move she was making, see each person she spoke with. His fear was now of her sudden indifference, change of mind—no longer of betrayal.

A pale grey light filtered into the room from the street. Through the curtains, the snow seemed no more than a blown powder that pattered against the glass. In an effort to stop thinking, he went to the bathroom. There was a razor on the glass-topped table. She had left blades, soap, talcum, ready for him. He shaved carefully, content with the reflection the mirror showed. The thick, bruised skin on his cheek bones was gone. As a face, he reasoned, there was nothing about it to distinguish it from a million others. No scars there—no oddity of feature—nothing that could help a cop without a picture to recognize him by. By itself, the General Description put out by the Yard meant nothing to a man on the run. To the public, the Flying Squad was a combination of Dick Tracy's and Sherlock Holmes. Granite-jawed supermen and characters straight from a book by a lady author of fireside skullduggery. But of ten wanted men who were caught by the Squad, nine of them were put away by their associates. *Friends*, he amended.

He eased himself into the steaming tub and relaxed. A farm-house on the side of a mountain was a long way from places like Cameron's club. The rat-race of the West End of London. With food, heat and water, he could last there indefinitely. For as long as it took to straighten out his thinking—to prepare for that one last touch that he had to make before leaving England. A sheep-farm, Bridget had said it was that. He saw steep mountains with sheep pastures sloping to streams that ran quietly on a pebbled bed. It wouldn't be the first time that he'd had the remote countryside as a shelter.

Those first two years of the war, he'd been on a course over similar terrain on the west coast of Scotland. The " Kill-or-be-killed course ", they'd called it. The sergeant-instructor was a full-blooded Ontario Indian, a hunter in peace and in war. The way to deal death to an enemy was his birthright. All the skill of modern technique had been added. John Baptist passed on his knowledge gladly, driving his pupils to savagery with simple pleasure. The course had been a prelude to the Dieppe Raid. The incredible blunder that was to have brought acclaim to a bored Canadian Army. For a year, Greg had been a permanent volunteer for any special assignment. He'd taken Baptist's instruction gladly. The team had consisted of five lieutenants and the Ontario brave. Parachuted from a Lancaster, they had dropped to the waste of the Lochiel highlands. Their job, to infiltrate through an alerted police force and Home Guard. Baptist had led them through the silent pine forests, rivers where the salmon rose to their footsteps, glens showing buzzards that flapped in alarm, wheeling as they caught their first sight of man. It had been a game with a difference—soon it would be played in deadly earnest. To learn the rules meant the chance that you'd live. They carried their iron rations, killing their meat as they went. Baptist read the trees, tracks and wind like a book, thin nostrils flaring as he sniffed out danger. They had travelled at night, sleeping in piled bracken, a deserted forest watcher's hut, the fork of a tree. It had taken five days before they walked into Fort William Police Station at midnight, to announce its technical demolishment.

He remembered the commendation that had come from the stiff autocrat who had been his colonel. " You've done well, Lieutenant. Not at all badly. We'll keep you in mind." They had, along with four thousand other Canadians who had charged up the streets of the old Norman city, the beaches, the woods on the outskirts. Of every ten men, nine had been killed.

He sat up in the bath and soaped his body. He'd have no trouble in Bridget's farmhouse . . . He finished his dressing in the room at the front. The snow had stopped now. A milkman climbed the steps outside, whistling with professional cheerfulness. The setter barked. Instinctively, Greg held the dog, unwilling that there should be any sign that the flat had an occupant—a dog even. He heard the bottles clink as the man set them down, the retreating footsteps.

It was gone nine when the phone rang for the first time. The unexpected summons dragged him from his seat, the fear drumming in his head. He stood over the instrument, willing its silence. After a while, it was quiet. He looked at the clock again. There was time to catch the news. The need to know the worst persisted in him. He went to the radio in Bridget's bedroom and sat on her bed.

The voice was precise. ". . . to debate a motion tabled by Opposition members of the House." The man cleared his throat. " Police last night, using dogs and walkie-talkie outfits, raided an area outside Henley in a new hunt for Paul Gregory, the convict who escaped from Wandsworth Prison eight days ago. Roads leading to the neighbourhood were sealed while officers questioned motorists and householders. The search was concentrated on a wooded part of the Thames where Gregory had been seen earlier in the day. A police spokesman said it was possible that the convict was being aided by friends."

He listened to the rest of the news without hearing. Like an animal approaching a lure, he scented a trap. There'd been no more mention of Sloane—of murder—of the police wishing to see him about it. The failure to associate his name with Sloane's death, except in the stylized way that they did it in England, meant nothing. Here the law was jealous of pre-judgement. The bit about him being seen at Henley was crazy. There were plenty of people there who knew him by sight. Some eager bastard must have turned in a mistaken report. Not that it mattered—the more that happened, the sicker the cops would become of the false-pretence tips that must flood their office.

Suddenly he remembered Judith. Maybe the police had charged in the house again, scaring her with search warrants, unconvinced by the telephone conversation that must have been monitored. He moved his shoulders in resignation. She couldn't have it both ways.

He boiled an egg in the kitchen, standing at the stove to eat it. Bridget had been gone for an hour-and-a-half. For the first time, fear for her safety was as quick as for his own. The loud tick of the kitchen clock bothered him. Back at the window, he watched the street, hidden by the curtains. A door slammed upstairs. Then someone passed in the hall, outside. He heard the front door open then close. A woman walked rapidly down the steps, turning towards Sloane Avenue.

Again the phone shrilled behind him. That could be Bridget, he thought. Ringing to warn him of some sudden danger. The setter pawed hopefully at his leg but he pushed the dog aside, impatiently. Maybe she was at a phone somewhere, hoping that he'd ignore her instruction not to answer, waiting to tell him to leave the flat before it was too late. The phone went dead and he sat down again. "Christ!" he said once, aloud. The dog moved its ears.

It was after ten when the sound of the front door took him again to the window. A man with a brief case left the house. Greg was in time to see his back as he walked off, swinging his the bag at his side.

He dragged a chair to the window a smoked a cigarette without tasting it. Minutes passed and a Sunbeam-Talbot, being driven slowly, passed the front of the house. The horn was sounded once and he was able to see Bridget at the wheel. She lifted a hand and went towards Moore Street.

He found his hat and topcoat, searching the room for something forgotten. There was nothing. The setter was whining. Conscious of time being wasted, Greg scattered clothes, scarves and papers in the hall, ham-handed in his anxiety. The leash hung on a hook in front of him. Holding the dog by the collar he opened the flat door and stood at the bottom of the stairs, listening. Nothing moved.

TWELVE

HE pulled the front door shut behind him, and walked to the corner of Moore Street. Bridget was parked twenty yards away. The setter pulled as he saw the car. She had the door to the convertible open ready. The front seat was pushed forward. " In the back," she said.

He climbed over a square stove, a drum of oil, to a seat littered with packages. She slewed in her seat, smiling back at him. " You must have thought I was never coming. Are you still nervous—or has that gone now?"

" It's gone, *now*," he answered. For a moment, their eyes held steady. He was quiet, not trusting to words. She had tied a scarf, French fashion, round her hair. Her bare hands were smeared with oil from the drum. The whole car smelt of her scent. He leaned back. The only doors were in front. The canvas hood closed, masking the seat at the back. He was hidden from other cars, from the street. The dog sat next to Bridget, tongue lolling from an open mouth.

She broke the silence, a little awkwardly. " Everything's in the back. There's a duffle bag to stow the things. You can change as we go and we'll throw those clothes you're wearing away. Somewhere they'll never be found. I've brought food and a couple of Thermos flasks with tea that Roy had made in the bar for me." She brought the motor to life. " We should be there by eight. The A.A. say that the roads are clear except for bits over the Cotswolds." She put the car into Sloane Avenue, heading for Uxbridge and the west. " It couldn't be better," she added. " By the time we get to Coedmawr, it'll be pitch dark. I'll take the car up as far as we can and help you with all that stuff. You'd never find the farm by yourself in the daytime. At night, it would be hopeless."

He started to change into the lumberjack's shirt and fisherman's trousers she brought. He ripped the fastenings from the other packages, dumping the contents into the duffle bag at his feet. She had forgotten nothing. Soap, matches, towels, a bottle of brandy, a windcheater and blankets. There were cigarettes, razor, a combined knife-and-spoon. There was a square box of provisions next to the drum of oil.

His feet were warm in the oiled wool stockings and the low rubber boots fitted well. He took a deep breath. It was no longer that this *had* to work—it was going to work. Everything that this girl did for him bore the certainty of success.

She reached a hand backwards, over her shoulder. He took the dark glasses unquestioningly. " There's absolutely no reason for you to speak to anyone," she said. " But keep the glasses on. If we *are* stopped, I'll do the talking. You're Alastair Selkirk, my cousin, and blind."

He watched the movement of her strong wrists as she put the lively car through gaps in the traffic. A strand of hair had escaped from the scarf. She took a hand from the wheel, dabbing impatiently at her hair.

"*I never want another woman but you,*" he said silently.

Bridget was able to drive and talk. He leaned forward, resting his arms on the back of the seat as she described Coedmawr and her life there. It was a Georgian house in a park by a river, screened north and south by the Cambrian Mountains. Eleven miles away was Rhayader, a tiny town in the Elan Valley. This was the wild Wales—the coal-poor mountain country that remained remote. The wooded slopes down to the great houses of the valleys were broken by rough pasture where men farmed sheep in the way of their ancestors. Small dark men speaking English with hesitation. Each year, the valley lost its youth to the collieries, the shipyards, the factories of the south.

Unspoiled, Coedmawr had offered a gracious way of living to three generations of Selkirks. Now, General Selkirk and his wife found their home stability in a world whose values they no longer understood. Bridget's memories were an acceptance of the things that only great wealth could produce. She spoke of a house filled with treasures that had come from her ancestor's home in Scotland. Of glass, paintings, furniture, that her father considered to be no more than in his charge, to be passed on as he found them. But Coedmawr had no heir. Timothy, her brother, had been killed the year before in Cyprus.

High Wycombe had gone long since, they were skirting the spires and smoke stacks of Oxford. A cold driving rain washed the road, freezing in the hedgerows. Bare black trees stood like sentinel crows on the Cotswold Hills, guarding the frigid fields. On the high land, the crust of the snow had settled under the weight of the rain. The car whined on the wet road surface as it made better speed. Once, Greg lit a cigarette for her, close to the smell of her hair as he reached across.

" You'd have liked Timothy," she said seriously. " And he'd probably have liked you. He was bloody-minded—stubborn—and had nothing but contempt for conventional ethical values." She raised her head at the clear weather ahead of them, touching a button, silencing the wind-shield wipers. " Timothy hated the army."

Once in a long while, this happened, he thought. Generations of straitlaced parents, throwing back violently to some forgotten strain, producing children they were unable to understand. A dead rebel son, a daughter harbouring an escaped convict, a man the police called murderer.

" Why did he join the army—your brother? National Service?"

In front of him, she moved a shoulder. " The sort of obstinacy that makes one do something unpleasant. *Proving* something to somebody. Not that he ever convinced Daddy. Secretly, I think my father is pleased that Timothy's dead. The last of the Selkirks a hero! " She laughed shortly and he made a sound of sympathy, sensing the bond she had had with her brother. Catching the play of his hand in the mirror, she asked: " Those scars on your thumb, what are they?"

He told her, reliving the night at Sloane's flat—recalling the dead man's face, twisted and puzzled, on the bed. They were up now, in the lichen grey of the Cotswolds. Occasionally, a car or a truck passed in the opposite direction, the high whine of its motor flattening to a thud as it reached them. The hiss of their own tyres, the flap of the wind in the canvas hood, made a background for his growing security. They had seen no police since they had left London. Here and there, a yellow-slickered A.A. scout raised a hand in salute as they passed. Every mile that Bridget put on the clock, the conviction grew—he was going to pull out of this jam. He warmed to her, quickly, watching the line of her cheek as she looked for a suitable parking place. This was a new feeling to have about any woman. It was a need to belong, a wish to continue to be whatever it was that she found in him.

She pulled the convertible on to a lay-by. Opening the door, she let the setter out. Sniffing the thin cold air, it barked then skeetered in crazy circles. Bridget opened a basket at her feet and passed him sandwiches, a Thermos flask. She poured water from a bottle into a bowl, calling the dog. They ate in silence, sipping the hot, strong tea. She wiped the curve of her mouth with a tissue, carefully, like some small, well-mannered girl. He leaned forward, twisting her shoulder so that she faced him.

" Bridget—I've got to say this. I don't know how long I'll know you—it isn't going to matter. But when I do leave you, I'll be losing the most important thing that's happened to me. The best thing."

She stroked his cheek impulsively, tracing the lines of his mouth with her finger-tips. " No longer the man with the answers," she said quietly. " Like the rest of us, you are dependent on somebody else. For someone like you, it must be terrible."

He pulled away, denying the truth. " It happens that I meant what I said."

She nodded. " I believe you. In a few hours, it's possible to be closer to someone that you get to others in years. Do you remember what you said last night, Greg: ' This is a crazy thing '. You were sure of it, too. It's your safety that really matters to you. I'm just a means to an end. It could have been anyone, chance made it me." She turned, switching on the motor. " I'm your friend," she said quietly. " I promise you that. But you don't have to feel grateful about anything."

She turned the car back to the highway. She was silent, her eyes on the icy patches ahead. Beside her, the setter tucked his tail round his nose and slept.

" Shall I take the wheel for a while? " he offered. " There isn't a straw man up here, let alone anyone who's going to ask me for a licence."

" I've done it a hundred times," she answered. " I know every inch of the road. My brother used to say that this car knew its way back to Coedmawr without a driver."

He pulled the windcheater round his shoulders, settling low in the back of the seat. The wind thumped steadily into the canvas. He took of his glasses and shut his eyes. A means to an end. Maybe she was right—but she was becoming as important as the end itself. He slept until the jarring of brakes awakened him. Outside, it was dark now. The lights of a small petrol station showed. A man filled the tank and Bridget and the dog stretched their legs. Getting back, she drove the car over a small humped bridge, up a narrow street where tight-shut houses looked over a deserted market square. Out of the dreary town and north on a hard-top highway. He craned forward, looking at the clock on the dash. It was six-fifteen. He started rubbing his cramped legs.

" Where was that?" he asked.

" Brecon," said Bridget. The headlights were picking out a winding road with thick snow-topped hedgerows. " Builth Wells next," she added, " then about fifteen miles more to Coedmawr."

When the lights of the next town were behind them he felt the car swaying on the sharp curves. The slant of the fields and the hedges showed that they were climbing. The setter shook itself, nosing the window, whimpering. Bridget pointed over the dog's back.

" We're there. Coedmawr's behind that wood."

Caught in the lights, a grey squirrel leaped from the stone wall to the trees beyond. Greg had a glimpse of an open white gate, a driveway that vanished between a black belt of trees. They went for another mile then she cut the headlights, taking a rough track that snaked through a ragged copse of firs. Spinning as she changed gear, the back wheels kicked a shower of stones behind them. She wrenched the jolting car from the ruts and changed gear once more.

The track had been made by dumping stones in a gully. Raw frozen earth sloped from the trees to the rutted foundation. She put the car up the incline, steering from one side to the other. The moon was up and its cold light sliced the trees in grotesque shadows. They jolted a half-mile to a clearing where an acre of larch, birch and willow lay where it had been felled, tumbled black streaks on a glittering background.

She stopped the car where the track ended and pulled on a pair of rubber boots. " The rest we do on foot," she told him. " There's another quarter-mile of it."

He threaded a stout cord through the handle of the drum of oil and knotted the other end to the stove. Passing the cord over his shoulders, he took the two loads, He carried the box of provisions in his right hand. Bridget led the way, carrying the duffle bag.

Sifted snow was loose on top of last year's leaves. As he struggled his load after her, his feet sank to the ankles. The dog had gone ahead, breaking ground with assurance.

" Rusty knows the way—we often come here." She was just

ahead of him, going easily under the weight of the bag she carried.

He made no answer, sucking in cold air through his open mouth. Pain in the injured rib dragged his body down to one side. He lowered his head, steadying the swinging stove and oil drum with the insides of his forearms. Bridget turned left, towards the sound of running water. A little more light showed in front of them. Striking through a break in the trees, the moon was reflected in a wide, swift stream. Lapping the twisted fallen trunks, the boulders washed down from some mountain height, the stream dropped in its course in a series of tiny waterfalls.

The setter stopped on the bank, its paw raised in uncertainty. " We have to ford it." Bridget said. He followed, the icy water spilling over the tops of his rubber boots.

In front of them, rusted sheep wire sagged from the trees, barring the way to yet another gully. They climbed over the wire, following the slant of the gorge. Freshets, trickling down the snowed sides, made a sucking hazard underfoot. Then came a break in the side of the gully. It led to a farmyard littered with broken equipment. The dark bulk of a stone-built barn and cottage made a rough T in the sheltered hollow. Beyond, over the roof of the cottage, Greg could see the slope of the mountain side.

The door of the cottage was in two pieces, like that of a stable. An old heavy lock held it fast. Bridget dropped the duffle bag and reached above the lintel. She opened the door with the large key. The wood creaked inward, leaving a drift a foot deep at its base.

He followed her inside, pulling the door shut behind him. There were windows on both sides of the room but it was impossible to see. She rummaged in the bag that she carried. As the pale light of a candle gathered strength, he saw the old-fashioned kitchen range and the stone floor. Through a doorway without a door was a room of the same size. The cottage was bare but it smelt dry.

" I'm afraid this is it." Bridget started unpacking the bag. " There's water from a spring in the yard that never freezes."

With the climb finished, the hammering in his chest had subsided. He helped her with the blankets, making a rough bed on the floor. They tucked the end of the bed into the empty bag, securing the bedding. It would be hard but reasonably warm. The small oil stove burned steadily.

" The only way anyone could know that you were up here

would be seeing smoke." She was by the door to the yard, the dog at her feet. " You can't light a fire, Greg. But water will boil on the stove and I've brought a kettle." She sounded uncertain. " Do you think you'll be all right?"

His shadow huge on the whitewashed wall, he moved across the room. He stood in front of her. In the candlelight, her eyes were dark and questioning. Very gently, he took her face in his hands. Bending, he found her mouth cool to his lips. She turned her cheek slightly and he lowered his hands, stepping back. Then suddenly her arms tightened round his neck, pulling as he sought her eyes, her mouth.

" Don't go, Bridget," he whispered.

They stood for a while that way, bodies straining. She shook herself free but held on to his hand. " I won't," she promised.

It was after eight by her watch. The fierce little stove pervaded the room with a reeking heat. She brought food from the box of provisions, heating soup that they ate from the tin, sharing the one spoon. They fed biscuits to the setter and drank brandy from the tops of the Thermos flasks. The dog flopped at the end of the bed, content in the warmth and their nearness.

They spoke quietly, almost impersonally, as if forced to deny an admission of changed relationship. It was Greg who blew out the candle. In the rough warmth of the blankets, he watched as she pulled her sweater over her head. In the yellow light from the stove, the skin of her back was amber. He felt the slight weight of her skirt as she threw it by his feet on the bed. Then her body was next to his. His mouth at her neck, he discovered the softness of her breasts, the long clinging length of her legs. The pain in his side forgotten, he took her to him fiercely.

A grey morning light filtered through the filthy panes. On an oak in the yard, a blackbird's song was bravely sweet. At the foot of the bed, the dog was still sleeping. With his outstretched fingers, Greg found the cool stone flags. He shivered, bending over the girl beside him. Under his mouth, her eyes opened and she smiled lazily, rubbing her instep against his leg.

" What time is it?" she yawned.

He turned her warm arm, reading the watch on her wrist. " Seven."

She closed her eyes again, bringing her finger tips to his cheek. He lay there watching. Her mouth relaxed, composed. But not with the laxity of spent passion, he thought. There was a faint suggestion of the professional nurse's smugness about the ease on her face. After a while, she dressed, washing in spring water that she warmed on the stove. She made breakfast and they sat on the bed, eating. The first cigarette of the day made conversation thankfully unnecessary. Finally, she stubbed out her butt and started to fasten the leash on the setter.

" I must go. It's nearly ten, Greg. I'll have to say that I left early this morning to avoid the traffic."

His hand gripping her arm, they went out to the yard. Now it was possible to see the terraced slopes that rose beyond the back of the cottage. Sheep pastures, dotted with trees, glittered under the bright winter sun. They walked slowly back down the gully towards the stream. It was a silent wood with an odd absence of anything that lived. A witches' wood from a child's fairy tale. Only round hard droppings showed where the sheep had broken through the fencing. There were badger setts but no tracks, no squirrel prints, even the trees were bereft of birds. As if warning, the faint sound of the blackbird came to them from the periphery of the wood.

From the clearing, they could see down and over the massed birch, fire and willows. The road beneath wound in the valley like a silver worm, its gradients exaggerated by their own altitude. Beyond the wooded park of Coedmawr, the pillared front of the house sheltered a straggle of outbuildings. At the back, a lane climbed a bridge over the river. Crossing it at right angles was a single railway track. Like a toy, a short train puffed its way south along the valley.

" One train a day," smiled Bridget, " and always empty. The line runs through our land. Since my grandfather's day, there's been a tiny station at the back of the farm. Our own station. If we want to stop the train, we telephone Rhayader."

He walked to the car with her. The setter jumped to her side. She hit the starting button and turned to Greg. " Don't wander," she warned, " no matter how much you feel like it. These mountain farms are eerie. You come across a place that looks deserted. Nothing is moving. But somewhere—behind a curtain, up in a hayloft—somebody's watching. They're miles from civilization but they know everything that happens, these people. It isn't that they're curious. They're defensive—afraid."

He nodded. It seemed to take more of this thin air to fill his lungs. Require more effort to suck it down. He tapped his short pocket, feeling for the phials of amyl-nitrite. Hauling that gear the night before had been agony. He wanted to be sure that he was able to stave off a fainting fit such as he'd had that night in the cab.

"When am I going to see you again, Bridget?" he asked, suddenly. He bent at the open window. Faced with her freshness, he was conscious of his own stubbled beard.

She tapped her teeth with a nail, frowning. "It won't be so easy. You see there's always something to do down here and people expect you to help. My family's no exception." She gestured at the snow-covered hills. "Saying I'm going for a walk would only intrigue them more."

He scowled, resentful of all that tied her to anything but him. "You can't just let it go at that," he objected. "These last few hours, I've forgotten who I was—why I came here. Now you're leaving, I'm going to remember. And it'll be that much worse."

In spite of the words, there was entreaty in his voice and she touched his hand quickly. "You're not to start all that again, Greg. Our little station—the one at the back of the farm—can you see it?"

He scanned the railroad, past fields where sheep were feeding on root crops and on to the halt, a tiny black box against the snow. "Sure. I can see it."

"Then be there at six," she instructed. "It'll be easier for me to slip from the house then—say I'm going to do something to the car. I'll bring some things that you'll need. Timothy's little radio. It'll be dark and all the dogs will be in the house. Will that be all right for you . . ." she hesitated. ". . . Greg?"

Almost, he thought, as if she were frightened to let even her voice caress him now. Not one endearment had passed between them yet last night it had been more than desire that joined them. "That'll be all right," he said steadily. "How shall I know the time?"

She slipped her watch, its strap still warm from her arm, on his wrist. He stood there as she turned the car then ran it down the gully track and into the woods. When he could no longer see her, he found his way back to the cottage. Yard, barn and cottage nestled hidden in a hollow. He crunched through the crusted snow bank to a crest. Ten yards away, a brown buzzard perched on an eyeless ewe. Her belly swollen in pregnancy, the ewe lay on her side, breathing heavily. As the great bird saw Greg, it flapped lazily to the top of a fir, a hundred yards further up the mountain. There it waited, honking metallically.

He slithered down the slope. In some way, the buzzard reminded him of Sloane. Evil—battening on the defenceless. The ewe's legs twitched in agony. About her, the snow was spattered with blood and wool. The crimson tracks of the buzzard showed where it had walked round the ewe, ripping with talon and beak. The ewe lay in its own filth, breathing spasmodically. For a moment, he was uncertain. Robbing the foul bird of its prey would have afforded a satisfaction that he must forgo. He had nothing with which to bury the animal and the buzzard was patient. He went back to the cottage and found the knife. The point was sharp. He whetted it on a slate and climbed back to the ewe. The buzzard still perched on the fir. Another, scenting death or attracted by the call of its mate, wheeled in the bright overhead.

He knelt at the animal's head, probing the greasy wool of its neck till he found an artery beating under the skin. Guiding the sharp knife point, he turned his head away and leaned all his weight on the haft. In a gush, the ewe's blood covered his hands to the wrists. The striken animal's breath rattled in her throat. Kicking a couple of times, she was dead. Mechanically, he wiped his hands and the knife in the snow. A stain showed on the strap of Bridget's watch and he dabbed at it ineffectually. Against his wish, he turned his head. Both buzzards were perched on the fir, waiting. He went back to the yard and fouled the clean snow with his vomit.

Inside, he brewed himself hot tea that settled his stomach. He used the rest of the tea to shave with, feeling his way round his cheeks with his fingers. The smell of Bridget was still in his bedding reminding him of her. He shook the bedding carefully and carried it out to the yard. The barn was in good repair. The hay in the manger broke, brittle, between his fingers. There was the persistent smell of cattle, long since gone. Uppermost on a pile of old newspapers was one with the headline:

KING EDWARD'S ABDICATION.

He had a strange interest in the people who had lived in this cottage—the story behind a track now lost in the wood. The tiny hollow gave a feeling of peace—of remoteness from the chase. It would be good, almost, to stay up there, living the life of a recluse. A life that could be partially shared with Bridget.

In the upper part of the hay loft, through the air slits in the stone wall, he could see the stretching valley, far below. Now and again, the sun caught the windshield of a car climbing the road. He went back to the cottage and slept, easing the insistent pain in his side.

It was five-thirty by Bridget's watch. The daylight had gone with the quickness of winter. He fastened the door, replacing the key above the lintel. Then he started down through the woods. With the coming of evening, the temperature had tumbled. Snow that had thawed during the day now froze again under his feet. He made his way to the clearing, using the old tracks in the snow as a guide. Down the steep-sided gully to the main road. Here, apart from the singing telephone poles, the highway was quiet. He slipped across it to the wall of Coedmawr. Lights showed in a lodge, a couple of hundred yards to his right. A dog barked. He topped the stone wall, dropping to the shelter of still more trees. Yew, larch and firs screened the approach to the lawns in front of the big Georgian house. He stood for a while where they ended, watching the great windows. Lights blazed through open curtains in half-a-dozen rooms. From behind the house came the sound of a steadily pumping motor. It could be light, he thought, or water. Both, possibly.

He skirted the lawn cautiously, ducking under the live cattle wire strung round its edge. On the left, the snow-covered grass sloped to a haha. He dropped to the bottom of the deep ditch, making his way to the kitchen quarters at the rear of the house. He passed a dovecote in the kitchen yard where pigeons murmured in the dark. Through a stable yard smelling of horse manure, and on to the bridge. Behind him, now, the darkened appendages of the big house spread over an acre of intricate yards, passages and outbuildings.

He crossed the humped bridge, the cold rushing water under his feet drowning all other sound. Here, fifty yards from the main part of the buildings, the unscreened lights were no more than a glow making it possible to distinguish a walled rose garden to his left. Ahead, the lane rose to the railway track. The halt was no more than a square box, the size of a couple of telephone booths, set on a granite ramp. He pushed the door. It was open. He struck a match cautiously. There was a wooden packing case in front of the empty fireplace. Across the top was stencilled:

GENERAL SELKIRK
SINGAPORE—SOUTHAMPTON
BOOKS

Old dust covered the top of the leather-edged table. He took one of the two chairs to the window. A hundred yards away, the line of the humped bridge was distinguishable against the dark rushing river, the snowed banks. He waited in the small silent room.

THIRTEEN

THE watch on his wrist showed six-fifteen before he saw Bridget crossing the bridge, hurrying up the lane. He stood by the open door and took her shoulders in his arms. She had no words for a moment, shivering in his tight embrace, her cheek cold against his. A little uneasy, he recognized her fear. " Now what? " he asked, anxiety cracking his voice. " What happened?"

Still holding his hand, she took one of the chairs and sat down. " Something terrible. The police have been here this afternoon. Not the ordinary police but a man called Prescott—he's Chief Constable of Radnorshire. He drove over from Presteigne and asked to see Daddy who's a friend of his. I was called into the library. I'm afraid, Greg."

He was on his feet again, ready to break for the door. Incapable of reason yet aware of its need. He wet his lips, forcing himself back to his seat. " Where are they now—what did they say?" He could not bring himself to take back her hand, unwilling to touch the disaster she brought.

She leaned towards him, giving her strength. " If you lose your head now, Greg, we're done for. Brigadier Prescott's gone. Everything that he told Daddy and me was under promise of secrecy. Scotland Yard phoned his office this morning for permission to come down to Radnorshire to question me." She moved her hands nervously. " It's something they do, apparently. Some ghastly protocol. They're arriving after dinner, I think, to see me."

" Why?" he persisted.

" The phone number at Cadogan Gardens. It was found on a piece of paper in the library at South Street, they say." She gripped his arm. " I *was* right—one of the maids came back to South Street unexpectedly. Prescott says that Scotland Yard found your fingerprints all over that house. An escaped convict, he told Daddy, wanted for murder. They think you may be here, in Wales. Your description was circulated this afternoon from Presteigne."

He pushed his shaking hands under his buttocks. The hunt

had never seemed so near. He tried to recall—a piece of paper with Bridget's telephone number on it, left in the Mackinnon home. He had no memory of it. He'd sat at the desk in the library, the phone book in front of him. And he'd found her number. There might have been a pad—an indentation of his writing on the top blank sheet. He found it impossible to take his mind back to the details of the scene. Had a maid come back to the house, calling the police was normal procedure. But nothing but the dollars from the safe had been stolen and the maid could hardly know about that. Unless they had a definite lead, it was improbable for the police to crawl all over the house, searching for prints.

He had a brief, unpleasant picture of cool, implacable men, plotting this thing like a mathematical equation. X plus Y : Z. That night, he had been recognized by the cop who had stopped him near South Street. Then Greg disappeared. A house nearby was broken into and showed signs that someone had been living there.

Unconsciously, he moved closer to her, letting his breath go. It was no fault of hers but his own. Only luck and courtesy between cops had prevented the Yard from springing a complete surprise on her.

" When are the police coming, you say?" He was conscious that his voice sounded flat, almost an accusation. He put his arm round her again, drawing her close to him. " I've got to get out of here in a hurry, Bridget. These guys aren't fools. They'll nose around, throwing trick questions at you. Chances are, they'll come here, ready to say that you know me. Can you stand up to that?"

" I think so," she answered quietly. " Daddy was wonderful with Prescott. Threatening to go up to London to see the Commissioner. To find out out why his daughter was being involved in a murder enquiry."

" Whatever happens," he said quickly, " you've got to deny knowing me." A memory prompted. " Did Prescott say if they'd found your address or simply the phone number? " He moved his shoulders hopelessly. " I can't begin to think what I wrote at that desk."

" He didn't say," she answered. " Only that they were coming here and why. But they must have been to Cadogan Gardens, I suppose. Greg . . ." There was a catch in her voice.

He got to his feet, dropping the words bitterly. " And there's nothing I can do."

She moved to his side, speaking urgently. " I *want* you to go. Now. Not for me but for you, Greg. I sat thinking about it this afternoon till I thought I'd go mad. And Daddy and Mummy, arguing whether they should give these detectives rooms for the night." She managed a laugh, warming him with her courage. " There *is* only one thing to do. You've got to take my car. You'll find one of Timothy's uniforms in it. There's some money, his passport, in the pockets. You've been in the army. In a place like this, nobody dreams of questioning an officer and there aren't any M.P.'s for a hundred miles."

He shifted his feet uncertainly. " What happens when somebody notices that your car's gone?"

" They won't," she assured him. " You can go out by the back lane, turn right at the main road. You'll be in Rhayader in no time. There are buses, trains, from there. Leave the car in front of the Wellington Hotel in the main square. I'll take the bus in, in the morning and pick it up." Sensing his indecision, she gripped his arm. " For *Christ's* sake, you must, Greg! If they catch you now . . ."

For two days he had followed where she led. Voicing his fears with the certainty of her rebuttal. Losing the hammering memory of personal danger in her strength. Now, suddenly, her competence was gone. The clutch of her fingers, the urgency in her voice, betrayed her own weakness.

Somewhere between this still countryside and London, he remembered, a squad car blazed headlights through the night. In the back sat the Murder Squad. Shrewd, experienced cops, blasé from the denials of a thousand interrogations. And still, Bridget's anxiety was for him, not for herself.

Glad in the decision, he pulled her to him roughly, putting his cheek against hers. " It wouldn't work. They're too near—too close to you. This is where I've got to take off, alone."

She pulled back, trying to read his eyes, and he knew he must lie. She must never know that for the first time, deliberately, fear for another was greater than fear for himself.

" It's the only way, Bridget," he insisted. " Your idea's hopeless. I wouldn't get five miles in that car. The only chance that I have is by myself." She moved restlessly and caught his arm again. " The police only need to find one person who saw me in the car with you. It'll be enough to bitch anything you say to get yourself out of this mess unless you work fast. It can't be any better for me if the police think you helped me willingly. Only worse for you."

Outside, the wind off the icy river searched the length of the lane, sending the door banging on its rusted hinges. She shivered. " What must I do then, Greg?" she asked quietly.

" Get your brother's stuff back to the house as quickly as possible. Make sure nobody sees you. Then tell your father as much of the truth as you think fit. Say I broke into your flat—was waiting there with a gun. You drove down here with a pistol in your back."

" And the farm, last night?" she asked.

He forced brutality into his tone. " What of it? Look, the police want me for murder. I've got no time to remember anything else. *Nothing!*"

She pushed her hands deep in the pockets of her coat. " No, of course. No time. I forgot. But I'm not asking you to remember, Greg. It's the *things* in the farmhouse I meant. The things that I bought. The stove, the bedding. If they're found, how could I deny helping you?"

" They won't be found," he assured her. " I'll take care of them. Your people still think you arrived here this morning."

She whispered assent.

" Then you drove me to Rhayader and left me there," he said.

" How can I say that?" She was moving nervously from window to door and back. " If you'd forced me to drive you here, I'd have told someone. The police. Daddy, at least."

Her objections went deeper than form and, deliberately, he sought to destroy her concern for him. " Forget the Girl Guide stuff," he said crudely. " You're in a jam and you've got to lie your head off to get out of it. You can only hinder me now. Get your father on your side. *I* can't tell you how to handle him. Your version's got to reach this man Prescott, somehow, before the men from the Yard arrive."

" Why should it have been me in the first place? " she asked. " Won't they want to know that? Why should you break into *my* flat? As far as they know, I'd never seen you before in my life."

" Why *any* of the places I've been?" he said savagely. " A man on the run doesn't conform to a pattern. You don't *know* why. Let them work it out. They'll know I was in Bishop's flat. I might have found your address there. They're ready to believe anything about me—just remember that. You've got to admit bringing me to Rhayader but deny doing it any way but at pistol point. Understand?" She made no answer and he crossed to the corner, wrenching her arm so that she faced him. "*Understand?*" he persisted.

Her head moved. " Goodbye, Bridget," he said at last. " And that means everything that the word stands for."

She was away from the pale light from the window and he was not able to see her face. But the sadness in her voice increased his own loneliness. " Just like that, Greg?" she whispered.

" Just like that," he answered.

" Goodbye," she repeated softly. She turned at the door. "*Bonne chance.*"

He watched as she came into the light by the bridge, He sat there for a while. Now that he knew what he must do, he was ready with the numbed calm that belonged to the eve of battle. Then he went out to the dark lane, ducking below the level of the stonework as he crossed. Past the stable. A hoof thudded against a door with sudden violence and he flattened himself against the wall. Then on through a passage, heady with fertilizer, into the kitchen yard.

A dinner gong sounded in the house. He stopped in the yard where the doves murmured over his head. He turned so that he faced the great lighted windows on the stairway. From the house, he could hear Bridget's name being called.

As he watched, she made her way slowly down the staircase, following an elderly woman with white hair. He was near enough to the house to see the armour in the wall-niches, the emblazoned shields that hung above them. Her shoulders were bare and her throat knotted with pearls. She smiled as she took her mother's arm and passed from his sight.

FOURTEEN

He climbed back as he had come, skirting the great house to the shelter of its wooded driveway. Over the wall that confined the park, across the highway and up the rutted track that led to the deserted farmhouse.

It was almost eight. The bright moon was high in the night. The slush underfoot had frozen again, crunching beneath his weight. He made his way through the silent spinney and stopped in the clearing for a while, leaning his weight on a fallen tree, easing the pain in his side. The hurt came in recurrent waves—an off-beat echo of his breathing. When he was rested, he wiped the sweat from his neck and went back among the trees. The urge to keep upright was no longer intense and he half-fell, half-slithered down to the sound of the running stream. He waded through it and climbed over the sheep fence, ripping the stuff of his trousers on the snagged wire, without strength to lift himself free. His flesh burned where the metal had notched the skin.

The farmhouse was quiet in the moonlight but no longer sanctuary, he remembered. Bridget's father would be in immediate communication with the Chief Constable, for his daughter's sake. Rhayader was only a few miles away. If they thought that he had been dropped there, the hunt might well extent to the neighbouring valleys.

There was a chance for him yet. A good chance, if he kept his head. The dollars and Sloane's cigarette gold case made a reassuring weight in his pocket. Forty or fifty miles to the south were the great ports of Wales. Cardiff, Swansea. There were enough provisions in the farmhouse to last him a week if he rationed himself. Blankets. He must travel by night, sleep by day.

He found the key above the door and went into the room that still held Bridget's presence, an unsubtle reminder of his need of her. Out in the barn, he bound newspapers round a stick, making a rough broom. Under the stacked journals was an old bus timetable with a crude map of the area. His direction was plain. Across the valley to the massed mountains that ridged to the south, like folds in the hide of an elephant.

He looked down at Coedmawr—a handful of tiny candles hanging in the dark beyond the trees and the highway. As he watched, the headlights of a car swept the lower slope of the mountain as it turned into the driveway. His eyes followed the white beam as it wound through the wood to the house.

Maybe it wasn't the police but he had to leave this place immediately. With the makeshift broom, he swept the room where they had slept, removing all trace of its occupation. He sprinkled the soft dust from the barn on the floor. Then he rolled bread and beans, chocolate, a can of corned beef and the flask of brandy in his blankets and strapped them on his shoulders. He closed the door to the farmhouse and replaced the key where he had found it.

The drum of oil rumbled its way down to the sheepwire. There he pulled the plug, letting the kerosene soak into the ground. Then he scuffed snow over the stained earth. Drum and stove, he hid in a tangle of undergrowth on the edge of the stream.

Once again he crossed the clearing. The moon hung high, giving a cold clarity to the night. Bare black trees threw sharp shadows on the snow under his feet. It was freezing hard and as he breathed, the hairs in his nostrils crackled. He tried to keep the movement of his lungs shallow.

He was working his way down through the spinney, avoiding the rutted lane, aiming to cross the highway a mile south of Coedmawr. Descent was easier on his injured rib but he bent from the hips to ease it. When he reached it, the highway was silent.

Beyond the thick hedge, he ploughed through the deep snow to the river. From Coedmawr, the swift water snaked through the valley to the reservoir. A few hundred yards to his right, the line of a rough stone bridge showed black against the glittering pasture. On the far bank, a deep-cut track mounted, hidden by hedges. He went over the bridge, into the frosty shadow of the gully. Stunted thorn trees in the banks above filtered the moonlight into strange shapes in front of him.

After a mile, the track curved in its climb, skirting a cluster of cottages, a chapel and manse. Lights burned in the hamlet and he struck out across the fields, making a detour round the huddle of houses. The going was harder in the yielding snow and he moved like a hinged doll, leaning forward into the rising ground. Leaden legs wearily pushed his body up the slope.

His breath came in shallow gasps, driving the agony in his side. He pulled the straps fastening the blanket roll to his shoulders and stood with the weight of cloth swinging in his hands. Suddenly his vision blurred and his legs gave way under him. He fell to his knees slowly then pitched forward, hands clawing at his shirt pockets.

He lay where he was, the powdered snow needling the skin of his neck. When his hand found the smooth glass phial, he forced his arm up, jerking his clenched fist nearer till he nosed his own flesh. Under the spasmodic grip of his fingers, the glass broke and the volatile liquid spilled over his mouth and nostrils. He stirred on his side, cupping his nose in his palm, sucking in the fumes.

The crusted snow was a dark, warm bed—a salt heady place that gave him back life. He opened his eyes, spitting the tiny glass splinters from a bleeding mouth. Pain still dragged at his side but his sight was clear. Using his legs like an animal, he pulled himself erect. Still swaying, he found the flask of brandy and unscrewed its top. He drank, searing his throat with the raw spirit. He refastened the roll of blankets round his shoulders. Salt blood still tasted on his mouth. He wiped his lips mechanically and, head down, stumbled up the slope.

No longer was he separate and distinct from the mountains and silver snow but a part of them. A couple of hundred yards beyond, a birch thicket bent gracefully. A white owl hooted once then flapped clumsily through the thin air, the scream of its beating wings loud in the silence. He moved cautiously now, smelling out danger like a suspicious animal. There was something about the birches—they were young trees, no more than a dozen years old. Someone had planted them there as a windbreak.

Among the trees, the drifts were shallow. Here and there, rusted pieces of farm equipment jutted from the surface. A pile of rotting tins cans spread like a rash at the edge of the thicket. He stood there motionless for a while, looking out through the fringe of wood. This was the first crest of his ascent. The ground before him dropped briefly to a small valley a quarter-mile wide, a mile long. The track he had forsaken at the hamlet followed the line of his journey, joining the valley at its far end. In this last loneliness, a stone-built farm and its outbuildings showed in the clear moonlight. He looked at Bridget's watch. It was eleven-thirty.

The farm stood square in the bed of the dip, like the bridge of a ship on its deck. Sheltering behind it, the outbuildings straggled on for thirty yards. Beyond the still house and its barns, trees rose in steep progression on the far side of the valley, ending in a black ridge, etched sharply in the pale cold light.

He knew he must rest. The drive of the two powerful restoratives was gone. Like a sick dog, he needed a corner and sleep. His eyes followed the line of the pasture land that dropped to the valley. A stream trickled down from the trees to the farm. In a matter of hours, there would be people moving about down there. Animals would be tended, chores done.

He looked up at the sky. The stars were sharp and brilliant, the moon clear. No fresh snow would fall before daybreak. Any tracks that he made would be there in the morning, warning the farmer of trespass. He picked his way carefully through the heap of rotting cans to the stream. In places, the water ran deep. He pulled off his socks and boots, lifting his trousers. Carrying the boots, he stepped into the icy brook and followed its course down the slope.

In one of those outbuildings, there'd be a place to hide, to rest, till nightfall. He was leaving no tracks to betray him. He walked clumsily in the bed of the brook, slipping on the slime. Already, his feet had lost all sense of touch. He moved them, indifferent to the sharp stone edges, the bruising pebbles. A hundred yards down the slope, at the flat of the land, the stream ended in a shallow pond. He waded out to the thin ice at its edge and squatted in the frozen mud round the wallow. There, he rubbed the movement of blood back to his feet and legs. He was in a wide yard at the back of the farmhouse. Sheep and cow tracks, their droppings, were frozen in the grey muddy earth. His footsteps would never register on this surface.

He got to his feet. With the farm, the outbuildings made a hollow square, enclosing the yard and the pond. Sixty feet away stood the barn, the lines of its dry stone walls and massive quoins sharp in the moonlight. As he moved towards it, the warning cackle of a goose came from the side of the house. He flattened himself in the shadow of the barn till the bird quietened. The heavy door opened easily under his hand. He closed it behind him, standing in the dark that held the sickly-sweet reek of cattle. He sensed rather than saw the patient heads turn towards him. After a while, his eyes were able to make out the stalls at the end of the barn. No longer curious, the cows faced their mangers.

Away from them was a platform stacked with fodder and cake. At its side, a ladder was erect to the dark of a storage loft.

Up there, he would be safe. There was enough fodder down in the barn to last the cattle for a week. Nobody was likely to climb to the loft.

He went up the rungs with difficulty, hauling his weight with his forearms. Fine dust settled in his nostrils, making him cough. The sudden salt in his mouth stirred him to effort. He dragged himself through the open hatch to the rough plank floor. He turned his body, the rolled blankets propping his shoulders. Sweat broke out, making cold patches in the heat of his loins, his back. When the nausea had gone, he sat up, unfastening the blankets from his shoulders.

Vents slashed the thick stone walls on each side of him, throwing a pale light on the loft. Piled hay and straw reached to the slanted roof—storage bins stood against the walls while from the rafters hung green blackthorn staves, ready for shaping, ploughshares and scythe blades.

Head first, he burrowed his way into the sweet hay, pulling the blanket roll after him. He curled like a dog that settles its bed, pulling the dried grass to seal his entrance. After a while, he slept.

He woke to the sound of a barking dog. He sprawled in the warm shallow burrow. Parting the hay, he crawled out cautiously. Bright sun slanted through the wall vents, the dust of his movement thick in the rays. He inched on his belly towards the head of the ladder. Below, the cattle were feeding stolidly, content. It was eleven a.m. by his watch. Still crouching, he peered from the slit in the stone wall.

A few hens scrabbled in the yard beneath while a dozen geese were busy by a trough at the side of the pond. He faced the back of the farmhouse. The door was hidden by the sweep of a porch. the curtained windows shut tight. Some cloths flapped on a line in the sun. He went to the opposite wall. Now, he could see the near end of the valley. Five hundred yards away, sheep, their fleece dingy against the brilliant snow, milled round a tractor and cart. With almost lazy ease, a man was trundling what looked like turnips to the ground from the cart.

Greg moved from the wall, flexing his shoulders, picking the sharp stalks from neck and hair. He was still tired. First he would eat then he would sleep again till nightfall. His route lay through the massed birch, holly and elder on the far side of the valley. When it was dark, he would move. With luck, he might cover ten miles that night. He sat on the floor, chewing the stale bread and greasy meat.

By now, Bridget had seen the police from Scotland Yard. Had told her story. He went over it, seeking to still his fear for her. There was a loyalty of class that was stronger than civic duty. Prescott was not just Chief Constable, he was General Selkirk's friend. Both men would believe Bridget's story for the alternative would be preposterous to them. The account that she gave to the men from the Yard could never be shaken as long as she stuck to it. With Prescott there and her father's support, she would tell it with her old competence.

Vaguely, he sensed that in refusing Bridget's last help, he accepted disaster. Her safety and his failure made the pattern complete. Without the second, the first was merely an empty gesture. He moved uneasily, rejecting the train of thought. He'd *still* beat the bastards. As long as he didn't panic, he'd beat them.

This was suddenly an intensely personal struggle with no room for outsiders. His freedom was his life. For the first time, he recognized his absolute isolation. He was beyond all help from anyone.

He put the food carefully back in the paper. He had to fill the Thermos with water and he needed a drink now. The need grew greater with the thought. By the porch at the back of the house, he had seen a pump. He dare not risk crossing the yard in the daylight. But there would surely be water somewhere in the barn below. He took one last look at the scene outside. It was unchanged. The farm seemed to be in the care of the animals. Far off, the man was still spreading food for a fresh flock of ewes.

He took the Thermos and, leaving the blankets in the hay, lowered himself down the ladder. The barn was ankle-deep in clean straw. Through the open door to the yard, he could see the steaming manure heap. Someone had mucked out the barn without him hearing. He looked along the length of the wall. Beyond the platform piled with fodder, a pump dripped water into a trough. He pushed towards it, past the open stalls. An old man sat near the wall, his back resting against the side of a brown and white cow. He had a blackthorn stave in his hands and was whittling its end with a keen, hooked blade.

As he saw Greg, the old man stopped, knife in mid-air. He

rose creakily from the milking stool, his language outlandish in Greg's ears. Greg shook his head, pointing first to the pump then the Thermos. It was impossible for the old man to have seen him come down the ladder. Greg would bluff as a stranger who had strayed to the yard, then the barn, in search of water. Again, he pantomimed drinking—filling the flask.

The old man's hooked blade was set in a hornbill haft. He snapped it shut, polishing the haft on dirty trousers. His face, brown with the glaze of earthenware, seemed to hold timid resentment. Almost furtively, the old man circled Greg to the door. As if afraid to turn his back, he called over his shoulder to the house, the lilting Welsh echoing in the barn. The cattle stirred ponderously, their heads curious.

The only way out was past this old fool and through the doorway. As Greg reached the yard, the door at the back of the farmhouse opened. A woman of thirty stood there, wiping her hands on a cloth. Greg pushed past the old man who smiled timidly, standing aside. Again, he said something in Welsh to the woman.

"Are you looking for water?" she called.

He scanned the line of the farmhouse roof, the stone walls with their tracery of dark, dormant creeper. There was no sign of a telephone wire. Here, in this remote valley, they could know nothing of him.

She was a tiny woman with dark smooth hair dragged in a bun at the back of her neck. Only kindness showed on her scrubbed face as she repeated her question.

"Was it water you were looking for?"

He crossed the yard, followed by the old man. "If you'd let me fill my flask . . . There are three of us—camping in the woods back there." He threw a vague hand at the mountains, sure of the rightness of what he was saying. Three men were less sinister than one, a solitary traveller. "We're hiking to Abergavenny." He chose the name at random.

The woman seemed indifferent, clucking as she saw the rent in his trousers. "Hiking! That must be surely cold, this weather." She shook her head at the folly of men and opened the door to the kitchen. "Was it water or tea, now, that you really wanted?" She smiled archly, showing teeth that were strangely good. "Sleeping in the woods! It'll be tea, surely. And some to take back for your friends."

A wall-eyed sheepdog rose to its feet, laughing. Time had burnished the wrought-iron front of the old fireplace. Hooks hung in the brick chimney. A dresser, dark with the care of generations, was set with pewter and china.

He sat in a wheelback chair as she busied herself at the stove. The old man dropped in a settle by the fire, talking softly to the dog at his feet and watching Greg with a child's curiosity. The woman poured water from the great iron kettle and put a rough clean towel and soap by the basin.

" You'll get no hot water in the woods," she smiled. " By the time you get to Abergavenny, you'll all be looking like tramps."

He thanked her and washed the dirt from his neck and face. As he lifted his arms above shoulder level, pain tore at his side. He put his hands on the sink, steadying himself. The heat of the fire, the singing kettle and the old man's voice dragged at his weariness. He wanted to stay where he was—unknown but accepted. A stranger to be sheltered and warmed. He plunged his head into the basin and dried with an effort, the coarse towel rasping his skin.

He took a seat at the table and drank the hot sweet tea. Somehow, he had to retrieve his food and blankets from the loft, unobserved. The woman filled his Thermos, bright with the chatter of one who hears her voice too seldom. The door to the yard opened. Without bothering to rise, the sheepdog switched recognition with its tail. This was the man who had been in the pasture. He had bright eyes under crumpled lids that he turned casually on Greg, then in enquiry towards his wife. The old man spoke from the fire and the woman nodded. The farmer hung his jacket on a hook and turned back his short sleeves, showing long, stringy arms. He cocked his head as his wife continued in rapid Welsh. Back turned, he sluiced face and hand in the bowl before he faced Greg again.

" You must be daft, mon, walking the woods in this weather. Sleeping in the open! " His smile robbed the words of offence. He spoke quickly to his wife in Welsh and she made a sound of distress, lifting her hands.

" There's silly of me! You'll take something to eat with us? There's plenty . . ." She pointed where the lid on a great pot was lifting regularly. The smell of the bubbling stew brought the water to Greg's mouth, its savour tempting him to accept the invitation. But what was it Bridget had said—you could never assume that a Welshman's heart was won because he smiled.

In a few minutes, these people would be at their meal. If he went now, he could sneak to the loft for his bedding while they were at their food. " No thanks," he said, hefting the Thermos flask in his hand. " My friends will be waiting for me."

The farmer shrugged indifferently. He looked round the kitchen, slapping his pockets. With a word to his wife, he went into an inner corridor. Greg buttoned his collar, oddly tense. They were in a group, the woman, the old man and the dog, watching him expectantly. He turned his head to the window. A long icicle, fluted and catching the sun, hung there. Beyond the barn, he could see the massed trees, climbing the mountain side. Suddenly, he wanted to go.

He was by the window, a dozen yards from the door to the yard. As he moved towards it, the inner door opened. The farmer cradled the barrels of a shotgun in the crook of his left arm. He had the fingers of his right in the trigger guard. He covered Greg, pushing the door shut with his elbow.

" Don't move!" He instructed. He inched between Greg and the door to the yard. " The wireless, mon, I heard," he said. It was as if he were impelled to justify himself. Their eyes held for a second then the farmer nodded. " You'll be Paul Gregory," he said simply.

" No!" But the words made no sound. Events and people had shrunk in perspective leaving only this room and its problem. " No," he repeated. This time his voice sounded, cracking. He concentrated, trying to force the babble of words from brain to mouth.

The farmer squared the shotgun watchfully. He spoke sharply to the old man who went out to the yard, followed by the dog. " You better sit down." It was as though the man had respect for the end of a hunted creature. " You must see Edwards, the police. Must see Edwards," he said again. His bright eyes unwavering, he sat on the edge of the table. " Get him a chair to sit, woman!" he ordered.

She crossed the room, the tall-backed chair in her hands. Her eyes were unafraid, still kind. He tried to read more than compassion there. Useless. There was nothing. If he stayed here, he was finished. To these people, police surely meant the hamlet in the next valley. A slow-thinking countryman, set apart from them only by his uniform. There'd be a phone in that cottage. Once the old man had reached there, a call to headquarters would bring every mobile unit in the county, converging on this valley.

He took the chair from the woman, twisting his body as if to sit. Then he lunged, using the heavy wood as both shield and lance, throwing it at the pointing barrels. The chairlegs caught the other man's arms, pinioning them. His fingers crooked on a trigger and the kitchen resounded with the blast of the explosion. Shot from the twelve-bore tore into the wall, spattering the room. The weight of the flying wood forced the man to his back on the table. The shotgun clattered to the stone flags. Greg picked up the gun.

The woman stood whimpering but unhurt by the fire. Shamefaced, the man crossed to her side. The smell of burnt powder was acrid in the confined space and the man coughed, bending his head. Greg kicked the chair aside. The second cartridge in the gun meant his freedom. He shoved the barrels towards the frightened pair.

" Do as you're told and you'll be all right," he gasped. " Where's that old man gone—for the police?" The farmer nodded, putting an arm round his wife's shoulders. " How far?" said Greg. "*How far?*" he shouted, incensed by the man's slowness.

" Three miles."

" Where's your cellar?" The man pointed at the door he had used. " You first," ordered Greg and followed the pair into the chill passage. The man stopped at a stout plank door, fastened on the outside with staple and hook. " Open it!" said Greg. The man hesitated and it was his wife who undid the door with shaking fingers. It swung out to reveal a short length of steps to a darkened cellar. " Where's the other way out of it?" demanded Greg. They stared at him, not understanding. " Go on then, get down there! Get!" he shouted.

Again, it was the woman who was first to move, pulling at her husband's arm. The man followed her.

Greg waited a second at the head of the steps. He could hear them moving about in the darkness—the man's voice soft with reassurance. Greg shut the door, securing it with the stout hook. He ran out to the yard. Fowls and geese foraged the frozen mud, unconcerned. A sow led her brood to a warm patch by the steaming dung-hill. Taking the shotgun by the barrels, he swung the stock against the wall, shattering wood from metal.

He retrieved the roll of bedding from the loft. In the larder, he found more food—bread, cheese, meat and butter. He packed these securely with the Thermos in the blankets and strapped them to his shoulders. There was a rough, stained topcoat hanging on a wall and he took it. He crossed the farmyard at a shambling run, his head dragging down to the injured rib.

The ground was flat to a slight depression at the entrance to the woods on the far side of the valley. Once there, he'd be safe for a time. There, the drifts were shallower and there were bare patches of ground among the trees. Streams, maybe. There'd be the chance to cover his tracks. Some sheep huddled at the edge of the wood, muzzling the sparse green that showed through the snow at the base of the trees. As he neared, they wheeled in front of him. Now the ground rose. Holly, birch and ash crowded the side of the valley. He pushed in, slowing to a walk, pumping his legs steadily. Dead snarls of briar grabbed at his arms, his body, as he passed.

In there, it was colder. Only now and then did the sun struggle through the canopy of interlaced boughs overhead, throwing a pale light on the sharply rising ground. Twice, he slithered up a hundred yards in the wet of a stream that trickled down through moss and dead leaves. He was leaving no tracks now for them to follow.

It was an hour before he heard the baying of dogs, faint, behind him. It was the deep, bell-tone of hounds and it came from the valley beneath. He ran a few aimless steps, his head swinging wildly like a bewildered animal. Bloodhounds. The full-throated sound of a hound on its line pealed in the valley, echoing thinly in the woods. He had to see. Someone down there was using hounds. He had to know who they were, where they were. A fir offered both vantage point and easy access. He hoisted himself up, treading the horizontal boughs like the rungs of a ladder. Up, till his weight sent the slender top swaying.

Half-a-mile below, the length of the valley was a white expanse broken at one end by the farm and its buildings. At the other, three trucks were parked on the track that led to the hamlet beyond the opposite hill. A line of men, the blue of their uniforms black in the distance, was working its way across the flat ground towards him. He could hear their shouts, the sense lost but the sound plain. In front of them, police handlers followed two pairs of bloodhounds. The black and tan hounds ran free, working carefully, casting for themselves. Fascinated, he crooked an arm round a bough, leaning far out to follow the scene. Bloodhounds were able to hunt the line of a man, many hours cold, without changing to a warmer scent. And he was no more than forty minutes away. The hounds moved confidently till they came to the spot where Greg had entered the woods. Here, they cast in wider circles, apparently baffled. He remembered the sheep. They must have returned, fouling his line, confusing the hounds.

The great dogs puzzled their way back towards the parked trucks, pausing at the place where Greg had broken from the farmyard. They rechecked their impression of the scent. One hound turned, putting back its head to bay. Then, silently, the four beasts swung along in the direction of the woods.

He dropped to the ground. The hounds would outstrip their handlers. Unless he queered the line, they would catch up with him. Bloodhounds rarely attacked a human but they pointed pursuit to the scene of the find, keeping the fugitive at bay. He started to run laterally, at right angles to the advancing line of police. The men were spaced at twenty-yard intervals, covering three or four hundred yards. He could outflank that line and work his way down through the trees to the valley. By the time hounds and men had reached the zenith of his climb, he would be on the flat. On the track that led from the valley, three trucks were parked, unattended.

He went at an awkward jog-trot, one foot higher than the other on the steep-sloped ground. Arms outstretched in front of him to fend off the whipping branches. Once, he looked at his watch, checking time against distance. He stopped. He had been running for fifteen minutes. Even at this slow speed, he should be clear of the flank of climbing police.

He strained his ears, trying to catch the sound of pursuit. But the woods were silent save where an overweighted fir branch tore from its trunk to the ground. He started to run down the mountain side. So dense were the trees, so steep the slope, that he could go no more than twenty yards at a time, slithering to the ground to check his descent. No longer able to control his need for oxygen, he sucked air into his lungs in great gulps. He got up, spitting, staining the ground red with his blood.

Through the trees ahead, the snow was bright under the sun. He dropped to the ground at the edge of the wood, wriggling his body into the cold wet till his head was clear of the tree-trunks. Smoke curled from the farmhouse but there was no sign of life. Five hundred yards to his left, the scuffed tracks of the police showed dark in the white expanse to the trees, then vanished. The three parked trucks stood, one behind the other, a hundred yards into the valley in front of him. There was no sign of movement there, either. At the angle he lay, it was impossible to see into the backs of the trucks, but the cabs were empty.

Between trees and vehicles was a stretch of glittering pasture. No cover. Once in that clear bright light, he could be seen from the farmhouse or from any point where lookouts might have been posted. There was no certainty that the trucks were empty—that the ignition keys would be in them. There was no certainty of anything but the hounds and the men behind him.

He threw away the faded topcoat and pulled the straps tighter on his shoulders. Head down, he broke for the line of vehicles. He seemed to be covering the ground in great strides, outstripping all chance of pursuit. Blood drummed in his ears and a new pain, like the hurt of extreme cold, bore in between his eyes. The trucks were only yards away, now. At the first, he tore at the door to the cab. It was unlocked and he pulled himself up painfully to the floor. His vision was blurring again. Just a little time and he'd be all right. A little time to rest. A glint showed in the black instrument panel over his head—the glint of a flat ignition key.

Now movement was all. The sense to plan, to reason, was gone. Even the consciousness of its need. Desperately, like an old man whose every step has become a hazardous adventure, he willed his hand to the key and turned it. A tell-tale bulb glowed red on the panel. The S on the starting button grew big and he jabbed at it. The motor caught, roaring as he sank the accelerator. He threw the truck into gear, wrenching it off the shoulder of the lane. The vehicle lurched as the powerful drive spun the back wheels on the frozen road surface.

There was a shout from behind, almost lost in the clattering cab. In the driving mirror, he caught brief sight of a uniformed figure that ran from the back of the last truck. It vanished as he sent the big vehicle round the first bend. He shut his nostrils against the reek of vaporized petrol. The truck was swaying, fighting his control as he took the curves dangerously fast.

A hoarse, catching whistle bothered him till he recognized the sound of his own breathing. No longer did his brain acknowledge pain, concentrating only on survival. He was at the top of the defile, dropping down to the hamlet in the next valley. Past that hamlet, lay the bridge and the main highway. He had a start on the man in the truck behind. Once on the main highway, he could run the truck up one of the mountain roads to the woods and leave it.

The ponderous vehicle careered down the rough track, bucking the curves, roaring in the straight. He accelerated through the quiet hamlet with a sudden sense of power, of lightning reactions. The stone bridge was below, a hundred yards down in a straight line. He changed down, meshing the gears clumsily.

Something moved in the side mirror. His eyes swivelled to the bracket. The high blunt nose of the following truck showed in the glass. Slowly, he fed the motor petrol till his foot was flat on the boards. The stonework of the bridge came up to meet him. A meaningless jumble of grey on black, hurting his eyes. He closed them gratefully, his hands coming up to join over his chest. Gathering speed, the truck slammed into the parapet, tearing through the loose foundation. For a second it hung on its chassis. Then, almost lazily, it turned over its length and plunged into the swift, dark river.

www.ingramcontent.com/pod-product-compliance
Ingram Content Group UK Ltd.
Pitfield, Milton Keynes, MK11 3LW, UK
UKHW022314280225
455674UK00004B/303

9 781471 905599